Love Finds You in *Romeo* COLORADO

BY GWEN FORD FAULKENBERRY

summerside
PRESS

Love Finds You in Romeo, Colorado
© 2008 by Gwen Ford Faulkenberry

ISBN 978-1-934770-46-7

All scripture quotations, unless otherwise indicated, are taken from the HOLY BIBLE, NEW INTERNATIONAL VERSION®. NIV®. Copyright © 1973, 1978, 1984 by International Bible Society. Used by permission of Zondervan. All rights reserved.

Scripture quotations marked KJV are taken from the King James Version of the Bible.

The poem, "a question of returning," is from the poetry collection *As Orion Falls*, Ghost Road Press, 2005. Used by permission.

The town depicted in this book is a real place, but all characters are fictional. Any resemblances to actual people or events are purely coincidental.

Cover and Interior Design by Müllerhaus Publishing Group | **www.mullerhaus.net**

Published by Summerside Press, Inc., 11024 Quebec Circle, Bloomington, Minnesota 55438 | **www.summersidepress.com**

Fall in love with Summerside.

Printed in the USA.

DEDICATED TO JAMES AND JANIE FORD,

PARENTS EXTRAORDINAIRE.

....

a question of returning
....

is this possible
are migratory monarch butterflies
and a woman humming
only slightly out of tune
in the next room over
metaphors for the same thing
can there be too many words
in the trees
too many butterflies
in the mexican pines
resting with the sum
of north american summers
under their wings
is that really the tree groaning
the weight of all that airiness
creaking in a soft breeze
head down in a mexican summer
God bless those butterflies
and what is left of memory...

—Aaron A. Abeyta

Chapter One

....

She left the marble tile and fluorescent lights of Old Main and stood
for a moment outside its austere facade. Walking over to the grand steps
at the front of the building, where carefree students were ascending
and descending, Claire resisted the urge to run past them and down
the cobbled pathway that snaked through two rows of giant oaks.

Instead, she took a deep breath, inhaling the aroma of fall in the San
Luis Valley. The oaks, which seemed to reach out and beckon her, looked
in the midmorning light like a group of old ladies gathered for tea.
Except for one—the diseased tree that maintenance was in the process
of cutting apart—they were all decked out in their best September finery.

Returning to her office, Claire plopped a heavy pile of papers onto
her desk and sighed as she sat down. Two large sections of Composition
One back-to-back was a lot of work. She took a quick look at her watch
and noted that Graeme would soon be eating his lunch with the rest of
his class at Manassa Elementary School.

Her screensaver—which she'd not bothered to change since arriving
a few months ago—showed another lovely, old walkway on the campus,
which was carved between rows of giant oak trees that surrounded it like
silent witnesses. The perspective of the photograph, Claire supposed,
was meant to draw potential students. It invited the viewer to step onto
the narrow path and stroll in the shade of the oaks. A heading above the
picture read, *Adams State College: Great Stories Begin Here.*

Claire was pondering the irony of that statement in light of her own
situation when the phone on her desk rang once. It was the long, single
ring that signaled an intercampus call.

"Hello, this is Dr. Caspian."

" 'Dr. Caspian…' I do so relish the sound of that." It was Dr. Oscar Norbert Gunther III, Claire's mentor and something of a father figure in her life.

Claire smiled. "Hi, Oscar. How are you today?"

"Very well, thank you, if a bit weary of sophomores. I've just come from my sophomore lecture and been reminded again, for the thirty-fifth year in a row, that they certainly are a bunch of—"

"Wise fools?" Claire smiled as she finished his sentence, remembering his back-to-term speeches to the Honors College every year. As director, he personally addressed each class.

"Indeed. True to the Greek meaning of the word. They think they know everything."

"Well, be patient with them. If they are anything like I was—" Her voice drifted off.

"You and Rob were some of the best kids ever to come through the program, and two of my personal favorites, I'm not abashed to say. I'm just glad we could get you back here after everything—oh, I didn't mean to say that."

Claire knew there were probably blotches popping out on his neck like wild strawberries, and she imagined he was taking a furious puff on his pipe.

"I'm glad to be here, too, Oscar. And I wouldn't be, without your help."

He cleared his throat.

"Well, what's say we go to lunch? If you're not too embarrassed to be seen in public with a decrepit old man."

"You will never be old, and I'd love some lunch. How about I pick you up in the courtyard?"

Ten minutes later, Claire spotted Oscar sitting cross-legged on a bench and smoking his pipe. He had on navy pants and a tweed jacket with a white shirt and a red bowtie. His skin was smooth and tan, barely wrinkled, and striking underneath his immaculate grey beard and mustache. He peered at her approvingly with keen hazel eyes. He was wearing tennis shoes.

"Feel like walking?" she asked him.

"Ah, always," he said, standing to his feet. "I delight in peripatetic exercise."

Claire loved the smell of his pipe. She held out her hand to him, and he squeezed it tightly.

* * * * *

After lunch and some lively conversation with Oscar about Sartre's *No Exit*, which a group of Honors College students were performing that week, Claire returned to the English department. She left her office door open in case a student came by needing help and sat back down at her desk to grade essays. Checking her watch again, she saw that it was one thirty, which meant Graeme should be out on the playground for recess. Claire hoped he'd remembered to put on his jacket.

As she took out her red pen, she glanced at the picture of Graeme that sat in a frame by itself, like a little soldier on her desk. It was his school picture, taken just this year when he started kindergarten. He was dressed in a linen shirt of pale green—the color of both his and Claire's eyes, only several shades lighter. His dark, unruly hair was curled around his face, and his skin, always olive, was tanned from the summer's sun. He still had all of his baby teeth, and they looked like tiny white diamonds in his bronze face. He was smiling, if reluctantly.

Rob was right, she thought. *He does look just like me.*

Claire set down her pen and gazed intently at Graeme's smile, studying it. Running a hand through her jet-black hair, she caught a small section between her fingers and gently twisted.

Mariposa.

The word came to her through the years like snow falling on the desert. It was quiet, like a whisper. And as Claire closed her eyes and breathed in deeply, giving in to a rare indulgence, she could see Graeme with Rob a few feet away from her in a patch of wildflowers, Graeme toddling toward her with a fragrant bouquet.

Then suddenly Rob was behind her, kissing her neck and whispering.

Mariposa. Mi bella mariposa.

His rugged hands, cupped, and then opening in front of her face. . . The tiny Silvery Checkerspot butterfly fluttering up, right before her eyes, and quivering away toward the water.

"Dr. Caspian? Dr. Caspian? Are you okay?"

From somewhere far away, Claire heard the voice of her student assistant, Christina Salazar, and opened her eyes. Christina was persistently knocking on her office door, and Claire realized that the phone on her desk was ringing—two quick rings each time. An off-campus call.

She grabbed the phone, breathless. "Claire Caspian."

"Dr. Caspian, I'm so glad you answered. I've let it ring several times within the last few minutes. I didn't want to leave a message."

"Yes?" Claire recognized the caller as Julieta, the secretary at Manassa Elementary School, and her heart began to pound.

"Your son Graeme has been taken to the emergency room in La Jara. He's having trouble breathing—"

"What? Why? Did you use his inhaler?" Claire's mind was racing. Graeme had mild asthma, and she had made sure there was an inhaler for him at school in case of an emergency. He very rarely used it, but it was there when he needed it.

"Yes. It didn't work very well. The school nurse has taken him to the hospital. I called ahead. I'm sure Bonita is taking good care—"

Claire dropped the phone, grabbed her keys, and bolted out the door.

* * * * *

Conejos County Hospital, in La Jara, was fifteen miles due south of Alamosa and Adams State College on Highway 285. It was only twelve miles north of Manassa, where Graeme went to school. And yet when the school nurse pulled up at the emergency room with Claire's little boy, Claire was already waiting.

"Graeme, Mommy's here!" Claire threw open the car door and grabbed a frightened Graeme, who was gasping for air.

A team of nurses and technicians were right behind her and ushered them in through the big open doors of the ER.

Claire, Graeme, and Bonita, the school nurse, were whisked into a smaller room where the head ER nurse took Graeme out of Claire's arms. He placed Graeme on the exam table, hooked up a machine with a tube, and administered an Albuterol treatment to him within seconds. The gasping stopped. Inhaling the vapor, Graeme gradually began to breathe normally. Claire could see his little face and shoulders relax, and he even attempted to smile at her with the tube in his mouth.

The ER nurse beside Graeme was tall and burly and had a braid that hung all the way down his back. "So, big guy, looks like you scared your momma half to death. What were you doing, jumping jacks or something? Is that how you got out of breath?" The nurse patted Graeme on the back with a brown hand the size of a bear's paw. Then he turned to Claire.

"You okay? You're little boy's going to be fine."

Claire relaxed her own shoulders a bit and met the nurse's eyes for the first time. They both saw a flicker of recognition.

"*No lo puedo creer!* Are you Claire Caspian—the Caspian C?"

Claire blinked and stared at the man in front of her. He vaguely resembled an old friend from high school, only the Carlos she remembered had worn his hair short and was considerably slimmer.

"Carlos Caballeros?" she asked tentatively.

"At your service." The ER nurse, still holding the breathing apparatus up to Graeme's mouth with one hand, folded the other hand across his enormous waistline and bowed slightly.

"Well, you certainly are my knight in shining armor!" Claire beamed.

Bonita, who'd been all but forgotten up to that point, interjected, "You two know each other?"

"Well, yeah. You heard the lady, I'm her shining *caballero*. And, she's the famous 'Caspian C' of Manassa High School's glory days. She won the State Geography Bee when we were in tenth grade. Put Manassa on the map!" Carlos grinned facetiously.

"Oh, Bonita, I'm so sorry." Claire turned to her, blushing. "I haven't even thanked you for taking care of Graeme and bringing him here. I was so worried, and everything was happening so fast. But it does seem he's okay now—don't you think?" She turned back to Carlos, who was taking the tube out of Graeme's mouth and disassembling the breathing treatment machine.

"I think he's great. Aren't you, *hijo*?" Carlos helped Graeme down and shook his hand. "Hey, that's a nice grip you've got there."

Graeme smiled at him and scrambled up into Claire's lap. He leaned his head onto her shoulder, spent.

Carlos brought some paperwork for Claire to fill out, and Bonita stayed to help with the details of what occurred at school. She left when that was done. Carlos, however, sat back down with Claire and Graeme in the room while they waited for the doctor to come.

"So, *amiga*," he began in his own San Luis Valley version of Spanglish. "What are you doing back in this area? I haven't seen you since the day we graduated. That was over twenty years ago! Where've you been? What have you been up to?"

Claire looked into Carlos's kind face. "Well, I went to Adams State for undergrad and then to the University of Arkansas to get my PhD."

"Arkansas? Are you crazy? Why did you go there?"

Claire couldn't help but laugh. "I don't know. Adventure, I guess."

"Adventure? In Arkansas? You always were a little *loca*, Caspian C," he joked.

"Well, I was interested in seeing a different part of the country and they had a great program for what I wanted to study, so I thought, why not? My husband's family is from there. And it actually is a beautiful place."

"What did you study? Hillbilly music?" He pantomimed playing a guitar with his beefy arms and oversized hands. "Redneck art forms?" Carlos clearly could not imagine the brainy Claire Caspian in Arkansas.

Claire grimaced at Carlos's generalization.

"No, comparative literature. My main focus was literature written by Spanish-speaking people who have immigrated to the United States."

"Oy. Over my head. Where'd you find this little guy?" Carlos tapped the toe of Graeme's tennis shoe.

"I found his father at Adams, where he was in pre-law. We got married and moved to Arkansas for grad school, and Graeme was born a few years later, while I was teaching at the university and his dad was working for an international law firm. What about you? Didn't you go to Colorado State?"

"*Si, amiga*, I did. I had a football scholarship at the *collegio grande*. Played for the Promise Keepers guy—that was a hoot. I got my degree in nursing and came right back home to work. You know, giving back and all of that. It's fulfilling," Carlos declared matter-of-factly.

Claire remembered the rusty trailer where Carlos's large family had lived and how she'd suspected—though Abuelita never told her—that her grandmother gave them money from time to time.

"Well, you seem to have done very well for yourself. I'm happy for you."

"I never was one of those who wanted to get out of this area—" Carlos's gaze suddenly shifted to the doorway, and he rose to his feet. "Hi, Dr. Reyes!"

"*Hola*, Carlos!" a dark-complected man responded warmly. He wore a white coat and worn, tan Birkenstocks.

"I'll see you later, Claire. Take care of that boy!" Carlos gave her a pat on the arm as he left, closing the door behind him.

"Stephen Reyes." The doctor held out his hand to Claire as he sat down on the stool across from her and crossed his long legs.

Claire noticed that he had a square jaw and big, brown eyes with long lashes. She reached out, gripping his hand firmly. "I'm Claire, and this is Graeme."

The hand he offered her was warm and strong. Big veins rippled across it, hidden just below the surface. *Like Michelangelo's* David, Claire thought.

Graeme opened his big eyes sleepily and rolled them toward the doctor before laying his head back down on Claire's shoulder.

Dr. Reyes smiled at this, and Claire observed that one of his front teeth was chipped ever so slightly.

"Do you need me to wake him?"

"No, not now; I don't think so." He was scanning through the chart. "It sounds like a pretty textbook asthma attack. Has this ever happened before?"

"Well, we lived in Arkansas when he was smaller. He had one scare, sort of like this, when I rushed him to the doctor. He'd been playing in the leaves in our yard. They thought it was allergy related." Claire shifted Graeme's body weight in her arms. "He had to be on a steroid for three days, and after that he took Singulair. That was in the fall. After a hard freeze that winter he didn't have any other serious problems. We've just used his inhaler ever since—a time or two here and there—if he was having trouble."

"Hmm." Dr. Reyes was writing on the chart. His head was turned to the side, and she could see just a hint of curl that reminded her of Graeme's hair. Also like Graeme's, the style was neither long nor short.

"But today the inhaler didn't cut it," he remarked.

"No, apparently not."

"Can you think of any potential allergens at his school? It says here that the attack came on at recess." Dr. Reyes' brown eyes shone as he questioned Claire.

"No. To be honest, I assumed any allergy problem would be gone when we moved to the desert."

"Well, it's not technically a desert here. But you're right. It's logical to believe there would be fewer allergens here than there were in Arkansas." He stood up. "Go ahead and lift up his shirt in the back so I can listen."

Claire noticed that Dr. Reyes's hands were gentle as he touched the stethoscope to Graeme's skin. Graeme flinched slightly at its cold surface. The doctor listened, obviously looking for something specific, but he didn't seem to find it. He motioned to Claire to shift Graeme so he could listen in the front.

"Nothing there either," he said. "That's good." He unhooked the stethoscope from his ears and let it fall around his neck.

"What were you looking for?"

"A heart murmur, wheezing, anything else abnormal."

Stephen looked at Claire for a long moment and then sat back down on the stool. "I think we better set your son up with a pulmonologist."

Claire felt the color drain back out of her face. "Why?"

"With the history you've described, it seems to me that Graeme may be developing a more severe form of asthma. It's not uncommon for this to surface at his age. I can't tell just by listening, so we'll need to let a specialist look at him and determine treatment. If his inhaler no longer works to control his asthma, he could be in danger pretty quickly—just like he was today."

Claire rested her chin against Graeme's head. "Oh."

"Would you like me to set up that referral for you? I know it's a drive, but I'd really recommend you take him to Salida. There's an excellent pediatric pulmonologist there."

"Sure," she said. "I guess."

Stephen turned from the chart where he was scribbling some notes and peered curiously at Claire. She looked down then, and while her right arm was holding onto Graeme, her left hand stroked his back, up and down between his shoulder blades.

He spoke softly. "Your little boy will be okay. I just want to get him the best care I can. That asthma is mean stuff."

Claire looked up at him, and they stared at each other for a long moment.

"Thank you," she said, meaning it.

"I'll have Carlos call in the referral right now if you'd like. Is the first available appointment all right with you?"

"Yes."

He stood to leave. Claire noticed that he wasn't wearing a ring, but not because she was looking for it. She was looking at the gentleness in his hands.

Chapter Two

....

When his shift at the family practice clinic across from the Conejos County Hospital ended late that afternoon, Dr. Stephen Reyes changed into farm clothes and got into his truck, a black Ford F350 King Ranch Diesel. Stephen liked to joke with local people that the truck was named after his small ranch. Even with his limited knowledge of Spanish, he knew his last name meant "kings."

After stopping at the feed store in La Jara for some dog food and bulk sunflower seed, he headed south on Highway 285 toward home. Stephen could feel himself unwinding as he drove, windows down, the seven or so miles from La Jara to the village of Romeo. He didn't pass anything or anyone, unless he counted a small herd of antelope beside the road. No fence was keeping them in. Stephen slowed to count the herd and admire the rust-red color of their coats. One of them looked at him with large, inquisitive eyes before darting away into the great expanse of field and flatness that bordered the highway. For a moment, Stephen remembered his earlier encounter with Claire Caspian. *Those eyes. And she wasn't wearing a wedding ring.* He decided to put those thoughts on a mental shelf and move on.

Just before reaching the grain elevator that stood like a sentinel on the outskirts of Romeo, Stephen turned onto County Road 7. He passed a white clapboard house belonging to his neighbors, the Patricks, before turning across a cattle guard and onto his drive. A John Deere Gator was approaching at top speed from the direction of his place, kicking up dust behind it. The driver was Nell Patrick, in her nightgown and robe.

"Nell, what's wrong?"

"It's that old cow, the Charolais. She's been tryin' to have her calf for two days and can't. Gene's with her right now, but he called the house while I was in the bathtub. He told me to jump out and try to fetch you. He's afraid we're goin' to lose her."

Stephen turned off his engine, hurried out of the truck, and climbed into the ATV beside Nell. He noticed, as she stamped on the gas, that her feet were in pink rubber boots. Her gray hair, carefully pin-curled, was working its way out from under a red polka-dotted scarf, and when she raised her right arm to tuck a piece of it back in, the sleeve of her blue terry-cloth robe slapped Stephen in the face. She smelled of lemon verbena.

"Where are they?"

The Gator practically hurdled the cattle guard and went up on two wheels as Nell turned back onto the county road.

"On our north forty. You'll have to get the gate." Nell slowed the Gator but didn't stop, as Stephen jumped off to open the bright orange metal gate across the road from the Patricks' house. Nell plowed through, and Stephen pulled the gate closed without latching it before sliding back into the Gator just as she sped off. They quickly cut across the acreage following a well-worn cattle trail.

The sun was setting, and as they approached the lone tree on the horizon, Stephen could make out Gene's lanky silhouette beside the cow's. She was on her side, her white-gray abdomen swollen like a giant balloon, and Gene was bent over it, pushing and prodding. Stephen jumped off the Gator, more than a little relieved to still be in one piece.

"I'm glad you could make it, Steve; I've tried all of my tricks, and ain't nothin' workin' for this old girl." Gene patted the cow's belly and squinted at Stephen with his small blue eyes. His face looked like wrinkled parchment.

Stephen thought he could see the faint outline of the calf's hooves against its mother's skin. "Have you tried to turn it?"

"I've tried twiced, but I can't get 'er done. Guess I'm turning weak in my old age." Gene stood to his feet stiffly, taking off his straw cowboy hat and running a finger through his steel-gray hair. "She's been laborin' since yesterday."

Stephen took off his work shirt, threw it to Nell, who was still on the Gator, and rolled up the short sleeve of his white V-neck T-shirt. "This isn't going to be pretty," he said.

"It never is." Gene squatted back down by the cow's head and rubbed her neck soothingly. She was breathing hard. "Steady, old gal."

As gently as he possibly could, Stephen reached his hand into the suffering cow. First, he was up to his elbow; then his arm disappeared up to the shoulder. He found what he was looking for. "It's too late to turn it," he said. "We'll have to try to pull the calf out breech. Gene, do you have a chain and a rope in your truck?"

Gene hurried over to his '78 Chevy. Old Blue, he called it. While Stephen pulled on the calf's hooves, working with the cow's contractions, Gene backed up Old Blue as close as he could get. He got out of the truck, fished a rope and a chain from under the seat, and brought it over to Stephen. Stephen wrapped the rope around the calf's hooves and tied it to the chain, which Gene was fastening to the trailer hitch.

"On my go, Gene," Stephen said, still holding onto the calf's hooves and motioning Gene back into Old Blue. "One, two, three!"

Gene edged the truck forward just a few inches. The cow heaved, and a few inches of the calf's lower back legs appeared.

"One, two, three!" Stephen called again.

They repeated this process with the truck until most of the calf was delivered. Finally, it was time for the shoulders and head to come out. Gene unhooked the chain from Old Blue, and Stephen took the calf's posterior in his arms, hugging it from behind. He pulled with all of his might. First the shoulders and then the head popped out, like a cork, and Stephen fell back into a mixture of cow manure, blood, and amniotic fluid. The calf's front legs slid out next, as though an afterthought. Gene came over to tend to the calf while Stephen got up and scraped out the mother's placenta.

When all was said and done, the mission had been an incredible success. Stephen, recognizing more than anyone the odds they'd surmounted, was thankful that either animal had survived and amazed that both appeared to be thriving. Gene and Nell were very pleased, though not surprised. They'd depended on Stephen's expertise more than once since he'd become their neighbor ten years ago. As the exhausted cow nursed her traumatized-yet-hungry calf, Stephen loaded himself into the back of Old Blue. And, with Nell leading the way on the Gator, they all headed for the house.

* * * * *

Back at the Patricks', Nell insisted that Stephen stay for dinner.

"No, Nell, thanks. I feel nasty, and it's nine o'clock. I still need to feed my animals." Stephen looked at Gene. "Would you mind taking me home, though?" He was still in the back of Old Blue and, filthy as he was, would rather walk the half-mile length of his driveway before he got inside his truck.

"Go home hungry after what you just did? No sir, Gene'll feed your stock for you, won't you, hon?" Nell had parked her Gator in the carport and was headed for the door that led into the side of their house.

Gene nodded. "You get out of the truck and get cleaned up. I know where everything is. I'll be right back."

Stephen chuckled to himself as he obeyed. No matter that he was a forty-year-old doctor who was used to giving orders all day. None of that meant beans to Nell and Gene Patrick, who treated him like he was their son. After Gene left, Stephen stood where the truck had been by the shed, thinking about what to do and not wanting to get anything dirty.

"Is it too cold for the hose?" Nell had just returned from inside the house with a pair of Gene's boxers, sweatpants, and a T-shirt. Stephen's clean work shirt was still on the seat of the Gator.

"Uh, well…" Stephen hated to say yes.

"Here. Stand over here in the light and let me spray you off real good. Then you can go behind the shed and change."

She's not kidding, thought Stephen. He edged under the bright fluorescent light that illuminated their driveway like a disinclined actor entering center stage. His clothes, boots—even his hair was covered with evidence of what they'd just done.

Nell broke into a peal of laughter. "Son! I had you going, didn't I?"

Stephen relaxed when he realized she was joking. He began to laugh, too.

"Now, you just leave your boots by the door and take you a shower in Gene's bathroom there off from the laundry. You can leave your clothes in the utility sink—and here." She remembered the clothes in her hand. "I'll set these on the washer. I need to get you a pair of socks, too." Grabbing his shirt off the Gator as she passed, she ran back into the house, robe flying. Stephen followed her.

After getting him settled, Nell headed across the house and out the door to the front porch. "I'll just sit out front and wait for Gene, and then when you're done we'll have us some coffee and I'll warm you up a plate."

* * * * *

The coffee—decaf Folgers—was surprisingly good to Stephen. Nell bustled around the kitchen in pink slippers, fussing over him, and Gene sat beside him at the low bar. Until that moment, Stephen hadn't realized how hungry he was, but he and Gene both ate like starving men. Nell kept heaping plates in front of them—of roasted lamb and mashed potatoes, with corn and peas recently harvested from the garden.

"Nell, this is delicious."

"Ain't she something?" Gene beamed. "She's been feeding me like this for fifty years. It's a wonder I'm not round as a barrel!"

Nell smiled her thanks at both of them. "It's because you work so hard, hon. Now, don't forget to take your blood pressure medicine."

She cleared their plates, poured more coffee, then escorted the men into the living room. Gene kicked back in his blue recliner while Nell sat down in her mauve one and rocked. Stephen was across from them on the flowered couch, elbows on his knees, holding the warm cup of coffee in both hands.

"Your hands sure do look better now than they did a couple of hours ago," Nell commented tenderly.

Gene laughed a deep, throaty laugh. "That's one story that could chase a few women off your trail."

"Yeah," Stephen consented. "It would."

"Not if they're the right kind, though," Nell reminded him, eyebrow raised.

"Well now, that's the problem, Nell. Most of them just don't seem to be the 'right kind,' as you call it."

" 'The right one will come along at the right time—when you least expect it.' That's what my daddy told me," Gene interjected. "And he was right. I was minding my own business, hauling grain down there at the feed store, when up walks Nell. 'Hey, Mr. Romeo, you know where I can use a telephone?' she asks me. She was here to watch the migration of the cranes, but when they migrated on, she stayed with me. The rest is history."

"That's right, babe." Nell took a sip of her coffee. "I didn't know it at the time, but it was a divine appointment."

"Mr. Romeo and Miss Juliet—your story is straight out of a book.

I don't think that kind of thing is going to happen to me." Stephen leaned back, crossing one leg and smiling at them. "But I'm pretty happy with Regina and the Duchess." They were his two Labrador retrievers.

"Well, I'm still prayin' you'll find yourself a wife," Nell declared.

Stephen was thoughtful. "If I ever married again, she'd need your prayers. I don't think I have what it takes to make a woman happy."

"Well, now, just a minute." Gene eyed him, squinting. "Nobody can do that for somebody else." Straightening his skinny shoulders, he turned to Nell mischievously. "Even all the man I am."

Nell smirked and rolled her eyes at Gene's feigned machismo. He looked back at Stephen. "Can't nobody keep a woman happy all of the time unless she's already happy in herself."

"I've not met too many of those, unfortunately. Maybe there's still one out there, but the girls I've been around lately all seem to want something. They see I'm a doctor and want money or something else."

"They're after your good looks, too, kid—don't fool yourself," Nell told him.

Now it was Stephen's turn to feel embarrassed. He rose to go. "Well, it's been fun," he said affectionately. "Don't get up."

They grinned at him.

"Thanks again for all you done. I sure do appreciate it." Gene shook Stephen's hand from the recliner.

"Anytime."

Nell saw him to the front porch, and they heard Gene clicking the TV on to *Headline News*.

"Thank you again for the wonderful supper. I'll get these clothes back to you in a day or two."

She hugged him. "No hurry. You take care."

Stephen's truck, across the yard and through a barbed-wire fence from where he and Nell stood on the front porch, was barely visible.

Wish I had a flashlight, he muttered to himself after stepping in a hole about midway. He heard Nell shutting the front door behind her and felt oddly alone.

Suddenly, the door opened again and Nell reappeared with a spotlight that lit up the whole yard. Stephen waved his thanks. He climbed through the fence, started his truck, and was home in fewer than five minutes.

That night as his head hit the pillow, Stephen's bones ached. He was too tired to think about anything that had happened that day. Except for the antelope. And the eyes.

Chapter Three

....

Claire peeked out at the sunrise from behind the handmade Italian drapes Abuelita had chosen for her room. They were dark brown and green—a light, soft hue of green that matched the walls, which were trimmed in brown. It was Abuelita's idea to redo her room before she moved back, and Claire was glad. Even though Graeme said it reminded him of Andes mints, his favorite candy, Claire preferred that to other memories. There were plenty of those here to contend with, even with the curtains and new coat of paint.

It was a damp morning. The lawns were shrouded in fine mist, and Claire could just make out the spires of the tall, wrought-iron gates that guarded the entrance to La Casa de Esperanza. *The House of Hope.* Her great-grandfather, Francisco Rodrigo, had acquired the two-thousand-acre ranch just outside Romeo and established La Casa as a safe place for his family after Mexican-American War. Named for his only daughter Esperanza, who was Claire's abuelita, the house had served as a refuge for many others throughout the years.

Beyond the gates—far beyond them—were the San Juan Mountains. In the faint sunlight, Culebra, with its long, snakelike ridge, appeared to her dimly through the fog, as though behind a veil. She couldn't see it, but she knew that just north of Culebra was Blanca, the sacred peak of the Navajo. On the west was Conejos , which she could see driving to work in Alamosa. *He hems us in behind and before, just like the mountains*, Claire could almost hear her abuelita saying. Abuelita was full of analogies like that.

Graeme tugged at her nightshirt, and she lifted him up.

"See the sunrise?" She pointed out the window to show him the sun. It was just beginning to appear on the horizon, like a pat of butter on top of the foggy mountain.

Graeme grinned. "That's pretty."

"That mountain is Culebra, remember?"

"I remember. The snake."

"*Bueno*. Ready for some hot chocolate?"

"Yep." He hopped down. Hot Mexican chocolate was his morning ritual.

Downstairs, Abuelita was already in the kitchen preparing breakfast tacos. Her long, grey-black hair was pulled back in a loose bun, and she was dressed in a white lace gown that came to her ankles. Graeme's warm chocolate was waiting for him on the stove.

"Abuelita!" He ran to her and wrapped his arms around her small, sturdy frame.

"How's my little *nieto* this morning?" Abuelita's dark eyes danced when she saw her great-grandson, and she reached out to hug Graeme with her free arm. With the other, she stirred scrambled eggs with a wooden spoon.

Claire kissed her on both leathery cheeks. "*Buenos dias*, Abuelita."

"Help me put these together, *hija*. There's bacon and beans and cheese."

Claire began assembling the tacos.

Graeme stood on his tiptoes to watch. "Yum!"

They moved to the breakfast room and sat at the table, a round, Pre-Revolution antique made of walnut. After prayer, which she led, Abuelita clapped her hands and inquired, "So, what's happening with everyone today?"

"I'm staying home in my pajamas," Graeme informed them, before taking a big bite of his taco.

"Oh? *Chistosa*, Graeme! On a school day?" Abuelita scolded him, charmed.

"Graeme is going to school, and I'm going to work. It's Friday, so I'll be coming home early and can pick him up. We're planning on going to Mickey's game tonight. Want to come with us?"

"No, *gracias*. These old bones won't be sitting out on those cold bleachers."

"What are you going to do?" Claire asked her.

"I was thinking of going over to Abe's in town. I've heard they have great weekend dances—*corridos* and country."

Claire gaped at her, incredulous. "What? Are you serious?"

Abuelita laughed naughtily. "Nah, I'll probably play chicken feet," she answered, pouring cream into her coffee. "Louisa and Pablo invited me."

Claire shook her head.

"Mickey's the new Manassa Mauler," offered Graeme over his cup of chocolate. "That's what Billy Sanford told me."

Claire and Abuelita exchanged looks of amusement.

"Is that so?" Claire asked him. "Who is the old Manassa Mauler?"

"Jack Dipsey, of course. That famous boxer."

She didn't correct his pronunciation of Dempsey. "What else did Billy Sanford tell you?"

"Oh, nothing, just that our team was going to kick the Sand Lizards' butts."

Abuelita, trying to suppress a laugh, spewed out some of her coffee.

"I see." Claire smiled at him and put down her fork. "Well, since Sand Lizards have tails, let's say 'tails' instead of 'butts,' okay, buddy?"

"Okay, Mom."

* * * * *

Although Graeme had a bedroom of his own across the hall, which Abuelita had lovingly prepared for him, he didn't spend much time there. This morning, like every morning, he came into Claire's room to get dressed. While he buttoned up his polo shirt and pulled on his jeans, she was in the adjoined bathroom with the door open, applying her makeup. Graeme often watched her draw on her eyes and brush her cheeks, like an artist. He said she was as beautiful as a movie star.

Graeme didn't like to be far away from his mother. In the evenings, unless he was playing with his toy train or looking at a book from the bookshelf in his room, he'd rather be in Claire's room where she was. He took his baths in her big claw-footed bath tub and dried off in front of her fireplace. And when it was time for bed, he curled up beside her while she read to him and slept snuggled beside her in bed. They'd slept that way for almost as long as Graeme could remember.

"About ready to go, Graemesy?" Claire called from the bathroom. "Be sure to get your jacket and backpack."

Claire put on a fitted black suit and her favorite jasmine perfume and then met Graeme in the hall. They bounded down the stairs together holding hands.

On their way out the door, both kissed Abuelita. She was still sitting at the breakfast table, reading her worn Bible.

"The Lord bless you," she told them as they waved good-bye.

In the backseat behind Claire, Graeme buckled his seat belt and then arranged his backpack beside him. "Why does Abuelita always say that?"

"What?" Claire asked.

"The Lord bless you."

"Oh, it's just a nice saying. It means that she wants us to be safe and happy, and that she loves us." Claire put the car in Reverse and backed up. Then they started forward down the painted brick drive.

"Are you happy, Mommy?" Graeme looked at her in earnest.

"Well, yes, honey. I'm happy that I have you." Graeme's question both startled and saddened Claire—saddened her because he had to ask. She held out the remote. "Want to push the button?"

Graeme pushed the button to open the gates, something Abuelita had updated several years ago. "What's your greatest fear?"

"My goodness, Graemesy. Where are all of these questions coming from?"

"I don't know. But what *is* your greatest fear?" he persisted.

Claire had always tried to be honest with him, and she was now. "Losing you."

"That's mine, too," he sighed. "And after that, it's scorpions."

Claire had to laugh. "I don't like scorpions either!"

When they reached his school, which was just a few minutes away, Graeme leaned forward to hug her.

"I'll pick you up after school, little man. Love you!" she said.

"The Lord bless you, Mommy." Graeme slung his backpack over his little shoulder and shut the car door behind him.

Trekking back past the Casa before turning onto Highway 285, Claire drove straight through the heart of Romeo. She slowed down as she went through town and paid homage to its deteriorated buildings, some of which housed ghosts from her past life.

There was the Romeo Fire Department, labeled by a crude sign someone had painted with a can of black spray paint and seemingly deserted. Its discolored plywood doors looked so tired that Claire could not conjure an image of a fire truck racing through them to perform a rescue. Were there still volunteer firefighters in Romeo, like her grandfather had been? Claire didn't know.

Next to the fire department was a seedy-looking liquor store. It had bars on the windows and a chain on the door. A woman who looked to be in her fifties was working on the lock with a key. The woman acknowledged Claire with a nod of the head when she lifted her hand in a wave.

On the other side of the liquor store was an abandoned building with several windows broken out. It had a rusted tin roof, with layers of brick, mortar, whitewash, and stucco all exposed, and Claire thought briefly that the building had character. A sign on the door, with peeling paint, still read "Curl Up and Dye." Claire sighed. That place used to be a beauty shop, where Abuelita had taken Claire to get her first perm.

On the corner was a white stucco building with three logs protruding from the face at the top. It wasn't labeled anywhere, but everyone knew the building as Abe's Bar. Below the logs were tinted windows, which at night were lit with glowing signs that advertised Corona and Budweiser. Claire smiled when she saw one that said *Tecate*. She'd been teased mercilessly in high school for asking Carlos Caballeros who "Tea-kate" was.

In the center of the windows was a set of double doors. They opened onto the sidewalk, which was just inches off the road. Had they been wooden and swinging from hinges, it would have seemed more appropriate somehow.

Claire remembered the time she'd witnessed a fight right in front of those doors, like a scene from a Western movie. She was with her abuelita, when they had gone to visit a sick person in one of the trailers. Claire remembered that Abuelita had put her arm around her as they drove by and told her not to look, but Claire had looked anyway. She couldn't resist. The look in the fighting men's eyes had scared her, and so had the crowd that was cheering them on.

Another time, Claire and her best friend, Martina, had been scared to death by a drunk coming out of those doors. He yelled nasty things at them at them while they passed by in Martina's Camaro. Claire never told Abuelita about that incident. There wasn't much to do in those days other than cruise the town, unless you went up to Salida.

On the other side of Main Street, another white stucco building was decorated by a fairly decent looking mural, a desert painting of a wolf howling at a full, white moon. This was the meat-packing business owned by Abe's son, Jerome, who was a butcher and somewhat famous in the valley. Claire had been there once with her grandfather before he died, to purchase antelope and elk for a charity barbecue.

Next to the meatpacker's, between it and the next building, was a vacant lot. Shards of sheet metal were scattered about the lot, which was grown up with weeds. A broken plastic bucket and sheets of old newspaper rolled across it like tumbleweeds in the wind and stuck to the rickety wood fence that served as the lot's rear border.

Adjoining the lot was a building that her best friend, Martina, had recently purchased and was busy transforming into a restaurant. Claire slowed her car to inspect Martina's most recent renovations. The cinder-block building had been freshly painted the color of burnt clay. Directly in the center, where ugly wooden doors had been, Martina and her husband had installed glass ones overlaid with ironwork in the shape of a gigantic desert sun. The painted sign above the doors, in Martina's fabulous signature style, read "Art and Sol." Claire recalled Martina's plans to convert the ugly vacant lot next door into a garden patio for parties and wedding receptions.

Claire sighed, admiring her friend's creativity, her ability to transform something useless and broken into something beautiful.

She pulled away from the strip of buildings that marked the end of Romeo proper, if there was anything proper about it. The housing district, which was next, consisted of two gravel roads lined with old trailer houses. From the steps of scattered trailers, where dogs barked behind fences and toddlers played in the dirt, a few men and women gawked back at Claire as she drove past.

Passing out of town, she saw that the grade school of her childhood was abandoned. The community center, next to it, looked almost as bad. It stood in a field of weeds against the backdrop of overgrown trees, whose leaves looked like brownish lace pasted to a blue sky. The white stucco facade crumbled in disrepair behind more chain link and signs that said DO NOT ENTER. *What else can these people do? Where can they go?* Claire wondered fleetingly. She was glad that Martina was trying to make a difference and hoped that her friend's new restaurant would breathe some life back into their hometown. *And I hope it doesn't suck the life out of her*, Claire thought forebodingly.

The only thing that seemed to be thriving at the moment besides Abe's Bar was the grain elevator and its adjoining feed store on the outskirts of town. An older man with a sack of feed over his arm tipped his straw hat at her affably as she drove into the vast landscape that swallowed up Highway 285 and made Romeo a memory.

Before Claire on the way to Alamosa, highline wires stretched out on the shoulders of stripped pines. They looked like an army of toothpicks the further they extended ahead of her on the highway. She wondered what the land must have been like before this acupuncture took it over— and then remembered that acupuncture is supposed to heal a person, relieve her pain, and not add to it.

＊ ＊ ＊ ＊ ＊

Claire arrived at Adams State College fifteen minutes before her first class. Unlocking the door to her office, she unpacked her bag, sorted the papers she needed to hand back to her students, and decided to check her e-mail.

Her inbox was mostly full of advertisements and forwards, which she promptly deleted. Glad to have that tidied up, she saw a message from Martina and opened it.

Dear Claire,

Did you see in the paper that they are calling my Mickey the new "Manassa Mauler"? I'm not sure what to think about that! I hope you are still planning on coming to the game. The coach is in our home church group and he says it will be a great match. Meet us on the fifty-yard line. Jesus and I are looking so forward to seeing you!

XXOO
Martina

Claire giggled. *Jesus and I are looking forward to seeing you.* Of all of the men out there, Martina would marry a man named Jesús.

At eight fifty, Claire walked down to the room where her nine o'clock composition class met. On the board, she wrote five quotes for the week's journal reflections:

1. *"By words the mind is winged."* Aristophanes
2. *"Injustice anywhere is a threat to justice everywhere."* Martin Luther King Jr.
3. *"Beauty is not caused; it is."* Emily Dickinson
4. *"In spite of it all, I still believe people are basically good at heart."* Anne Frank
5. *"It is better to have traveled and gotten lost than never to have traveled at all."* George Santayana

As she was writing, the class started to fill up.

"Where do you find these quotes?" Ryan Sellers, a freshman athlete from Pagosa Springs, asked her as he ambled by on the way to his seat.

Claire answered him without turning around. "I read."

"Well, I read, too, but I've never read that, about the mind getting wings."

"Sounds like you need to read a little more," Claire teased.

The class sniggered.

Turning to face them, Claire picked up their journals and began to pass them out. "When I hand back your journal, start copying the quotes for the next week. Remember that I require at least a page for each of the five entries; other than that, there are no stipulations. You can write whatever you want, within reason. I just want you to write."

She took attendance by looking around, noting in her grade book whoever was absent. After giving them a few moments to finish copying the quotes, Claire told them to gather up their things. "We're going outside."

The students followed her out of the building and down the steps. She guided them past the Honors College, across the courtyard, and onto the pathway that led through the giant oaks and wound about the campus. Under the oaks, she stopped and told her students to sit down. They all found places either on benches or on the grass beside the walk.

"On our school's Web site we have a picture of this pathway under the trees, and there's a caption that reads, 'Adams State College: Great Stories Begin Here.' Your assignment is to write a great story that begins, literally, here. I'll take them up at the end of class."

There were a few groans, a few nervous laughs, and many sets of wide eyes staring at her.

"Get started!" Claire commanded with a smile and then waved at Oscar, who'd just come out to the courtyard to smoke a pipe.

* * * * *

Later that day, as Claire drove the thirty minutes or so it was from the college in Alamosa to Manassa Elementary School, she thought about the assignment she'd given her Composition students. She and Rob had first met under those same trees. *I never expected my own story to turn out like this,* she thought. Pulling up at Graeme's school and seeing him standing there, she knew he was the best part of it.

"Hey, buddy!" Claire said as he piled into the car.

"Hi, Mom!"

She took his backpack and set it in the front seat, while he buckled up in the back. "How was your day?"

"It was good. I got to be the leader in the lunch line." Graeme's green eyes were shining.

"That's cool."

"Yeah. We say, 'My hands are locked behind my back; I'm standing straight and tall. My lips are sealed so I won't talk; I'm ready for the hall.' "

Claire tried to hide her grin. "Wow."

"Can we get a snack at Sonic?" Graeme begged. "I'm starving."

"I just happened to bring you an apple." Claire held it back to him.

Graeme took it and sighed. "Gee, thanks."

Back at the Casa, where Claire changed into jeans and a lime-green sweater, there was a note from Abuelita. The scrawl was a mixture of Spanish and English explaining that she had gone to Louisa's and would be back "when I get there." Claire rolled her eyes when she read that, hoping her grandmother would be okay driving in the dark.

They left a little early to pick up burgers at Sonic—at Graeme's request—and arrived at the game just in time for kick-off.

"Claire! Graeme! Up here!" A green-and-gold-clad Martina was waving her arms wildly from halfway up the bleachers on the fifty-yard line.

Claire and Graeme made their way through the crowd toward them, alternately saying "Excuse me" and "Pardón." When they reached Martina and Jesús, there were hugs all around.

"Sit down, sit down!" Jesús moved over to make room for Claire and Graeme.

"How was your day?" Martina asked Claire, keeping her eyes locked on the field.

"It was good. I did something a little different with my students."

"Oh yeah? What's that?"

"I took them outside and—"

Martina broke into Claire's sentence with a roar. "There they come!"

The Manassa crowd stood up and cheered as their team entered the field, led by Mickey Rodriguez. The Grizzlies were fired up. As they ran in, dancing like warriors in green and gold, Claire noticed a black man, apparently the head coach, taking charge on their sideline. He was pulling his players together for instructions even as the team captains met in the middle of the field for the coin toss. Graeme looked at his mother with excitement and pointed to Mickey. "There he is! There he is! Number seventy-six!"

In spite of her usual lack of interest in sports, Claire found herself enjoying the game. Mickey *was* a wonder, seemingly stopping every offender who came into his path and blasting through the Sand Lizards' defense like a runaway train. By halftime he'd already scored two touchdowns for the Grizzlies.

"We're kicking their but—tails!" Graeme cheered, glancing sideways at his mom as the team trotted off the field.

"Want to go get a drink?" she asked him.

"Sure, and I need to go to the bathroom."

"We'll be right back, guys," Claire told Martina and Jesús.

They climbed down the bleachers holding hands. In front of the bathrooms, Claire told Graeme, "I know you won't like this, but I want you to come with me into the ladies' room."

"Why, Mom?"

"So I can keep you safe. I don't want you going in that men's bathroom where I can't see you." Claire had heard too many news reports about disappearing kids to let him out of her sight.

"Mom! I'm in kindergarten!" Graeme protested.

"Precisely my point. Now come on."

When they finished in the bathroom, Graeme pulled Claire toward the concession stand. Several people looked familiar to her and a few seemed to smile in recognition, but Graeme was in too much of a hurry for her to stop and talk.

"Can I have one of those giant pickles?" He pointed to a jar he could see on the counter.

"Okay," Claire answered, "but we have to get in line."

They took their place behind a tall, stout man with a bushy braid down his back. Graeme, on a five-year-old's impulse, reached out and pulled it. The man turned around sharply.

"Hey, big guy!" It was Carlos. "I thought I was going to have to take somebody out! What you doing playing with my hair, boy?"

Graeme was suddenly shy. "I'm sorry."

"Oh, Carlos, I'm sorry, too," Claire apologized. "I don't know what got into him—"

"It's okay, it's okay. *No problemo*, right, big guy? Give me five." Stooping down to Graeme's eye level, Carlos held out his hand.

Graeme gave him five, slowly coming out from behind Claire's legs.

"How are you guys doing? How's the breathing?"

"We have an appointment next week with the specialist in Salida."

"I see. She's good—*muy buena*. You'll like her," Carlos promised.

"Are you here to watch the Manassa Mauler? He's our friend," Graeme bragged, finding himself again.

"*Sí*, I am, *hijo*. I am a great fan of the Grizzlies, as I once was one myself."

"I'm going to play football when I grow up." Graeme confirmed what his mother feared.

"I bet you'll be a fierce player—Graeme the Grizzly!" With that, Carlos growled and held his hands up in the air like a bear's front paws.

Graeme growled back.

"Oh, look, Carlos, it's your turn," said Claire. *Thank goodness.*

* * * * *

On their way back to their seats, Graeme spotted Billy Sanford, a friend from school, standing by the fence that bordered the field. He asked Claire if he could talk to him and she agreed, saying she'd wait and watch him. The fence was only a few feet away.

Claire's eyes were glued to Graeme and his friend when someone tapped her on the shoulder. "It's Claire, right?"

She turned her face to see Stephen Reyes standing beside her. He was dressed in jeans and a green polo shirt with a leather bomber jacket over it that matched the warm brown of his eyes. He smelled of wood smoke.

Claire looked back at Graeme, who hadn't moved. "Yes, Claire. And you're Dr. Reyes." She held out her hand stiffly. "Forgive me; I'm just watching my little boy."

"Graeme." He took her hand, squeezed it, and released it. "That's quite all right. But you can call me Stephen."

"Thank you, Stephen."

There were people milling about between the fence and where they stood. Claire could not be distracted from watching Graeme. What if he got lost? But Stephen just kept standing there. Finally, she laughed softly at herself. "I'm sorry; would you like to go with me over to the fence? It's this crowd—I guess I'm paranoid about losing Graeme in it."

She moved to within inches of Graeme and his friend, and Stephen trailed behind, sidling up to the fence on her other side. The boys didn't notice him.

"Hi Mom, this is Billy."

"Hello, Billy. Graeme's told me lots about you." Claire smiled at him warmly.

"Hi." Billy had red hair, a cowlick, and an ornery-looking face that was covered in freckles.

The two little boys went back to their conversation about the game and the Manassa Mauler.

Claire turned her attention to Stephen.

"Do you live here in Manassa?" he asked.

"Just outside," she replied, "In Romeo. What about you? Do you live nearby? Do you have a son playing?"

"Uh, yes and no." Stephen kicked at the dirt with his boots. "I live in Romeo, too, and I'm a friend of Coach Riggins. He's my running buddy."

"Oh," said Claire. "I see." She was suddenly aware of how attractive this man was, standing by her side, and the awareness was not entirely comfortable.

"How's Graeme's breathing?" Stephen queried.

"Good, since that day we saw you. I'm anxious to get it taken care of, though. Every time he sighs I get nervous, and I worry about him at school now. It will be good to go to Salida next week."

"Maria is a first-rate pulmonologist—and great with kids. I'm glad you're going to see her."

"That's what everyone says. Thank you for the referral." She smiled at him, revealing the perfect alignment of her teeth.

"Mom!" Graeme was pulling on her sleeve. "I need to go to the bathroom again!"

She turned to Stephen. "I guess I'd better go. Thanks for saying hi—it was nice to see you."

"You, too, Claire," he said, sounding completely sincere.

Chapter Four

....

The next morning Stephen had to make early rounds at the hospital in La Jara, but he was back home in Romeo by noon. Placing his keys in the pottery plate on the table just inside the door of the mud room, Stephen was waylaid by Regina and Duchess.

"How are you lazy girls today?" He rubbed each one, in turn, on her face and behind her ears. Their tails beat the floor like a set of drums.

"Ready to go out?" They sped through the door and it closed behind them. Stephen took off his Birkenstocks. Heading across the wood floor and into the kitchen to find something for lunch, he noticed the red light on his answering machine blinking. He went over to his desk to listen.

Beep. "Steve, this is Maria. Hope you're having a good weekend. I didn't know if you were on call. I was going to see if you were interested in coming up for a movie. That one we were talking about—*Small Town Girl*—well, I borrowed a copy. I haven't watched it yet; I'm waiting for you. I thought we could get dinner and watch it at my place if you want to. Let me know."

Beep. "Are you tired of credit card companies who charge higher interest rates after the low introductory rate expires? If so, we can help…" Stephen pressed ERASE.

Beep. "Uh, yeah, Steve, this is Joe. I was just wondering if you're up for a run this weekend. I'm watching film this morning at the field house, but I could do it later. Give me a call. See ya, man."

Beep. "Well, I guess you're already at the hospital or somewhere. Gene and I are headed to Sam's. I just thought I'd see if you needed anything. We'll talk at you later." It was Nell. Stephen grinned.

He went over to the fridge and stared into it for a while. Taking out some organic greens, petite carrots, strawberries, an orange, and a pear, he placed them onto the counter. Then he grabbed a bag of dried cranberries, dates, walnuts, and almonds from the pantry. To Stephen, this seemed like the makings of a good salad. He congratulated himself on his heart-healthiness.

When the thought of Claire came into his mind, he tried to shoo it away. But the thought came back like a butterfly landing on his shoulder. He couldn't seem to shake it off. *Is she married?*

He washed the greens and fruit in the kitchen sink using a colander, and then, picking the greens off the fruit, wished he'd done them separately. Next he read on the bag of carrots that they were "washed and ready to eat." He mused for a while about this and decided to wash them himself anyway. While all of that was drying on paper towels, he cut up the fruit, nicking his finger in the process and getting a spot of blood on his kitchen towel.

Maybe Carlos would know. But Stephen couldn't ask him. *No way.*

He placed the salad in a bowl as a mental lightbulb went off. *Maybe it's on her son's chart.*

Resolved to look first thing on Monday morning, Stephen added the nuts and dried fruit to the bowl and tossed it. Then he stirred together a little vanilla yogurt and honey and drizzled it over the salad. Grabbing a fork and some water, he went out to his sunroom. He settled into a leather chair to eat, enjoying a distant view of the San Juan Mountains in front of him.

Stephen's eyelids were heavy by the time he finished his lunch. Shrugging off the temptation to lean back in his chair and nap, he rose to his feet abruptly. There was too much that needed to be done on the ranch. Placing his dishes in the dishwasher and turning it on, he quickly changed into work clothes and boots.

The sun was high and the sky a vibrant blue when Stephen headed out the back door.

"Hello there, Miss Kitty," he called affectionately to the calico cat who called his barn home. "Any mice today?" The cat purred as she wrapped herself around one of his legs and then the next.

He went from stall to stall, looking at the rest of his animals. They'd all been fed early that morning, but he checked their water again and talked to them as if they were his friends.

"Oreo, you are the fattest pig in the county," he said to the six-hundred-pound sow he'd had for seven years. "I'm never going to sell you, and I certainly can't eat you—what am I going to do with you?"

The black-and-white pig sauntered up to the rails that were keeping her in, and Stephen leaned over them to scratch her on the back. She grunted her approval, did a little dance around the perimeter of her oversized stall, and then lay back down on some clean hay, looking up at him contentedly.

Stephen moved into the next stall to examine a sheep whose leg he'd been treating for an injury. "Looks like you're healing up just fine, Woolworth," he declared. "Good for you!"

Gathering his tools, Quickrete, and some barbed wire, he left the barn and loaded the back of his truck. Regina and Duchess jumped in before he closed the tailgate, and he drove over the cattle guard and out to mend the fence that marked the southeast section of his property. It had been damaged over a month ago by a wild teenage driver.

He called Joe Riggins on his cell phone as he drove.

"Hello?" Joe's rich baritone voice boomed out of the phone and seemed to fill the cab of the truck.

"Joe, this is Steve."

"Hey, man! You got my message?"

"Yeah. I was making rounds when you called." Stephen could hear adolescent voices in the background—locker room banter—and it brought back memories.

"Oh. You working this weekend?"

"No, just this morning. I'm home now. I've got to fix some fence."

"Oh yeah, Farmer Brown. You want to go running?"

"Yeah—that would be great. I can do it this evening or tomorrow. Either one."

"You want to do both?" Joe asked.

"Well, sure. Let's go for it."

"What time this evening?"

Stephen suggested, "You want to come over here?"

"That'd be all right. I'm open."

"Why don't you come around five o'clock? I ought to be ready by then." Stephen stopped his truck and turned it off.

"All right, then. I'll see you at five o'clock."

"See ya, Joe."

Stephen snapped his phone shut, got out, and surveyed the damage to his fence. Even though it technically had been repaired, the fence line still sagged in places like ruined guitar strings. The girl had been doing sixty—at least—when she hit it. Her car, a sporty red thing (according to Nell), had gone right through it, taking out a section thirty feet long. It came to a halt in the middle of the field, with the girl and the car sustaining only scratches. When Stephen was contacted at the hospital, his first thought was that she needed a doctor.

"No, *amigo*," the Romeo police officer had chuckled. "She's fine. These teenagers. Maybe it scared her enough that she'll get off that cell phone and slow down. We're calling you about the fence."

"Oh," Stephen had been relieved.

"Her daddy said he'd fix that fence for you this afternoon, but I thought I'd better call and let you know so you could decide."

"Hmm. Well, I guess that's all right. I'll need to come home, though, and move some cows before then, or they'll get out...."

"Your neighbor—Mr. Patrick—he's got that covered."

Stephen had marveled at the role this officer was playing in the drama. "Is this a normal day's work for you?"

"Yep. Welcome to the life of a small-town cop. It's about like *The Dukes of Hazzard*—only we're out west." He had laughed good-naturedly.

Stephen had hung up the phone, thinking about his cows and reminding himself of all of the reasons he'd left the city.

And today, as he unloaded his tools and supplies from the back of the truck, he was reminded again of why he left that life. The splendor of the San Luis Valley wrapped itself around him like mother-love. Along with hundreds of other settlers through the ages who had come here seeking peace, he had found solace in the valley. And on this patch of three hundred acres, Stephen was home.

The air—fresh and full of sunlight—smelled like cedar. Stephen breathed it into his lungs and exhaled slowly, just like he told patients to do when he wanted to hear their heartbeats. In a rare moment, he thought, *This feels like worship.* He let the moment be.

Thankful for the space around him and the absence of noise, Stephen walked up and down the new section of fence put up by the girl's daddy. Her father had reset the cedar posts and strung new barbed wire, but Stephen thought the posts needed bolstering. He wriggled each one to test its strength.

Going back to the truck to mix Quickrete in a bucket, he saw that Duchess had chased a butterfly across the road. In that same moment, a red car came roaring toward them, seemingly from out of nowhere.

Stephen's heart was in his throat as he waited for the dust to clear. When it did, Duchess came ambling toward him, emerging from the dust like a Phoenix. She slipped under the sagging fence and nudged him with her nose. Stephen's face burned as he patted her head. *That was too close.*

He shook his head, wondering if it was the same red car—and the same teenage driver—who'd hit his fence.

By four o'clock, Stephen had shored up the wobbly cedar posts and restrung the sagging barbed wire. Driving along the fence row before he turned across the field toward his house, he took inventory of the new section of fence. Eyeing the order that he had restored—the straight lines of gleaming wire, the strong, honest posts standing erect like soldiers—Stephen sighed with contentment. Even his cows looked happier.

* * * * *

Joe arrived promptly at five o'clock. He banged on the back door of Stephen's house and then backed up a bit. When Stephen came to the door, Joe was stretching his hamstrings.

"I do have a doorbell, you know."

"Yeah, but I don't wanna wear it out."

Stephen joined him in the yard but didn't mimic his contorted position. "You're wearing *me* out. What kind of a stretch is that?"

"It's one I learned from Frieda." Joe switched legs.

"Frieda? Who's Frieda?" Stephen lunged right and then left, slowly.

"Man, she's the cheerleading sponsor at Manassa. I thought I told you."

"Oh! I see."

"She knows her stuff, too. She's made me a lot more flexible."

Stephen raised an eyebrow. "I bet she has."

"Flexible's good. You might ought to try it yourself." Joe finished his stretch and moved to knock Stephen over.

They wrestled around a little bit, ending in a bear hug. Joe, the massive former linebacker, lifted Stephen, who had been a quarterback, off the ground. Stephen slapped him on the back.

"Good to see you, man. I haven't run since last time we went. I hope I can keep up."

Joe smiled. "I'll go easy on you."

They headed down the driveway and then turned left on County Road 7 toward the Patricks' white clapboard house. Stephen waved to Nell, who was in her yard taking laundry off the line. He could see Gene through the picture window, leaned back in his chair with his boots still on. There was a faint blue glow to the window, which signaled *Headline News*, but Stephen couldn't see whether Gene was watching or snoozing. *Probably a combination of both*, he mused as he ran by.

At the end of the road, they turned right onto Highway 285, which would take them past the grain elevator and right through the middle of town. Their normal route was to follow 285 out of Romeo and turn around when they were half way to Antonito, at a mile marker celebrating the Cumbres and Toltec Scenic Railroad. This would give them a little more than seven miles, which to Joe was Tiddlywinks but to Stephen was like climbing the Matterhorn.

It was six thirty when they finally arrived back to Stephen's. He grabbed two water bottles from the fridge in his garage and sat down beside Joe on the back steps.

"I'm about to pass out. There's no way I can do that again tomorrow."

"What?" Joe kidded him. "You cryin', weenie?"

"We can't all be superstuds like you. Anyway, tomorrow's supposed to be a day of rest. Let's do it again, say, Tuesday."

"I've got J.V. games Tuesday night. It'll have to be early morning."

"How early?" Stephen asked him.

"Five o'clock. Let's do it at my place."

"Okay, I can handle that." Stephen finished off his bottle of water. "Do you want to hang out a little while? I've got some steaks we could grill."

"Thanks, man, but I can't. Prior engagements."

Stephen stared down at his shoes.

"What are you doing tomorrow?" Joe offered. "You want to go to church with me?"

"Oh, you know, I've got farm stuff, or I may go up to Maria's. She called. We're thinking about watching a movie."

"That's one good-looking sister."

Stephen ignored the remark. "Tell me more about Frieda," he quizzed.

"She's a good-looking sister, too."

* * * * *

Stephen didn't go anywhere the next day, and on Monday he went in early to work. He was digging through charts and files in the ER when Carlos Caballeros came in for his shift.

"What's up, Doc?" he asked glibly.

"Oh, ha, ha, very funny, Carlos. Where's your carrot?"

The doctor's irritation seemed to surprise Carlos. "Is something the matter?"

Stephen looked up and felt his cheeks burning. "No. I just can't find the chart I'm looking for."

"What chart is that? Can I help you?"

"No, no, Carlos, that's okay." Stephen turned to leave the room. "I'm sure it will turn up."

"What are you doing for lunch today?" Carlos asked him.

"Honestly, I haven't thought about it. But why don't you come over to the clinic whenever you get a break? There's a drug rep bringing us lunch over there and I'm sure there will be a spread."

"Catch you then," Carlos called as Stephen headed out the door.

Stephen jogged across the parking lot that separated Regional Family Care, the clinic where he worked, and Conejos County Hospital, which served the clinic and also housed the ER where Stephen was often on call. Entering through the back door, he stopped by his office to check his schedule and saw that it was packed, as usual. Stephen pushed the button on his phone for the front desk.

"Yes?"

"Irene, this is Steve."

"Oh, good morning, Dr. Reyes." The usually persnickety receptionist sounded syrupy sweet.

"How are you today?"

"I'm just fine, Dr. Reyes; how about yourself?"

"Well, I'm just getting started back here, but I looked at my schedule and saw that I am double-booked almost all day long."

"Hmm, let me take a look." He could hear her long, curled fingernails clicking on the keyboard as she pulled up his schedule. "Well," she said as though it was a revelation, "yes, you are."

"Irene, I know this is not totally your fault, but as the office manager, you are going to have to remind the rest of the girls that it's against my policy."

She snorted, and her voice rose in pitch. "But, Dr. Reyes, what can we do about it? Everyone requests you. You don't expect us to turn people away, do you?"

"I expect you to schedule my appointments with enough time in between for me to actually treat people. I did not come here to slight patients so I could generate extra money for a clinic."

"Well! I've never heard such—"

"Irene, it is in my contract. No double-booking unless it is an emergency."

"I'll see what I can do, Dr. Reyes."

"Thank you."

Stephen and his regular clinic nurse, Desirae, worked the double-booked morning in what felt like double time. He tried to give every patient his undivided attention, to listen to all of their stories, and to treat them each as people with individual needs. Stephen wanted to give patients a personal touch—to truly know the people he was serving, which was one of the reasons he had moved to a small town. It was one of the places it could still be done. But even here, if you weren't careful, you could become a cog in a machine that kept people sick. Sometimes he felt like traditional medicine was so messed up—and this was one of those days.

After working nonstop through lunch, Stephen spotted Carlos coming through the door and noticed by his watch that it was two o'clock. He decided to take a fifteen-minute break with Carlos in the lounge, and over the leftover takeout the drug rep had provided, Carlos eyed Stephen warily while Stephen rubbed his forehead.

"Are you feeling okay?" Carlos finally asked.

"I'm fine. A little exhausted, I guess."

"Steve, what's up? I mean, I've worked with you for years now. I know when you're not on your game."

There was a pause before Stephen looked up at him, shaking the cobwebs free from his mind. He blinked and seemed to see his friend for the first time that day.

"I'm okay—just double-booked."

"Oh. Are you sure that's all? I mean, no offense, but you were acting a little weird in the ER this morning."

Stephen laughed. He was busted. "Carlos, you're a good friend, and you're right. I can't believe I'm this distracted by a woman."

"Oh, a woman!" Carlos's eyes suddenly lit up and his face broke into a smile.

Stephen suppressed a grin.

"Who? Tell me! The hearts of all of the other nurses will be broken at this news. *El Rey* of Hearts finally falls!"

"Shh! You can't breathe a word. I don't even know her. I mean, we've hardly met. I don't know anything about her."

"A mystery woman. Oh, this is *muy bueno*. I love mysteries." Carlos rubbed his palms together, waiting. When Stephen didn't say anything, Carlos reached across the table with his bear paws, motioning to choke him. "Are you going to sit there all day, or will you tell me who she is?"

"She's apparently very intelligent."

"Hmm."

"Seems like a good person."

"That's important."

They pondered this a minute and then Carlos quipped, "Is she ugly?"

"No. Definitely not."

"*Bonita*? Pretty?"

"More than pretty." Stephen's face warmed at the thought of her, and he felt like a fifth-grader.

"Ahh. I see."

"You know her."

"I do?" Carlos raised his eyebrows.

"Yes."

"Well, that narrows it down. I know everyone around here." He set down his plastic fork.

"She's not from around here. Well, I mean, she's not been around here in a long time…but now she is."

Carlos's face registered bewilderment before it suddenly seemed to dawn on him. "Claire? The Caspian C?"

Stephen backed up from the table, crossed his legs, and put his hand up, waving it slightly. "Not a word to anyone, Carlos, really. I can't believe I'm talking about this."

"Claire Caspian! You're in love with Claire Caspian!"

"Shh!" Stephen got up and shut the door to the break room. "Not in love! Don't be ridiculous. Just interested. And that's probably as far as it will go because I probably don't even have a chance with her."

"Well, *amigo*, I hate to tell you this, but you've got that right." Carlos nodded his head and sighed.

"What?"

"She's married."

* * * * *

On his way home that evening, Stephen resorted to country music. He turned it up loud. With the windows down in his truck and his hair blowing in all different directions, he tried to pull together the pieces of the story Carlos had told him. It wasn't complicated, really. She was married to a lawyer. They met at Adams. Carlos remembered the picture and announcement in the paper. After the wedding they moved to Arkansas, of all places, where he went to law school and she got her PhD. Carlos said she taught there and her husband worked for an international law firm. The boy was born in Arkansas. He didn't know why they'd moved back, unless it was just to be near her grandmother. Her *abuelita*. "Now there's a character," Carlos had said. "The richest woman in the county."

Carlos didn't know why Claire was alone at the hospital or the ballgame, but "You know lawyers," Carlos had said. "He could be a jerk, or he could just be out of town."

Chapter Five

....

It was pouring rain as Claire turned into the parking lot at the Heart of the Rockies Regional Medical Center in Salida. She pulled into the empty space nearest the door, which was not near enough, and turned around in her seat to wake up Graeme. Though he was technically big enough to be out of a booster seat, Claire thought it best to keep him in one for now. You could never be too careful. She also had him ride behind her, on the driver's side, in the backseat. The rationale for that arrangement was this: If she were ever in an accident, her impulse probably would be to swerve to protect herself. If Graeme were on the passenger side, he'd be more likely to get hurt. By keeping him on her side, Claire reasoned, he was definitely safer.

Graeme was buckled tightly—so tightly that even though he'd fallen asleep, he was sitting completely upright. His head had fallen over at an uncomfortable angle, resting on his right shoulder, and his mouth was slightly open. Claire didn't like to look at him this way. It was a bit unnerving. She touched his cheek and felt a warming sense of relief as his green eyes fluttered open and he looked at her, his eyes adjusting to wakefulness with several long blinks.

"Are we there?"

"We're here. Get unbuckled. See how it's raining? We have to make a run for it."

Claire got out of the car, opened Graeme's door, and grabbed his hand as he slid out. She closed the door behind him. Then they ran, side-by-side, the thirty yards or so that it was until they were under the breezeway and in the door. Claire's heels clicked on the sidewalk like fingers typing on a keyboard.

"That was fun!" Graeme exclaimed, shaking the water from his hair as it began to curl around his face.

The receptionist sitting at a nearby desk grinned at Claire.

Claire smiled back, smoothing her own curling hair and damp suit. The navy crepe was splotched all over with raindrops, and Claire wished she'd brought an umbrella. "Can you tell me where Dr. Maria Marquez, the pediatric pulmonologist, is located?"

"Sure. Her office is on the third floor. You can take the elevator to your left."

The sign on the door read MARIA MERCEDES MARQUEZ, MD. When they opened it, however, they stepped into a rain forest.

"Wow, cool!" Graeme said.

There was an aquarium the size of Claire's car on the wall to their right. It contained fish of many sizes, shapes, and colors, obviously tropical. In fact, it seemed to contain a complete, if miniature, coral reef.

"Nemo!" Graeme cried as he pointed to a clown fish. "And look! There's a sea horse, and some angelfish, and even a shrimp here on the bottom!"

The ceiling was painted dark green. The blades on the fans circling overhead looked like dried banana leaves. The furniture was brown leather, the tables bamboo. Silk palm trees decorated every corner. Murals on the three other walls depicted monkeys swinging on vines, parrots perched on branches, and tiny poison dart frogs. Other sets of eyes, belonging to gorillas and other jungle creatures, peeked out from behind giant fern leaves. And mounted to one of the walls was a wide-screen television playing Disney's *Tarzan*.

Claire gave Graeme's name at the desk and filled out paperwork while Graeme explored the wonders of the waiting room. In just a few minutes, his name was called by a nurse in khaki scrubs who was wearing a safari hat. After she weighed and measured Graeme and recorded his information, she took necessary instruments out of a belt that had several zippered pouches. The last one was full of candy, which she offered to Graeme. He pulled out a red sucker and thanked her.

"I like this place!" he told his mother, skipping ahead of her into the examination room.

Shortly after they were settled, the doctor came into the room smelling like lavender. She had fair skin, brilliant blue eyes, and lush red hair that formed soft layers around her face and flipped up slightly at her shoulders. Underneath her white coat, which had Bugs Bunny embroidered on the pocket, was a bright salmon blouse that coordinated with her floral-print Capri pants. She wore white sandals, and her toenails matched her blouse. She offered Claire a white, immaculately manicured hand.

"I'm Dr. Marquez." She smiled, revealing a set of perfect teeth.

Claire found the doctor's hand to be soft and warm. "Claire Caspian."

"And you must be Graeme!" Dr. Marquez turned all of her attention toward the seat next to Claire, bending her knees and squatting to reach Graeme's eye-level. "How are you today, buddy?"

Graeme looked at Claire and then back at the doctor. His eyes were wide.

"Is that a good sucker?"

Graeme nodded, keeping it in his mouth.

"Why don't you tell me what happened the other day on the playground? Did you have a little trouble breathing?"

"Yeah, I had an asthma attack." He took the sucker out just long enough to say it. Maria Marquez laughed. "I see. Those are pretty big words you're using. Were you afraid?"

"No. Well, maybe a little."

"Did you use an inhaler?"

"Yeah, but it didn't work. That's when I got to ride in the ambulance."

Graeme made a spinning motion with his sucker. "We went fast! That was so cool! We got to the hospital in no time!"

"That *is* cool. I like to ride in ambulances, myself. Did you get to hear the siren?" The doctor's excitement made her sound like she was close in age to Graeme.

Claire took Graeme's sucker when it circled by her head. He started to protest but then thought better of it. He re-engaged with Maria.

"No, they didn't turn it on."

"Bummer!" Maria said.

"I know; it *was* a bummer."

"Well, what happened when they got you to the hospital?" Maria was still on Graeme's eye-level.

"They got me better. I had to get a breathing treatment. Mommy came."

"Did you like Dr. Steve?"

"Who's that?"

"You didn't meet Dr. Steve?" Maria glanced at Claire, who supplied the answer.

"Graeme was pretty out of it by then. I think he sort of slept though Dr. Reyes's exam, so he may not remember."

"Oh," Maria said thoughtfully. Then she turned back to Graeme. "Well, Dr. Steve sure remembers you! He said you were a brave little boy and that I need to take really good care of you!"

Graeme smiled at her sweetly.

"Want to see a picture of him?" Maria asked Graeme, handing him a small framed picture, which Claire had not yet noticed, from off the counter.

"Oh, yeah, I remember him," Graeme said, handing it back to her.

"How about hopping up here on the table?"

After half an hour's worth of listening to Graeme's lungs, tapping on his chest, and peak flow testing, Maria ordered X-rays. Then she set

Graeme up in an observation room across the hall, where he watched *Finding Nemo* while Claire answered the doctor's questions.

"Is there a family history of breathing problems?"

"No," Claire answered.

"Eczema? Allergies?"

"No, not that I know of."

"How old was Graeme when this started happening?"

Claire relayed the incident that occurred in Arkansas when Graeme was three, as she'd told Dr. Reyes in the ER.

"Hmm. So, the Singulair was effective back then?" Maria's pen was smoking.

"Yes. He just took the one month of it, and we never got the prescription filled again, because there was a hard freeze. He didn't seem to need it after that. The few other flare-ups he's had since then have been easily controlled with the inhaler." Claire stretched her neck from side to side.

"How often is there a problem?"

"Not often—once or twice a year."

"Is it worse with exercise or at night?"

"Maybe...I don't know. I guess. It's happened with activity, like in the leaves that time or on the playground. And it's happened at night a time or two, but only when he's already been sick with a cold."

Maria pressed. "Cough? Fever? Any recurrent pneumonia? Other recurrent infections?"

"He had fever one of the times. Never any pneumonia. No other infections. He's been a very healthy child."

"What about diarrhea?"

"No."

"Was he premature? Has he ever had RSV? Any hospitalizations?"

"No, no, no."

Maria looked up from the chart at Claire and smiled reassuringly.

"I think we'll try some Singulair again. Let's do that for a month, and then I'd like to see you back. I'll give you a sample of a new inhaler, too. Try three puffs if he has a flare-up. Tell the school nurse *three*. I don't think he will have any problem on the Singulair, but if he does, call me and we'll need to see you sooner."

Claire gazed across the hall at Graeme, who was lying on a leopard-print beanbag, engrossed in *Finding Nemo*. "So, do you think he has a serious asthma problem?" Her eyes were tearing up.

Maria touched her arm. "I think he's got asthma, and we've got to control it so that it doesn't interfere with a wonderful, active life!"

Claire nodded.

Maria stood to leave. "Did you know the Arkansas River flows through Salida?"

"No," Claire said, waking up from a dream. She gathered hers and Graeme's things. "I mean, I guess I hadn't thought about it. But I know it begins in Leadville, and well, yes. Now that makes sense."

"There's a wonderful restaurant right on the river called Rumors. It's Steve's favorite place to eat when he comes here. If it's not raining anymore, you and Graeme should check it out." Maria flashed her white teeth again in another big smile.

"Thanks," Claire told her. She'd suddenly had her fill of the doctor and her office and was ready to get out of there.

Chapter Six

....

Five o'clock is brutal, thought Stephen as he got out of his truck. His eyelids, like the rest of his body, felt heavy.

Joe, on the other hand, was bounding down the front steps of his house, smiling like he had just swallowed a piano.

"You've got some big teeth," Stephen told him. "They glow in the dark."

"The better to bite with!" Joe slapped him on the back, making chomping sounds with his teeth.

"I'll tell you what bites, Little Red Riding Hood. It's running at five a.m. How did I let you talk me into this?"

They stretched their calves on the tailgate of Stephen's truck.

"As I remember, it was your idea. I tried to get your lazy butt out on Sunday, but you put it off until today. I can't help it I've got a game this evening. Some of us poor folks have to work."

Stephen smiled at him. "You know you love it."

"How far we going?" Joe finished stretching and then danced around Stephen like a boxer under the street lamp.

"You're the coach."

"Ah, that's what I like to hear. Let's go."

They turned left out of Joe's driveway and headed west. The town was still asleep, except for a few people in stray cars here and there who were either leaving for work in one of the bigger towns or returning from a graveyard shift. The only light was provided by street lamps, which cast an eerily phosphorescent glow.

Joe said he'd clocked a new route for them that would make nine miles, if Stephen was up for it.

"What if I'm not?" Stephen asked him, gasping for breath.

"I guess that's too bad." Joe grinned and stepped up the pace a little bit.

"That's what I thought."

They passed Dempsey Park, which honored Jack Dempsey, the town's most famous son; then they passed the Catholic church and the church of the Latter-Day Saints.

"Hey, you know how Manassa got its name?" Joe asked Stephen.

"Isn't there a Manasseh in the Bible?" Stephen managed to ask in between heavy breaths. "He was one of Joseph's sons."

"Aren't you the scholar," Joe ribbed him. "There sure is. The LDS who named this place named it after him—the dark-skinned boy—and his lost tribe."

"Ooh. I didn't know that."

"It used to be a big deal out here. There was a rivalry between Manassa and Sanford, which was named for one of their heroes. He was a white boy." Joe talked like he was lying in a hammock, while Stephen's cells were pleading for oxygen.

"Well, good thing Sanford doesn't have a football team, or they'd be in for some Manassa maulin.'"

"You got that right."

They ran in silence for several miles, and Stephen was thankful for the time to catch his breath. It was a great feature of their friendship that they'd always had, this ability to be quiet in each other's presence and feel perfectly comfortable. But there was something he wanted to talk to Joe about.

"Well, I hadn't mentioned anything to you, but I met someone last week and thought I was interested in her."

Joe almost tripped over his feet. "Are you kidding me?" He stopped and stared at Stephen, who blew past right him.

"Calm down, and come on. It was over before it started."

Joe caught up quickly and was back beside Stephen.

"What do you mean?"

"This woman came into the ER with her son, and I don't know—she just seemed amazing. Different. She wasn't wearing a ring, and then I ran into her again at your game on Friday. We talked a little bit. She was with her son, and I didn't see anybody else around, but then I found out on Monday that she's married."

"Oh, no, man. No way!" Joe's face made a painful expression, and he shook his head.

"Yeah."

"Are you sure? How'd you find out?"

They turned onto Joe's street and started walking to cool down.

"Well, you know Carlos Caballeros, the nurse who works with me."

"Yeah, yeah, I know Carlos."

Stephen panted. "Well, he knows her. Grew up going to high school with her in Manassa, in fact. Her grandmother's sort of a legend around here, at least to Carlos—a real rich lady. And I guess this woman and her husband just recently moved back here to be close to her. Get this—he's a lawyer."

"A lawyer? What's her name?" Joe asked.

"Claire. Claire Caspian. She kept her name, I guess, because the boy is Graeme MacGregor. I stooped to looking it up on his chart." Stephen laughed.

Joe turned and slapped Stephen on the shoulder. "Well, my man, I've got some good news for you, then," he declared with a broad grin.

Stephen couldn't possibly imagine why he was grinning. "What?"

"She ain't married—not anymore."

"How do *you* know?" Stephen's heart rate began to escalate again.

"Well, it's crazy, but you know what small towns are like. Manassa's no different."

"What is it?"

"Somebody tried to set me up with her."

"You?" Stephen didn't even try to hide his surprise.

"Wait a minute, man, what are you saying? She could do a lot worse!" Joe chided. "In fact, if she ends up with you, well…" He raised his eyebrows.

"Who tried to set you two up?"

"A guy with the hots for Frieda, who happens to be in the booster club."

"Sheesh, this sounds like a soap opera." Stephen shook his head.

"You're telling me. You ought to live here, coach here. I love it, but it gets interesting sometimes. Anyway, I said *no way*."

"Why?" Stephen asked him. "I mean, are you that tight with Frieda?"

"I'd like to be. If I can keep from messing it up. And your girl's not my type, if you know what I mean."

Stephen did. "Well, good for me."

Back at Joe's, he spread out a couple of towels he'd brought to protect his seat from sweat and climbed into his truck.

"Have a nice one, man!" he called to Joe.

Joe waved on his way up the steps. "You, too, Romeo!"

Stephen drove through Manassa just as most of its residents were starting to brush the sleep from their eyes. He pulled back onto Highway 142 toward Romeo and slowed, as much as he dared, when he drove by the Casa de Esperanza—the House of Hope. The sun was rising. He'd passed by this place a hundred—maybe a thousand—times in the years since he'd moved to the area. The extensive grounds, the white stucco mansion with its terra-cotta tile roof, the outbuildings and the great iron gates that encased it all—these had been of mild interest to Stephen in the past. He'd admired it from the window of his truck and occasionally when he and Joe had run by. But this time he studied it with greater intensity. Somewhere in his heart, something tiny stirred like a seed buried deep in long-fallow ground. *She isn't married—not anymore.*

Chapter Seven

....

It was early September, the time Rob's family in Arkansas called "Indian summer." Rob was leaving for a business trip to New York on Monday so they'd committed themselves to "doing nothing" over the weekend. "Doing nothing"—a term they'd affectionately coined during grad school—really meant that they were free from other demands and could do whatever they wanted.

"Let's check it out," he had said that Saturday morning over coffee when she pointed to the advertisement in the paper. And just like that, they packed a picnic, loaded Graeme in his car seat, and took off.

For about two hours they drove scenic highways from northwest Arkansas, where they lived, to the Arkansas River valley and a town called Paris. The highest mountain in Arkansas—a mere hill by Coloradan standards—was there, and the town was hosting its annual Butterfly Festival in honor of the many species that call Mount Magazine home.

They found a spot by Cove Lake, the small but pristine lake at the foot of the mountain, and spread out Abuelita's butterfly-patterned quilt. It was Claire's favorite quilt, and Rob poked fun at her for bringing it that day. "Leave it to you to be thematically correct," he'd joked. She fished a book on butterflies out of the basket and gently whapped him on the arm with it. "And who brought this?" she'd retorted playfully.

Graeme took Rob by the hand as he toddled toward some wildflowers that were growing nearby. Her guys. Claire admired the outlines of their shoulders. Rob's were broad and sturdy underneath his denim shirt, and he leaned over slightly to reach Graeme's hand.

Graeme's shoulder blades curved like little angel wings under his white T-shirt. As Rob ran his free hand through sandy blond hair, which was thinning, she smiled at Graeme's mop of dark curls. "You've got twice as much hair as your daddy," Rob had joked that morning when he gave Graeme a bath.

They began gathering sunflowers, black-eyed Susans, white zinnias and aster, along with a few orange flowers Claire couldn't name, which were sprinkled like confetti along the water's edge. As she unpacked the wine, cheese, and Gala apples, a delicious breeze caressed her, and she breathed it in, fixing the scene in her memory.

Graeme ran back to her on chubby legs, beaming, with a bouquet of the flowers. She kissed him and thanked him, arranging them as the centerpiece of their picnic. He sat bouncing on her lap, and she looked down for a moment to spread peanut butter on a piece of wheat bread. She was adding banana slices to make eyes and a curved row of raisins for a smile when she felt Rob's breath on her neck.

"*Mariposa.*"

Rob's hands. Cupped, then open. The calluses on his fingertips from years of playing guitar. His wedding ring.

The Silver Checkerspot flickered for a moment right in front of her face before floating in the direction of the water. Claire could smell Rob's aftershave, and she turned to kiss him, to see his face. But he was gone from her, too. Just like the butterfly.

She clutched Graeme tightly in the dark. Her pillow was wet when she awoke.

Claire tiptoed into the bathroom, so as not to wake Graeme, and splashed water on her face. The ornate clock on the vanity showed a little after six o'clock, which meant it was seven in Arkansas. Grabbing her cell phone out of the bedroom, she noticed the sun was rising. A lone truck was slowly passing by on Highway 142 near the front gates. She returned to the bathroom and closed the door gently behind her. She sat down on the rug and dialed a number she knew by heart.

"Hello?" A cheerful voice answered. "Hello?"

Claire's jaw was frozen shut.

"Hello? Is anyone there?"

Claire opened her mouth, but nothing came out.

The person on the other line said "Humph" and hung up.

Claire's hands were shaking as she dialed the number again.

"Hello?" the voice answered again, this time edged with irritation.

"Moira?"

"Claire? Is it you?"

"Oh, Moira, I'm so sorry."

"Claire! No, no—it's okay! You know you can call me anytime. I'm so glad to hear your voice. How are you? Has something happened? Is Graeme all right? Tell me what's going on." Moira's voice was soothing.

"I had a dream. It's been a few months since I've dreamed about him, but he was there. Right there beside me."

"In the bed? Was it like the old dreams? Were you in his hospital bed with him?"

"No. It wasn't that. It wasn't a nightmare, really—well, except for the end."

Moira sighed her relief. She'd stayed with Claire at night for six months during the last stages of a disease that had killed her brother. "Tell me about it."

"We were on a picnic. Rob and Graeme and me. On Mount Magazine—by the lake. There were flowers and butterflies—it was so beautiful." Claire's voice cracked.

Moira waited, then affirmed, "I remember you telling me about that day."

"It was before the diagnosis. Months before. We didn't have a clue anything was wrong. I was happy—so happy. I don't even know that person anymore—the person I was in my dream." Claire tucked her knees up under her chin.

"What happened in the dream? What happened in the end?"

"Graeme brought me a bunch of flowers. He sat down on my lap and I was making him a sandwich, and Rob came up behind me. He kissed me on the neck. I could smell him, Moira!" Claire reached for the roll of tissue and blew her nose.

Moira, too, remembered the rugged, clean smell of her brother. "I know," she said to Claire.

"Then—then he held out his hands in front of my face. They were strong and full, like they used to be—and his ring was on. It still fit. They were cupped around something. He opened them—I could see his calluses. A little butterfly flew out of his hands. It was so delicate and playful. Graeme giggled and reached for it when he saw it. I turned around to see Rob—to kiss him—but he vanished." Claire's voice sounded desperate now. "And then I woke up. I wanted to sleep forever and stay in that place with him—to try to find him again—but I woke up!" She closed her eyes like a dam, to try to hold back the tears.

Moira spoke slowly. "What a blessing."

"What do you mean?"

"I mean, this is the first time you've called me after a good dream. What a blessing it is to hear of this beautiful memory—this wonderful day that can never be stolen from you."

"But he vanished. He's gone!"

"I know. And we must wake, and live, and go on. And I believe you are doing that. I believe even this dream is a part of that."

"But it hurts. It still hurts so much."

"I miss him, too. We will always miss him. But we honor his life when we choose to live. I know it's what he would have wanted for you, for Graeme, for all of us."

The bathroom door opened and Graeme stumbled in, rubbing his eyes. His hair was sticking up in every direction, and he was wearing Batman pajamas.

Claire pulled him into her arms, and he snuggled into her lap there beside the bathtub.

"Is that Aunt Moira?" he asked.

"Yes," Claire answered, handing him the phone.

Chapter Eight

....

Stephen dialed the number, not thinking about the fact that it was only six fifteen in the morning. A groggy voice answered.

"Hello?"

"Maria? It's me. Did I wake you up?"

"Yep."

"Oh, sorry. I wasn't thinking about the time. I've been up since four-thirty."

"That's why I'm a specialist and you're insane," she told him. "But your rounds aren't usually *this* early, are they?"

"No. I went running with Joe. He's a slave driver."

"Oh. Well, you're both insane." Her voice was still sleepy.

"Look, I really am sorry. Why don't we get off and you can go back to bed?"

"Oh, no, it's fine, babe. Fine. I need to get up anyway. Besides, I'd better talk to you when I've got the chance. Did you get my message on Saturday?"

Stephen felt a twinge of guilt. "Yes—sorry I didn't call back. Busy weekend."

"Were you on call?"

"Uh, no." She sounded like his mother. "I had a lot of stuff to do on the ranch."

"Okay. Well, what about the movie? Do you still want to see it?"

"Yeah, sure. How about this weekend? Do you have anything going?"

"The symphony on Saturday."

"What about Friday night?" Stephen asked her.

"That would be fine. When can you get here?"

"I'll check the schedule, but I think around six. Is that good for you?"

"Perfect. You want to go to Rumors?"

"Sounds great."

He could hear her rustling around on her bed. He knew she often fell asleep reading and was probably looking for her glasses.

Maria offered, "Are you going to stay over?"

"Maybe—I'll have to see what's going on Saturday. But that would be cool. You could make us pancakes for breakfast."

"Or you could," she countered.

"I'll call you when I check the schedule, just to make sure."

"Okay—talk to you then."

"Love ya."

"Love you, too."

* * * * *

That evening after he finished up at the clinic, Stephen grabbed a bite to eat and drove north to Alamosa. Pulling into a parking space marked Visitor in front of the Student Union at Adams State, Stephen turned off his truck and grabbed his backpack from the passenger's seat. Rummaging through it, he found the brochure titled, "Talk to Me: A Seminar in Bilingual Education for Modern Medical Professionals." There was a map on the back which directed him via sidewalk from the Union, past a small chapel, to the imposing red brick building that housed the Honors College. The building bore the name Gunther.

Even though it was dusk, the grounds were well-lit and Stephen located the building without any trouble. Passing through the broad double doors at the entrance, he saw a sign that pointed to the auditorium. He followed the arrow and soon found himself in a room

full of people. The only seats left were in the front. He sat down in one
of them just as the seminar started. A woman with great legs in red heels
was walking toward the podium.

"*Buenas tardes. Soy Claire Caspio, profesora del inglés aquí en Adams.*"

Stephen's heart skipped a beat when he heard her voice, her name.
He looked up to see her face, and she met his gaze.

"*Me han pedido hablarles esta noche sobre la importancia de la
educación bilingüe en el campo de la medicina. Pero primero, necesito
advertirles que soy ex-convicta y acabo de escaparme recientemente de la
carcel. Tengo una condición mental seria. Todos ustedes están en peligro
grave, y deben llamar a la policía. Cuántos de usted pueden entender lo
que estoy diciendo?*"

Two or three people besides Stephen raised their hands. An older-
looking man laughed, and a woman glanced in the direction of the door.

"Great." Claire walked toward Stephen. "Dr. Reyes, can you tell
everyone else what I just said?"

"Well, I didn't catch all of it, but I know you said your name," he began.

"That's good, Dr. Reyes."

Everyone laughed.

"Then you said you're an English professor here and you were
going to speak to us, something about using two languages in medical
practice."

"Okay, fine. What else?"

"Then you said you were hungry and in danger of starvation, and we
should call in a pizza. Something like that, I think."

"That's actually close, Dr. Reyes." Claire smiled at him and walked
back behind the podium.

Stephen sensed he was being teased.

The older man who had also raised his hand cleared his throat.
"That's not exactly what she said." His hair was pulled back into a

ponytail and he looked like he just stepped out of a Louise Erdrich novel. He wore several big turquoise rings.

"That's true, sir. What is your name?" Claire asked him.

"Henry Banks. I'm semiretired, but I work in the wound clinic here a few days a week."

"Okay. Well, what can you tell us?"

Dr. Banks sat up straight in his chair. "You are an escaped convict with a mental condition. We are all in grave danger and need to call the police!"

Claire smiled at him and Stephen colored.

"Excellent! I think we've just illustrated the point of how important clear communication can be—and that pertains especially to the medical profession, where many of you deal with life and death situations."

* * * * *

During the break, Stephen walked up to the table where Claire was getting a cup of coffee. Her red suit buttoned down the front and the skirt ended just above her knee. Her nails were short with square edges. She wore neutral polish. With a glance, Stephen confirmed that she wasn't wearing a wedding ring.

"Thanks for embarrassing me," he joked.

"Oh, that. Well, I'd have to say you accomplished that all by yourself," she answered teasingly. She looked at him with her emerald eyes and then cast them down to her cup. He noticed that her lashes were long and full.

"I didn't know you were leading this seminar. You're doing a great job. Usually Continuing Ed is so boring."

"Thanks." She didn't look up.

"You're right, you know, about communication being important. I was trying to explain something the other day to one of my Hispanic patients, and I felt like an idiot. She had a cyst on her ovary, and I think I described it to her as a balloon full of blood. It was so embarrassing. I had to get Carlos in there to help me."

Claire laughed. "Well, at least you tried. Have you had much Spanish?" She took a sip of coffee and studied him from over her cup.

"No. I mean, well, my dad is Puerto Rican, so I heard some Spanish from him growing up, but not a whole lot. My mother is Irish and we lived in Oklahoma. There just wasn't a lot of opportunity."

"Did you visit relatives in Puerto Rico or take any Spanish in high school?" Claire smoothed her skirt, and Stephen was secretly jealous of her hand.

"We only went there once to see my grandparents. I've had a few classes, but—as you can tell—I'm not too good at it. I get by around here, but not as well as I should." Stephen shifted his feet.

"Well, you could take a few classes at Adams," she offered.

"Do you teach them?" He looked up, maybe too eagerly.

"Uh, no. I don't teach Spanish. I teach Comparative Literature though, for bilingual students."

Stephen looked disappointed.

"Probably the best thing you could do is go to Spain or even Mexico for a few months, to immerse yourself. We offer immersion courses here."

"Actually, my brother-in-law is doing that right now. It's a sort of mission trip, but he's getting immersed in the culture as a bonus."

"Really?" Claire said, and Stephen thought he saw a shadow pass across her face. "Interesting." She looked at her watch.

"Hey, listen, I know the break's almost over, and I've taken most of your time. But, if you don't mind, um, can I see that mole on your leg?" Stephen bent down for a closer look.

"What?" Claire backed away from him.

"It's just that—well, I noticed you have an irregular mole on your shin. I'd like to see you get that removed."

Claire looked like she didn't know whether to thank him or slap him.

He stood up and laughed softly. "I'm sorry. I just—"

"It's okay—thanks. I'll think about it." She turned away from him to throw away her cup and returned to the podium.

Stephen thought she seemed a little stressed as she gathered her notes, and he hoped he hadn't caused it.

* * * * *

"An irregular mole? How lame is that?" Maria was laughing so hard that she almost fell out of her chair. They were sitting on the patio of their favorite local restaurant beside the Arkansas River.

Stephen stared at her.

Maria laughed even harder. She was wiping her eyes with a napkin now. "Definitely original, Steve. Not your usual pick-up line." She cackled some more.

"Gee, thanks."

Maria opened her menu and held it up to her face, concealing a grin. "Let's see, what am I going to order?" She pretended to be engrossed in the dinner offerings at Rumors.

"Is it that bad? I mean, yeah, I was staring at her legs. That's true. But she does have a bad mole. Was it wrong to tell her about it?"

"No." Maria suppressed more laughter. "Certainly not! It was your Hippocratic duty. What a dedicated professional you are. I am very proud of you!"

"You're impossible."

"Seriously, knowing you, she probably found it very charming. Plenty of women would love to show you their legs."

"I don't think she's that type."

"No, me neither." Maria agreed.

"But do you think I offended her? By how I handled it, I mean?"

Stephen wished he could take the words back as soon as he said them, but she was already reared back, guffawing.

"Handled it? Let's see, how exactly did you *handle* it?"

"Honestly, Maria, I'm going to pitch you into that water. Let's just change the subject." Stephen smiled in spite of himself and then asked, "Have you talked to Mom or Dad lately?"

Chapter Nine

When Claire got to work on Monday morning, she looked up the number for Stephen Reyes, MD., in La Jara.

"Well, ma'am, it looks like he's booked up all this week with regular appointments. Was it something urgent?"

"Uh, no," Claire said. "He just suggested I come in to have a mole removed."

"The doctor suggested it?" asked the receptionist.

"Yes. I saw him recently at a seminar and he noticed it."

"Oh—I see."

Claire could hear the clicking of keys on a computer keyboard.

"Well, ma'am, since the doctor suggested it, why don't we get you in today? I can work you in after eleven o'clock."

"I'd have to be back in Alamosa for a class I teach at one o'clock. Do you think that's possible? Otherwise, I'll just take the next regular appointment."

"I'll make a note of it. I think it can work if you're here right at eleven thirty."

"Okay, thank you."

* * * * *

The towns of Alamosa, Estrella, La Jara, Romeo, and Antonito are dots on the map of southern Colorado. When they officially sprang up in 1880, it was the railroad that connected them, because trains had to stop for water every seven miles. Today, one connects the dots by driving Highway 285.

Claire was not nearly as frantic this day as she'd been the last time she'd driven from Alamosa to the hospital in La Jara. That was the day of Graeme's asthma attack and the first time she ever laid eyes on Stephen Reyes. He'd been a certain, albeit small, presence in their lives ever since. And now here she was, meeting him again. She didn't even know for sure where his office was, though she assumed it was near the hospital.

Just a block before she reached the hospital, on the same street, Claire noticed a clinic she'd totally ignored the other day. A sign read, REGIONAL FAMILY CARE and among the three doctors listed was Stephen Reyes, MD. She parked her car and went in. It was exactly eleven twenty.

The receptionist looked much like Claire might have imagined her. She was in her late fifties, with dyed black hair, penciled eyebrows, and reading glasses on the end of her nose. They were attached to a silver chain that hung around her neck.

"May I help you?" She looked up at Claire over her glasses, which featured multicolored rims. Her nametag read IRENE.

"Yes. I'm Claire Caspian. I'm here to see Dr. Reyes."

Irene, studying Claire's cream satin blouse, black palazzo pants, and pearls, smiled. "Of course." She handed her a clipboard. "Fill this out for me, honey, and I'll need your insurance card."

After exchanging the needed information with Irene, Claire plopped down in one of the chairs in the waiting room. Unlike Maria Marquez's office, Stephen's was as plain as they come. There were a few nice Ansel Adams prints on the walls—Claire recognized the Grand Tetons and the Snake River—but other than that it was bare. The furniture was standard, and the only distractions provided were an assortment of magazines scattered about the place. Claire thought the selections testified of a varied clientele: the current *Time, Newsweek,* and *National Geographic* shared table space with various editions of *People; Fur, Fish and Game;* and *Better Homes and Gardens.* Claire pulled *On Chesil Beach,* the novella by Ian McEwan, out of her purse and opened to her place.

Her cheeks burned a few moments later when her name was called, as if the nurse could sense what she'd just read about a tortured couple on their honeymoon. She shoved the book into her purse and stood, smoothing her pants.

The nurse's nametag said DESIRAE, and Claire inwardly cringed at the corrupted spelling of the French word. Desirae was a friendly girl in her midtwenties, however, who had graduated from Adams State.

"Let's get your weight real quick," she said, ushering Claire down the hall toward the scales.

"Ooh, that's no fun," Claire told her. "Is it totally necessary?" She removed her black slingback pumps.

"I'm afraid so." The nurse laughed. "But what are you worried about?"

She recorded Claire's 135 pounds and measured her height at five feet six inches.

"We'll put you in exam room one."

The exam room featured a print of a red poppy by Georgia O'Keefe. After answering a few questions, Claire settled into another chair—this one a bit more comfortable than the one in the waiting room—and opened up *On Chesil Beach* again.

Dr. Reyes came in quickly, looking somewhat flushed.

"Claire. Dr. Caspian. How are you?" He smiled at her, showing the slight chip in his front tooth. Then he sat down across from her.

"Fine, thank you, except for my mole."

"Of course. I'm glad you came in." He looked towards her purse. "What's that you were reading?"

"Oh, that. It's a book by Ian McEwan. He's a British author, most famous for—"

He finished her sentence. "*Atonement*. I love that book."

"You do?" Claire felt oddly surprised and pleased.

"Yes. Not crazy about *Saturday*, though."

"Me neither." Claire paused. "Though I think he was using that novel to continue the conversation he opened up in *Atonement*—you know, concerning modernism."

Stephen looked at her quizzically.

Claire went on, scraping polish off her thumbnail as she spoke. "Well, in the way he addresses the question of a writer's responsibility in literature."

Claire realized she was talking to Dr. Reyes as if he were one of her students.

Stephen smiled at her admiringly. "I don't think I quite got all of that from *Atonement*. But I did think it was a great story. I was actually very touched by it." He looked down.

"Me, too." Claire looked down at the book in her hand. "And this one—well, I'm not far enough along to know yet whether I love it. It feels a little bit like another experiment. But it's better, so far, than *Saturday*."

Desirae came back in with a tray that held supplies.

"Oh, thanks, Desirae. But I'm not quite ready to begin. Could you give us a couple more minutes?" Stephen stood to take the tray.

"Uh, sure." Desirae looked a little confused, but she exited.

Claire felt a little self-conscious when the door closed again. "I'm sorry—I got into my English teacher mode."

"No—don't be. I mean, I like talking to you." Stephen looked right into her eyes. Then he looked at her chart for the first time. "I guess I do need to get you out of here on time, though; it says here you need to get back to Alamosa for a class at one o'clock." He held up Irene's yellow sticky note.

Claire relaxed her shoulders. "Well, if it's possible."

He explained the procedure, which amounted to placing a miniature cookie cutter around her mole and pressing it out. "I have to do it that way to get enough tissue for the lab to test it—for melanoma."

"Melanoma?" Claire's eyes glistened like a deer's in front of headlights.

"I don't think it's anything, but we want to be sure." He opened the door and motioned to Desirae, who came in to assist.

With Claire seated on the exam table, they pulled out an extension in the front so she could fully straighten her legs. She rolled back her wide pants leg on the right side, to just above her knee, and rolled down her fishnet stocking. The imprint of the stocking carved little diamonds into her skin, and one diamond perfectly framed the mole, which was midcalf and almost directly on top of her shinbone.

Desirae handed Stephen a syringe.

"This is the only thing that will hurt," he told her, gently administering the Lidocaine to the tissue surrounding the mole. It felt like a wasp's sting but subsided much sooner.

Desirae took the empty syringe and handed Stephen the punch biopsy. He placed it precisely over the mole, taking in about two millimeters of the tissue around it so that the total circumference was similar to that of a pencil eraser. His hands were steady and assured.

Claire was intrigued to watch, to see herself being cut while feeling no pain.

Stephen pressed the end of the punch biopsy, and there was a tiny *pop* as it extracted the mole. He set it on the tray and then immediately applied pressure to the incision site with a piece of gauze doused in aluminum chloride. As Claire watched in fascination, he pulled the skin together with two perfect stitches.

"I'll take these out for you in ten days, if you'll come by," he said.

"I think I can do it myself." Claire smiled at him.

"Have it your way." He placed the bandage over her stitches as if he were handling a piece of fine china. "But don't pull that stocking back up."

"Okay."

He helped her down as Desirae left the room with the tray.

"We will call you with the results from the lab," said Stephen. "It can take up to two weeks, but it'll probably be sooner than that."

Claire held out her hand bravely. "*Gracias*," she told him.

"*De nada*," he took it, smiling, and then he added, "Take care."

On the drive back to Adams, Claire found herself going over the details of her doctor visit and smiling. Then she remembered Maria.

Chapter Ten

....

Desirae, who was filling out papers at her work station, looked up and eyed Stephen with suspicion when he came out of exam room one.

"What?" He tried to suppress a grin, but she could see the crinkles around the edges of his eyes.

" 'Oh, thanks, Desirae, but we're not ready yet. Could you give us a couple more minutes to chat?' " she crooned, flapping her arms like a chicken.

"Did I look that ridiculous?"

Desirae arched her eyebrows in response.

"I didn't say *that*, did I? I surely didn't say 'to chat'?"

"Well, maybe not; I don't remember. But that *is* what you were doing, isn't it?" Her eyes bored holes through him.

"What's wrong with it if I was? I try to talk to all of my patients, you know, to get to know them. It's called *good bedside manner*. You should try it sometime!" He poked her in the side with a tongue suppressor.

"You won't suppress my tongue that easily," she said and then whirled back around in her chair to face her desk.

* * * * *

Stephen worked through lunch, and he was peering into little Suzy Phillips's left ear with an otoscope when the emergency room called.

"They need you over there *now*," Desirae's eyes said "urgent" when she popped her head through the door.

"Call Suzy in a prescription for Augmentin—ten days. Bobby at

Medi-Quik will know the dosage." He scribbled something on the chart.

Desirae nodded and turned to follow his instructions.

Stephen paused in the doorway to address Suzy's mother.

"I'm sorry; I have to go to the ER, but I saw infection in that one ear. Desirae will call something in right now so you won't have to wait around for me."

"Thanks, Dr. Reyes," said a grateful Libby Phillips to his back.

Like a mother hen, she gathered up Suzy, the twins, their suckers and shoes, and their bag full of books, toys, crackers, and diapers. She followed him out of the exam room and then stopped at the front desk to pay.

"There's no charge," Irene said through pursed lips.

"Oh, no, there must be some mistake," Libby opened her checkbook. "He was in a hurry. Remind me—what's the usual office visit? I should remember." She smiled pleasantly at Irene and shifted Jake to her other hip while Johnny pulled on her leg.

"I said it's no—"

Suzy knocked over a container of pens on Irene's desk, spilling them all over the floor.

"Oh, I'm so sorry! Here, let me get those." Libby bent down, trying to pick up the pens, while Jake wailed at the inconvenience and Johnny joined him. Suzy stared at Irene, who stared back at her over her glasses. "Help me pick these up!" Libby told Suzy.

When the pens were settled safely back onto the desk, Libby brushed back several stray hairs, shifted Johnny, and asked Irene again, "What's the charge?"

Irene showed her the chart, pointing with a pen to Stephen's distinctive scribble. *No charge.*

"I have to follow the doctor's orders," Irene told Libby, sounding like she regretted it.

* * * * *

Stephen ran on foot to the emergency room and got a briefing from Carlos before the ambulance arrived. Matt, the EMT who had called ahead, said the prognosis was not good. There was no pulse and the chest compressions weren't working. But nothing could have prepared Stephen for what he would see.

The girl's hair was blonde—or had been before it was soaked in blood. Her face was deathly white and scratched in places. Stephen recognized her as the neighbor girl, Sydney Evans—the one who had mowed down his fence with her red car. He sighed. This was what hurt about working in a small-town ER. Recognition was unavoidable.

In the few seconds it took for Carlos to gingerly cut off the girl's clothes, Stephen struggled to keep his clinical mind dominant for the visual exam. It was hard. He could hear a woman crying in the waiting room. Sydney's pink T-shirt, now in tatters on the floor, had a horse on it, much like the one she often rode with her dad down their dirt road. She wore Wrangler jeans, which were tough for Carlos to cut through, and Stephen could see a phone number written in pen on her hand. When Carlos got the jeans off, Stephen, who was now at her feet, noticed that she had a tiny butterfly tattoo on her left ankle.

Carlos prepared the chest shocks, and they tried them. But nothing worked.

He knew she was technically DOA, but that didn't stop Stephen from trying to bring her back. He worked with her body for two hours. The fear and grief of her parents—whom he knew were waiting in the next room—weighed heavily on him, spurred him on. But in the end he could not save her. The flesh was not willing—her spirit, long gone.

When Stephen emerged from the girl's room, he felt a hundred years old.

"Mr. and Mrs. Evans?"

The attendant at the desk motioned toward the tiny chapel, a room set aside for prayer and times like this.

Stephen opened the door quietly. A couple was huddled together on the front bench with their backs toward him. Light poured through a stained-glass window, illuminating the single wooden cross that hung on the front wall.

Marsha Evans, the girl's mother, flinched as if Stephen had hit her when he opened the door. She turned around and looked into his eyes, wildly searching for signs of hope. Stan Evans rose, and Stephen motioned for him to sit back down. He could see that they were holding hands.

Stephen walked forward and knelt on his knees in front of them. He put his hand over both of theirs and bowed his head. A large tear rolled down his cheek and hit the burgundy carpet, darkening the spot where it hit for a moment as it soaked into the fibers, then disappeared. He raised his head to look them in the eyes.

"Your daughter is gone."

* * * * *

That night, instead of staying home, Stephen drove over to Joe's. When he parked his truck in the driveway, he noticed that the yard was freshly mowed and everything as usual was neat as a pin.

He beat continually on the door until Joe finally answered in a fluffy white towel. The towel was stretched around his waist, and water glistened like diamonds in little droplets all over his huge dark shoulders and chest. His face was half shaved, and he held a razor in his hand. Stephen had a sudden flashback of Apollo Creed from one of the *Rocky* movies.

"Man, you crazy?" Joe asked.

"Yep."

Joe stepped aside and Stephen walked through the door, shoulders sagging. Joe shut the door behind him and ushered his friend into the living room. He pointed to a black leather couch.

"Sit down, sit down. You all right, man? You look like you've seen a ghost or something."

Stephen smiled weakly. "Well, you are quite a sight in that towel."

"You okay?"

Stephen nodded. "You're dripping. Go finish your shower. I'm just here for Bible study."

Joe smiled, showing teeth that matched his towel and shaving cream. "Whoo, boy. God's answered my prayers!"

When Joe was dressed, Stephen helped him make coffee and boil water for tea. Just as he had done when they were roommates, Joe kept everything in perfect order in his kitchen, and it was easy for Stephen to find things. They set out juice and a bucket of ice and several mugs and glasses with napkins on the tiled bar.

"You'd make somebody a good maid!" Joe punched Stephen in the ribs as he spread store-bought cookies on a plate. They had just finished up in the kitchen when people began to file through the front door.

Joe introduced each person who came in to Stephen, describing him as his best friend from college. He seemed particularly happy to introduce Frieda, a small, sleekly muscular woman with skin the color of dark chocolate. Her almond-shaped eyes gleamed with what Stephen perceived as inner delight, and her hair was a perfect explosion of tight curls, layered smooth and long around her oval face. Nimble fingers squeezed the hand he offered and shook it earnestly.

When the introductions were done and drinks served, the group meandered toward the living room, where they formed a circle around

Joe's big round coffee table. Stephen lingered back, refilling his coffee before joining them. Frieda, leading the way, plopped down in a red-and-black-striped chair that swallowed her, and she put her feet up on the ottoman. Joe heard the doorbell and went to get it.

On the coordinating loveseat, which had a geometric pattern, a Mexican couple named Martina and Jesús settled in. A white couple named Sue and Jerry took the couch. Across from the couch was a rocker, which was empty until a Native American with a salt-and-pepper ponytail came in and sat down in it. Stephen recognized him as Dr. Banks from Claire's seminar.

"Last but not least!" Joe slapped Dr. Banks on the back. "Glad you could make it, bro!"

Joe got a chair from the dining room and offered it to Stephen. When Stephen refused it, Joe pulled it up beside Dr. Banks in the rocker. His hulking form dwarfed the dining chair. Stephen sat down instead on the fireplace bench, just outside of the immediate circle. He sat quietly, lost in his thoughts, observing this group that seemed as eclectic as a patchwork quilt.

"Well, I'm glad you all could come tonight," Joe began. "It's good to be with God's people, and I'm glad to have you here in my home."

The group members nodded their agreement, exchanging smiles with Joe and each other. Stephen noticed that Frieda looked especially comfortable in her chair, as though she was right at home.

Joe continued, "You know, in the book of Acts, Christians came together in homes, and the Bible says they broke bread and prayed. So, we've broken bread—or cookies"— everyone laughed at this —"and now I'd like to pray."

Joe bowed his head. He paused, breathing deeply. Stephen, eyes open, observed that Frieda held out her hands as if to receive something. Dr. Banks stared at a knot in the hardwood floor. Martina looked up but closed her eyes. She was gripping her husband's hand. The others, like Jesús, bowed their heads and closed their eyes.

Joe's voice, always strong, was softened around the edges as he spoke. He sounded as if he was addressing an old and honored friend.

"Thank You, Lord, for this day. Thank You for the life You live within us. Thank You for bringing us together in this place and meeting us here." He opened his palms in front of him and leaned back his head. "We look to You to lead us tonight, and invite You to do Your will among us. Come, Holy Spirit, and fill us. Teach us about Jesus and make us more like Him. In His name."

Joe didn't say "Amen."

There was a charged silence.

Then Frieda, in a voice like deep water, began to sing: "I love You, Lord, and I lift my voice to worship You, oh, my soul, rejoice. Take joy, my King, in what You hear. May it be a sweet, sweet sound in Your ear."

One by one, each member of the group joined in the chorus, and they repeated it several times. Martina and Frieda lifted their hands. Joe stood and raised his to the sky. They sang together like strings on a harp—each voice blending into the others and quivering with the same soulful longing—but also separate, sounding their own distinctive notes, telling their own personal stories of love.

Jesús whispered, "*Sí, Dios.* Yes."

Dr. Banks, his eyes not moving from the spot on the floor, said, "Hallelujah. Thank you, Father."

After a meaningful quiet, Joe sat back down in his seat, and the people in the group slowly opened their eyes and shifted in their seats, settling in.

"Well," Joe said, "who is in need of ministry tonight? What is the Lord speaking to our hearts?"

Martina said, "I'd like to ask prayer for my friend—the one Jesús mentioned? She's really going through a hard time right now. She lost her husband a few years ago and just recently moved back to this area. She has a small son who is having a few health problems—nothing serious, I don't think—but now she had to get a mole removed today because of possible skin cancer. It's probably benign, but, well, she just needs our prayers."

Stephen's skin prickled.

"And let's pray for that poor family who lost their daughter today in a car wreck." Sue reminded everyone of the news that was all over town.

Stephen bowed his head and listened while the others took turns talking to God.

After the time of prayer concluded, Joe asked, "Well, does anyone have a word they'd like to share?"

Jerry grabbed his Bible from the couch. "I do." He read aloud from Psalm 107.

"They cried to the Lord in their trouble, and he saved them from their distress…He stilled the storm to a whisper; the waves of the sea were hushed. They were glad when it grew calm, and he guided them to their desired haven."

Jerry looked at Sue. She beamed at him, even though her eyes were full of tears.

"You know we've tried for years to have a baby. Some of you have been with us through it all—the hoping, the heartache, all of the doctors."

Martina and Frieda, eyes as big as Frisbees, practically danced with anticipation.

"We're having twins!" Sue shrieked. "I'm past the first trimester!"

The whole group erupted like a volcano full of joy. The women squealed with delight, hugging Sue, and the men smiled, pumping Jerry's hands and patting him on the back. Stephen saw Jesús wipe away a tear.

"Praise the Lord!" Joe cried. "God is good!"

* * * * *

That night before turning out the light, Stephen picked up the Bible on his bedside table and brushed the dust off its worn leather cover. He turned to Psalm 107 and read:

"Some wandered in desert wastelands, finding no way to a city where they could settle. They were hungry and thirsty, and their lives ebbed away. Then they cried out to the Lord in their trouble, and he delivered them from their distress. He led them by a straight way to a city where they could settle. Let them give thanks to the Lord for His unfailing love...for He satisfies the thirsty and fills the hungry with good things."

Chapter Eleven

....

"On Monday, we discussed Zora Neale Hurston and *How It Feels to Be Colored Me.* Many of you did a great job with your analyses of her brown bag metaphor, which she uses to describe the view that people of all races are basically the same on the inside."

Claire walked up and down the rows of the classroom in a plum-colored suit, passing out their graded essays. Her black high heels clicked on the tile floor.

"Before we dismissed, I told you we were going to have a "Brown Bag Special" in class on Wednesday."

Most of the members of the class smiled, exchanging glances with one another.

Claire continued, "So, for the Brown Bag Special, you were all to bring a paper bag with you to class today. In these bags, you were supposed to place three miscellaneous things that represent pieces of your life and be prepared to share them. By doing this, we will test Hurston's view as well as learn a little more about one another. Did everybody bring a bag?"

She could see that most of them had bags on their desks, but a few reached into backpacks to pull theirs out. Ryan Sellers held his up, shaking it.

"Did you bring a bag, Dr. Caspian?" he asked her.

"As a matter of fact, I did," she answered, revealing hers from behind the podium and setting it on top. "Now, who would like to go first?"

"I will," said a dark-haired girl on the back row.

"Okay, Lauren."

"Well, you can see I painted my bag half red and half white, since my mother is Ute, and my father is Anglo." She held up the bag.

"Interesting. What's inside?" Claire inquired.

Lauren reached into the bag. "The first thing is this pen, because I like to write and my dream is to become a writer."

"Great. I'm glad to know that. What's next?"

"This is a picture of my favorite place." Lauren held up a postcard of Scotland. It featured the Edinburgh Castle.

"Edinburgh?" Claire swallowed hard.

"Yeah. Well, Scotland. That's where my father's family is originally from. I think I'd like to live there someday."

Claire forced a smile. "Okay, what else?"

Lauren reached into the bag again and held up a mirror. She turned it around so that Claire and the others could see the back of it, which was printed with the name THELMA.

"Okay, does everybody see that? It's a mirror that says *Thelma*. What can you tell us about it, Lauren?"

"This was my grandmother's mirror. She carried it in her purse all the time before she died."

Lauren turned the mirror to her face and looked into it with her hazel eyes. Then she looked at Claire. "When I look into this mirror, I see my past—and my future."

The class broke into a few oohs and aahs.

Claire said, "Nice job, Lauren. Very thoughtful." Students like this made her love teaching.

"Who's next?" she asked, looking around the room.

Ryan Sellers, on the front row, raised his hand. His blue eyes were innocent, and he smiled with a slight underbite, which some girls found irresistible.

"Okay, Ryan. Show us your bag."

He made a great production of rustling his paper bag. The first thing he pulled out was red plastic, with gold metal on one end.

"What's that?" Claire asked him.

"It's a shotgun shell. I use these puppies to kill deer, elk, antelope, you name it."

Claire felt queasy and hoped it didn't show. "I see. Uh, what else do you have in there?"

Ryan pulled out a can of Skoal and presented it on his open palm.

Some of the class laughed, and Claire raised her eyebrows at him. "Thank you very much. And, just what, I wonder, could be the third thing in your bag?"

"You'll be proud of this one," Ryan declared coyly.

"Really? Why is that?"

"Well, you told me I need to read more. So I started on this book." He reached back into the bag and pulled out a large paperback, which he handed to Claire.

"*Pro Bass Fishing*," she read the title aloud. "That sounds like a real classic."

"What's in your bag?"

"Yeah, show us yours."

The class urged her, so Claire opened her bag. "I don't know if I can follow that," she declared, looking in Ryan's direction.

He was beaming like an opossum.

Claire's lithe fingers reached into the plain brown bag and pulled out a small, leather-bound book. "This is a copy of Shakespeare's sonnets that I bought in his hometown of Stratford-Upon-Avon. I keep it in my purse."

"Ooh, neat," someone said.

"Sounds like some light reading," commented Ryan, who looked at his teacher as if she were from Mars.

Claire set the book down on the podium. She pulled out the second thing from her bag, which was a red hog with an *A* painted on it.

"What's that?" Ryan stared.

"It's an Arkansas Razorback. That's where I went to graduate school." Claire set the figurine beside the sonnets.

"Can you call the hogs?"

"You bet." She could see that his respect for her had just grown. Claire pulled out her third item.

"This is a very precious stone." She held it out in her hand, and walked around the class so everyone could see it.

When she passed by his desk, a boy named Landon said what they were all thinking. "Aren't precious stones like jewels? That looks like a regular rock to me."

"This stone is more precious to me than a diamond, because my son Graeme gave it to me yesterday. He picked it up on the playground at school."

"Aw," Ryan cooed sarcastically, "isn't that sweet."

"It *is* sweet," said Claire, "and that's precisely why it's precious. Thank you for your keen observation, Mr. Sellers."

She let that sink in a moment before turning her attention to another student. "What's in your bag, Landon?"

When class was almost over and everyone had shared the contents of their bags, Claire stood behind the podium again to address them.

"Well, I'd say we proved Hurston had a point. Even though the insides of our bags revealed different objects, those objects represented the same things—love, memories, accomplishments, dreams. As diverse as we are in culture, gender, and age, our class has a lot in common, don't we? Hurston would say it's the same for all human beings.

"Consider Hurston's notion of humanity as you read Kurt Vonnegut's speech, 'Fates Worse than Death,' which starts on page five hundred of our books. Would he agree or disagree? Jot down your thoughts. We'll discuss

Vonnegut, and particularly his views about war, in the next few classes."

There were both groans and knowing smiles from respective students as she ushered them out of the class.

* * * * *

Back in her office, Claire emptied the contents of her paper bag. She placed the Razorback figurine back in its home on her bookshelf and the book of sonnets into her purse. She was rubbing the precious stone from Graeme between her fingers when the telephone rang. It was the quick, double ring of an off-campus call.

"Hello."

"Uh, yes. I was trying to reach Dr. Claire Caspian." It was a man's voice, but Claire couldn't quite place it.

"This is Claire Caspian."

"Oh. Okay." The guy was stammering. "Claire, this is Stephen Reyes."

Claire felt the blood drain from her face. She hadn't allowed herself to worry—not too much—about the mole. *Surely, surely it was benign.* She'd told herself that over and over. *But why did the doctor sound nervous?*

"Yes, Doctor?"

"Call me Stephen."

"Okay—Stephen—what is it?" Claire didn't mean to be short, but she wished he'd get on with whatever he had to say.

"Your mole was benign." He sounded almost as relieved as she felt. "Nothing to worry about."

"Oh, that's good." She sighed and turned the stone over in her hand. "Thank you very much for calling me."

"Sure. You're welcome." He paused.

It was just then that Claire realized that *he* was calling and not his nurse.

"Claire?"

"Yes, Stephen?"

"Are you busy Saturday night? I mean, would you like to go out to dinner?"

He sounded so nice, so earnest. But Claire was appalled.

"I'm sorry, I can't. I have…plans." She hated him for putting her in this position.

"Oh," he said, sounding hurt. "Okay."

She hung up the phone, thinking of Maria, who had been so good with Graeme. *How could this man be such a jerk? He even recommended Maria.* Claire wouldn't be going back to *his* clinic.

* * * * *

When Abuelita arrived with Graeme from school, Claire was waiting on the steps in front of the English building. She jumped into the front seat of Abuelita's white Cadillac and buckled up just as Abuelita sped off.

"Watch out for that speed bump!" Claire hollered, and Abuelita's car cleared it, airborne.

Graeme bobbed up and down in his booster seat. "Yee haw!"

Abuelita glanced back at him in the rearview mirror. "You're showing your Arkansas roots, Graeme!" she told him.

Abuelita was wearing a long, gold skirt, a cream-colored blouse, and a matching crocheted shawl. Her hair was swept into a French twist and held in place with tortoise shell combs, which matched her huge sunglasses. A big diamond ring glinted in the sun as she gripped the steering wheel, and she tapped her fingers as though keeping time with some secret music.

Claire reached back to tighten Graeme's seat belt. "How was your day at school, honey?"

"It was good. Billy Sanford brought this awesome lizard for show-and-tell. It was so cool. I wish I had one."

"Your mother used to catch them *en la casa*, on the patio. They would hide from her in the cracks between the bricks and under flower pots. She could show you. She was a great lizard catcher in her time, that one." Abuelita nodded affectionately toward Claire as she wheeled out onto the main road in front of Adams State.

Claire smoothed her skirt and straightened her shoulders. "That's right! He just doesn't know that yet because there's a shortage of lizards in Arkansas—at least compared to here." Turning toward the back she asked, "What else happened at school, Graeme? What did you learn today?"

"I learned two plus two, but I already knew that."

"Did you learn anything new?"

"I learned that Ms. Lopez doesn't like lizards."

Abuelita reared back her head and laughed, and Claire couldn't help but join her.

* * * * *

"I can't believe how time flies!" Dr. Maria Marquez held her arms out wide when she walked into the exam room, and Graeme leapt into them. She was wearing an earthy brown dress with a turquoise belt and a necklace with huge turquoise beads. Graeme fingered it. Maria shifted him to her left hip and held out her right hand to Abuelita. It was adorned by a dangling turquoise bracelet. "Are you Graeme's grandmother?"

"Great-grandmother," Abuelita smiled at Maria and took the younger woman's hand in both of hers.

"This is my abuelita," said Claire, inhaling the fresh scent of lavender. "We live with her."

Maria nodded respectfully at Abuelita.

"Yeah," said Graeme, as Maria set him down on the exam table. "She's got a big, big house, and a goldfish pond, and a pool."

"Well, that sounds neat," Maria said to Graeme, as she looked into his ears. "I don't see any monkeys in there today," she reported. "What's your favorite thing to eat?"

"Breakfast tacos and hot chocolate. Abuelita makes it for me before school."

"Really? Well, let me see in your mouth. Open up and say, *Ah.*" Maria pressed gently on Graeme's tongue with a grape-flavored stick. "Wait a minute!"

Graeme's eyes got wide.

"Open a little wider!" Maria ordered. "I think I see a chocolate frog in your throat!"

"Like on Hawwy Pottuh!" Graeme exclaimed, still holding his mouth open wide. "Thosth ah magic!"

"They can also appear when a person drinks lots of hot chocolate. But chocolate frogs are very elusive. Ooh—he disappeared!" Maria feigned disappointment. She moved the stick all around Graeme's mouth, as though searching for something. "We lost him, Graeme!" she exclaimed and took the stick out of his mouth.

Graeme searched her eyes, smiling. The quizzical look on his face said he wasn't quite sure if she was kidding or not.

"Are you going to dress up for Halloween?" Maria asked him.

"I'm going to be Peter Pan, and my friend Gabbie's Tinkerbell," Graeme explained.

"Super cool. Just watch out for Captain Hook!" Maria curled her index finger like a hook and held it up."

"If we see him, I'll slash him with my sword!" Graeme said, pretending to do just that.

After faking her demise as Captain Hook, Maria morphed into the doctor again. "Can you take some deep breaths for me?" She placed her stethoscope on his back. "That's good—breathe in, then out." They repeated this several times.

"Everything sounds good. How has the Singulair been working?"

"He hasn't had any problems, but then again, he really wasn't having obvious problems before. The other episode was sudden," Claire explained.

"What about the sighing?" Maria probed. "Is he doing that as much?"

"No. I'm not noticing it near as much."

"Me neither," Abuelita agreed.

"Well, that's great. I'd say the Singulair is working. Let's stay on that until winter; then we might be able to take a break until spring."

"Do you think he's going to have to take it routinely? Always?" Claire asked Maria.

"My guess is that he'll need it for a while—but let's take one step at a time, okay?" She smiled her perfect smile at Claire, who observed that Maria's eyes were the same color as her beads.

Abuelita interjected, "You know the other doctor, Dr. Reyes? He removed a mole from my granddaughter's leg."

"Really?" Maria seemed taken aback by this sudden shift in the conversation.

"Yes. You can understand my concern." Abuelita tilted her head regally, holding out her hand in an inviting gesture. "I would like to know your outlook. He says it's benign, but should we get a second opinion on this?"

Claire turned crimson, then scarlet, then ruby-red. She looked out the window, longing to disappear.

Maria smiled warmly at Abuelita, and her eyes were as lovely as the Caribbean Sea. "Well, I may be prejudiced when it comes to my brother, but I'd trust him with my life."

When Abuelita heard this, she dropped her purse, spilling its contents onto the floor. Claire was grateful for the distraction, as she was suddenly overcome by a coughing fit.

"Water," she sputtered in Maria's direction. "Can I have a glass of water?"

Chapter Twelve

....

Stephen would never understand women. Claire had rejected him, just when he thought he was being a gentleman. Wasn't that what they were supposed to like? It was downright confusing! He couldn't pity himself too much, though, when he thought of the Evans family who had lost their daughter. No.

After his abysmal week, Stephen was looking forward to a quiet weekend. He wrapped things up at the clinic, changed into his farm clothes, and walked out to his truck. There was a note on the windshield, lodged under the left windshield wiper. It was on hospital letterhead.

"Call me sometime!" the note said and listed a phone number. The signature read "Ashli," and the "i" was dotted with a heart.

Stephen rolled his eyes. He remembered a former colleague from Colorado Springs. Pete had willingly perpetuated a myth about himself, started by spurned nurses, that he was gay.

"You're crazy," Stephen had told him in the cafeteria one day over coffee.

"You'd understand better if you weren't married," Pete had countered.

Pete had turned out to be right.

Wadding the piece of paper into a ball and tossing it into the passenger's seat beside him, Stephen sat down in his truck and sighed.

After he dropped off a bundle of his scrubs at the cleaner's in La Jara, he drove through McDonald's. Ordering a Big Mac Combo made him feel slightly like a rebel. Neither Joe nor Maria would believe it, if he told them. He hadn't been to McDonald's since he read *Fast Food Nation*, which further impressed upon his psyche the ills of a drive-through society. In fact, he'd spent considerable energy avoiding McDonald's as well as other fast-food joints. He frequently counseled his patients to do the same.

But today he didn't care. He didn't care about corporate deception, exploited workers, mistreated animals, or even his own clogging arteries. He ate his burger and fries in silent dissent as he drove down the road listening to Johnny Cash.

* * * * *

"Stephen? Stephen Reyes? This is your long lost neighbor, Nell Patrick."

The clock on his nightstand read six o'clock. Stephen stumbled out of bed in his boxers and walked into the other room, where Nell's voice was practically yelling out of his answering machine. He could hear Gene in the background saying, "He's probably out feeding."

"Hello?" Stephen picked up the phone.

"Hey, stranger, are you ready to work some cows?"

Stephen had forgotten their plans.

"Nell! Oh—this is embarrassing. I forgot to pick up the extra stuff at the Co-op." He opened the door to let out Duchess and Regina.

"That's all right. I think we have enough anyway. If not we'll run to the feed store. Do you want to start here or at your place?"

"I guess it doesn't matter. What's best for you guys?"

"Well, come on down here. I've got breakfast ready. We can do ours first, come in and eat lunch, and then go do yours. That be okay?" Nell sounded excited.

"Sounds good. I'll be down there in a few minutes." He hung up the phone, marveling at how well she administrated the business of both of their farms.

Fifteen minutes later, Stephen stood at the Patricks' back door.

"Come in here, stranger!" Gene opened the door for Stephen, who immediately smelled coffee and bacon. He shook hands with Gene.

"How are you, my friend?"

"If I felt any better, I'd be in heaven."

Stephen laughed. "That's a new one."

"A guy at my church says that. I thought I'd try it out on you." Gene smiled at him. He pointed towards the kitchen table. "Sit down, sit down."

Stephen obeyed as Nell set a steaming mug of coffee in front of him.

"Thanks, Nell." He sniffed appreciatively. "That smells good."

She put her hands on his shoulders and leaned over to kiss him on the cheek. Her curlers scratched him a little, and Stephen could smell lemon verbena.

"How you doing, hon?" Nell padded back over to the stove in fuzzy house shoes. She brought them a bowl of sausage gravy and a plate of flaky homemade biscuits and then returned to the kitchen.

"Man, I wish we could work cows more often," Stephen told her. "Nobody else ever feeds me like this."

"You know I'll feed you anytime you want me to," Nell smiled at him, plopping down a platter of scrambled eggs and bacon. She finally sat down after her last trip to the stove.

"Thank you, Lord, for these Thy gifts we are about to receive," Gene said as he filled his plate.

Nell added, "Amen."

"How are you guys doing? It seems like I haven't seen you all week," Stephen opened a biscuit and covered it with a rich helping of gravy.

"Well, pretty good," Nell answered him. "We've both felt good this week, but of course we've been up to the Evanses' place a time or two. I took some food, and Gene helped him with his cows on the day of the funeral."

Stephen's eyes dimmed and he set down his fork. "That was an awful deal."

"Yes, it was. It *is*." Nell stirred her coffee sadly. "They told us you were the one at the hospital." She poured in cream and stirred some more.

"Yeah," said Stephen. "It's something I'll never get used to."

"The Lord used you to minister to them, I believe," Gene offered.

Stephen kept silent.

"Well, what else?" Nell queried. "Are they working you too hard up there at the hospital?"

"Not too bad," said Stephen, "That one night was horrible, but I don't really have a right to say it was horrible for me. I can walk away. It's those parents who…" Stephen broke off.

Nell and Gene both looked down at their plates.

"Since then I've not been back to the ER. I've had to put in some long days at the clinic, though. One of the other doctors has been on vacation this week." Stephen tried a small bite of his breakfast.

"Did you go somewhere Tuesday night?" Nell posed, changing the subject.

He had to smile inwardly at the image of Nell in her bathrobe, watching out the window as his truck drove by.

"Yeah, I did. I went over to my friend Joe's to a Bible study."

"A Bible study?" Nell's voice was full of cautious energy.

"Good for you," said Gene.

"It *was* good. I was glad I went," Stephen told them. He took another bite of biscuit and washed it down with coffee.

"Do you want to tell us about it?" Nell asked.

"About what?" Stephen baited her.

"The Bible study. You know, you rotten thing. We've been trying to get you to go for years." She squinted her eyes at him.

"It was good," Stephen held, smiling at her. "I liked it."

Gene laughed while Nell scowled at them both. "Men!"

* * * * *

After breakfast, Gene and Stephen went out to the barn to prepare the vaccines, ear tags, and other supplies they'd need for working the cows. Nell finished cleaning up the kitchen, dressed herself in overalls and boots, and joined them. Stephen noticed that her hair was still in curlers under the red bandana she had tied around her head.

"Have you got a date tonight?" he kidded her.

"What do you mean?"

He pointed to his head.

Nell's hand went up to hers. "Oh, these? Well, you don't think I'd take them out for a bunch of cows, do you?"

Stephen grinned as he sharpened his pocket knife on Gene's whetstone.

"Beside, Gene and I do have a date. We're going to Sam's Club."

"Ooh, Gene, now that's romantic!"

Gene's eyes wrinkled like thin paper around his eyes. "I might even take her to Wendy's for a Frosty. You like those Frosties, don't you, hon?"

"Yeah, I like Frosties. I like dip cones, too." Nell picked up a bucket she was going to fill with water. "But, speakin' of dates, are *you* ever going to have one?"

Stephen looked at her for a moment as though he was deciding something. Then he answered slowly, "I was hoping to have one tonight."

Nell dropped the bucket. "You were?"

"Yep, but I got turned down." Stephen went back to sharpening.

Gene looked up and said, "You kidding me?"

The very idea seemed to make Nell angry. "She must have been blind *and* stupid."

* * * * *

Working the Patricks' cows went as smoothly as possible for a somewhat messy situation. The three ranchers formed an assembly line in the old corral. Nell's job was to prod the cows, using a stick, into the rusty chute. Gene stood on one side to put in their ear tags, and Stephen stood on the other to administer shots. Few of the cattle went through willingly, but most were manageable—until it came time for the bull calves. It was as if they instinctively knew what was about to happen. Nell reluctantly turned on her electric prodder for them.

As she got them into the chute, Gene put the ear tags in each one, and Stephen gave the shots. Then, using his razor-sharp pocket knife, Stephen neutered them as quickly as possible. Gene doused the area with Fulvicin spray solution to stop the bleeding and prevent infection.

When they released the calves after the cutting, their behavior was unpredictable. Instead of heading for the gate and open pasture, many jumped and danced wildly about the corral, as though demon-possessed. One calf kicked a slat out of the rickety cedar gate before exiting, and another time Stephen had to climb up on the chute to keep from being rammed.

"They don't like you," Gene said, grinning.

* * * * *

When the three neighbors were finished working all of Gene and Nell's cattle, they scrubbed their hands and arms in the yard. Stephen was glad he'd worn the plastic apron he brought with him. He held it up, and Nell sprayed off the blood and manure with the hose until the water ran clear. Then they hung it on her clothesline to dry while they ate lunch.

"We sure do appreciate your help," Gene told Stephen between bites of chicken salad. "I don't know if Nell and I could do it by ourselves anymore."

"Oh, well, it's my pleasure," Stephen told them.

"Your pleasure to cut those bull calves?" Nell looked like she might lose her lunch.

"You know what I mean."

"Tell me again just why that's the best way to do that. I trust you and all, but it sure didn't seem as horrible when me and Gene used to band them. And that was bad enough."

"Well," Stephen began, "they need their hormones to help them grow and develop to be good to sell. You can band them and then give shots with the hormones, but this way is more natural."

Nell's eyebrows furrowed. "Natural is not always everything it's cracked up to be—ask those calves. And ask me about natural childbirth!" She set down her fork.

"I know, Nell, and you and Gene can do it any way you want to. I'll help you band them if you want to go back to that. But in the end I think this way is better for the animal and for the people who will end up eating the meat."

Stephen took a bite of his sandwich.

Nell didn't look entirely convinced, but Gene said, "He's right, hon."

A few minutes later she served the apple pie she'd made that morning. "I guess we better be getting on up to Stephen's while we've got plenty of daylight," she said, scooping vanilla ice cream into their bowls.

Stephen, who had been quiet for a few moments, made a decision.

"Guys, I think I'm going to give you the day off." He pushed back from his plate. "I didn't get my cows up last night, and that's going to take some time to do. Could you come over tomorrow afternoon, if I get them up tonight?"

"Well, sure," Gene answered. "What time?"

"I know you have church and then usually take naps." Stephen grinned at them.

"We can miss our naps tomorrow," Nell offered.

"That's not necessary, Nell." Stephen rose and carried his dishes over to the sink. When he got back to the table, he looked into her eyes and smiled. "Thanks for feeding me. That pie was truly amazing."

Nell beamed. "We'll see you tomorrow, then, kiddo."

He bent down and kissed her on the cheek.

Gene stood up to walk out with him, and when they were out on the porch, Stephen reached into his pocket for his wallet.

"Will you do me a favor, Gene?"

"Depends what it is." Gene cut his eyes toward the fifty-dollar bill Stephen held out to him. "I'm not taking any of your money."

"This is a gift. Heaven knows I cost you and Nell enough in food today," he laughed.

But Gene didn't laugh. "You more than made up for that with all the work you done. We couldn't do it—I mean not near as smooth—without you." He hooked his fingers through his belt loops and gave Stephen a long, hard look.

"I can't explain it, Gene, not now—but I need you to take this. Take it, and you and your bride go out on a real date. Wherever she wants to go. Who knows? Give her that option and this may not be enough." He smiled into Gene's weathered eyes. "But at least it will be a start."

Stephen held the money out, but Gene just stared at it.

"I'm begging you to take it."

Gene shook his head, but the pleading look in Stephen's eyes finally overcame his pride.

"The kid really was begging. I could hardly turn him down," he would later tell Nell over filet mignons at Rumors, that snazzy little place in Salida they'd seen advertised on TV.

Chapter Thirteen
....

"Are you sure you want to do this?" Claire asked Graeme as they drove over to Martina's house on Saturday afternoon. Martina's daughter, Gabbie, was having a birthday party, and she had invited Graeme to sleep over.

"Sure, Mom. I mean, I can't let Gabbie down. Out of all of the people who are going to the party, she chose *me* to spend the night."

Claire thought he suddenly looked so big in his starched jeans and Rugby shirt, strapped down in the seat behind her.

He went on. "Aunt Martina let Gabbie pick out snacks just for us, and we're going to watch a movie and sleep in sleeping bags!" His green eyes sparkled with wonder.

"Graeme, you don't ever want to sleep in your own bed at home. I won't be there. Are you sure you can make it at Aunt Martina's in a sleeping bag?"

"Mom, this is different. I'll be with *Gabbie*. She's my best friend."

Claire smiled at him through the rear-view mirror. "Okay. Well, I think you're very brave, and this is going to be lots of fun. Just remember if you need me, I'll keep my cell phone on. You can call at any time."

"Okay, Mom."

They turned in by a mailbox that was decorated with pink balloons and pulled up to a red brick house with dated white shutters and a sagging single-garage door. More balloons were tied to the handrail of the front steps, and all along the weathered privacy fence that jutted out from the house on both sides, white lights were draped and gathered with clusters of more pink balloons.

They could hear squeals from the backyard, so Graeme headed

straight for the gate beside the garage. Claire followed him with his bag and helped pull up the rusty iron latch.

"Graeme!" A satin-and-chiffon-clad Gabbie ran toward them in plastic high heels. Rhinestone clip-on earrings dangled from her ears, and her black hair was tucked up in a bun encircled by a plastic crown.

"Happy birthday, Gabbie," he said with a big grin as he held out her present.

She took it and twirled around in her dress, a Disney princess costume. When she batted her brown eyes at him, her smile was full of innocent mischief.

Claire noted the innate charm in Graeme's voice when he told her she looked pretty and beamed at her in admiration. He was a natural prince. He reminded her so much of his father.

"Smile, *niños!*" Martina came up with her camera, clicking pictures of Graeme and Gabbie from every angle until they ran off and were out of her range. Then she turned her lens on Claire, who put her hand over it.

"Don't you dare!"

"Why not?" Martina peeled Claire's fingers off the camera.

"Look at me! I'd break your camera."

Martina rolled her eyes and said, "Hardly." Then she kissed Claire on both cheeks. "*Hola, amiga.* Are you staying?"

"I'd like to, but I think Graeme is needing a little space. You know how I tend to hover."

Martina suppressed a laugh. "You? Oh, no."

Claire made a face and stuck out her tongue at Martina. "I'd be hovering now if this party was anywhere else—and I certainly wouldn't think of letting him spend the night!"

"Well, thank you for your vote of confidence. After all, you have only known me about thirty years." Martina laughed and gave her a little hug. "But, of course, you *are* welcome to stay."

"I've got a date to do some grocery shopping—Abuelita's orders. But I will have my cell phone with me at all times, and I want you to call me—"

"We'll call you if Graeme needs anything at all. Try not to worry."

" 'Bye, Graeme," Claire called as she waved to her son. His head was down as he bobbed for apples in a tin tub that was manned by Jesús. He was surrounded by little girls.

Graeme raised his head, took an apple out of his mouth, and smiled and waved excitedly. "See ya, Mom!" he yelled.

Taking Graeme's bag from Claire, Martina put her arm around her friend. "Enjoy a little time to yourself tonight. We're gonna have a blast." She walked Claire through the gate and waited to shut it behind her.

"I'll try." Claire forced a smile. "See you tomorrow."

"See you then."

Gripping the steering wheel of her car before she pulled away, Claire closed her eyes and took a deep breath. As she exhaled she whispered, "I can do this."

* * * * *

There was no grocery store in Romeo—only a convenience store that sold a few staples—so Claire drove on into Manassa. The same family who had owned the store when she was a child still owned it, and it was surprisingly good for such a small town. Most of the meats were purchased locally, and the dairy section even offered organic milk and *créma* from one of the farms nearby.

After turning off the car, Claire pulled down her sun visor and took inventory of her appearance in the lighted mirror. She frowned at what she saw. She was wearing a rust-colored sweater with loose brown cords and a brown scarf around her neck. She hadn't felt like fixing her hair just to go to the store, so she'd brushed it out straight and pulled on a plain toboggan the color of oatmeal. She wasn't wearing a stitch of makeup. *I hope I don't see anybody I know.*

Claire grabbed her purse, depositing her keys inside, and shut the car door. Once inside the Market, as the grocery store was called, she fished out Abuelita's list. It was a jumble of Spanish and English, jotted down quickly in the sweeping hand of an old aristocrat. *Leche, créma, huevos,* bread. *Pollo.* Steaks. Chocolate for Graeme.

After hitting the meat and dairy aisles, Claire picked out some wheat berry bread and Mexican chocolate for Graeme then headed for the produce. She liked this section best and planned to purchase lots of fresh fruits and vegetables, which she was trying desperately to incorporate into Abuelita's diet.

Working methodically from bin to bin, Claire filled her cart. She chose apples, Gala for snacking and Granny Smith for pie, plus bananas, black grapes, Bing cherries, and several Ruby Red grapefruits from Texas. Graeme loved those. She was picking out the best navel oranges when she accidentally caused a small avalanche. About fifteen oranges came tumbling out of their bin and onto the floor, where they rolled like billiard balls in every direction.

Claire groaned as she stooped down, grabbing as many as she could at a time from off of the concrete floor.

"Here, let me help you."

Claire looked up and saw Stephen Reyes bent over, gathering several of her delinquent oranges into his arms like a mother hen.

She closed her eyes, ducking, and felt her cheeks grow hot and prickly. *Surely he hasn't recognized me.* She wanted to pull her hat down over her face.

"Uh, thank you," she said in a muffled voice, turning her back to him as she eased up to the bin in a sideways manner to deposit the oranges. Unfortunately, he stood up to transport his load before she could get away.

"Claire?" He craned his neck to look into her eyes as she replaced her oranges. "Is that you?"

"Hi," she said miserably.

He watched as she put each orange back into the bin and then he piled on the rest.

Claire noticed again how the veins in his hands were pronounced. *Like travertine marble.* Stephen was meticulous about the placement of the oranges, and Claire knew they wouldn't easily fall back down. When he was finished, he brushed off the sleeves of his leather jacket.

"Thanks for helping me," she muttered. She was looking at a drain on the floor, wishing it could suck her down like water and transport her far, far away.

"You're welcome."

Claire stood like a statue, wondering what he was thinking. Finally, she spoke. "Stephen?" She forced herself to look him in the eyes and found no encouragement in them. But at least he didn't look away. "I can explain," she said.

"There's no need for an explanation," he told her in a voice that was a little hard. He diverted his eyes, and the muscles in his jaw looked taut like a bowstring.

"I thought—" She tried to make eye contact before she told him of her mistake, but when she met his gaze, he interrupted her.

"Look, Claire, it's okay." His voice was a little softer this time. He even smiled a tiny bit. "I understand you had plans to get groceries. I can respect that."

The muscles in Claire's face relaxed into a grin, and she laughed just a little.

Stephen bowed slightly and moved to go.

He's letting me off the hook, she thought. On an impulse she grabbed his arm.

Stephen looked down at her hand on his arm, puzzled, and she removed it quickly.

"Could we talk?" Claire ventured.

Stephen tilted his head to the side, studying her. It seemed to Claire that he was trying to see behind her eyes.

"Well, I *did* have plans to get groceries, but—"

Claire laughed again, this time more heartily. She was impressed by this man's sense of humor.

Stephen responded with a grin of his own. "Where do you want to talk?"

"I don't know. I—well, I just need to talk to you about some things."

"We could go to the infamous Abe's," Stephen suggested. "That's about the only place in town."

Claire's hand went to her head, and then across her face and over her mouth, as a realization dawned on her. "I look awful," she said. "Maybe I could go home and change while you're getting your groceries."

"No!" Stephen said, impetuously. He looked straight into her eyes.

Both Stephen and Claire colored a little, and then he added, "I don't need many groceries."

Claire loosened her scarf, throwing caution to the wind.

"Well, then," she offered, "why don't you meet me in the front of the store when you've got what you need? I'll check out and wait for you."

* * * * *

Stephen followed Claire from the grocery store in Mansassa all the way to Abuelita's on the outskirts of Romeo. When she pulled into the garage, he parked behind her and got out of his truck. Claire was opening her trunk when he walked up beside her.

"Can I help you with your groceries?" he asked politely.

"You don't have to," she said, "but that would be nice."

He grabbed the heaviest bags in both arms, and Claire took up a couple of lighter ones. She held the door open for him and he followed her through the back entry and into the kitchen. The house was dark except for the evening light that came in from the windows all along the back. Claire switched on the chandelier that hung above the breakfast table, and a fluorescent light that illuminated the kitchen.

She put the cold items in the refrigerator, stooping down to deposit the fruit into a drawer, while Stephen stacked the other items on the marble counter. He made one more trip to the garage for the rest of the groceries.

"This is quite a place," he said as he set the remaining bags down on the counter and looked around. His eyes were drawn to the great room adjacent to the kitchen, with its dark wood floors, tall windows, and the majestic staircase that spilled into it.

"I could give you a tour if you'd like," Claire offered, surprising herself. It was amazing how comfortable she felt all of a sudden. She'd really only seen Stephen a few times, and now he was standing in Abuelita's kitchen with her, unloading her groceries.

I'm glad Abuelita is gone for the evening, Claire thought, even though she sensed that her grandmother would approve of Stephen.

He looked away from the great room and into her eyes. "I'd love to see the place, but maybe some other time." His words sounded like more of a question than a statement. Claire thought she heard something in his voice, but she was not exactly sure what. *Caution? Fear? Restraint?*

"Okay," she said, closing the cabinet door where she'd just put Graeme's chocolate. "I guess that's it for the groceries."

She scribbled a quick note to Abuelita, leaving it out on the counter, and they went back outside through the garage. Claire grabbed her purse from the front seat of her car and put down the garage door with the remote. When she turned around, Stephen was holding the door open to the passenger side of his truck.

Claire smiled her thanks and climbed in. The cab smelled like wood smoke, and she admired the color and feel of the soft brown leather seats. Stephen shut the door behind her and walked around to his side to get in.

"Do you still want to go to Abe's?" He turned on the engine.

"I'd prefer some place a little quieter, I think." *And less conspicuous.*

Stephen turned around and pulled slowly down the long, brick driveway. He stopped at the gate and looked at her with a question in his eyes.

"Why don't we drive up to the park? I haven't been there in years," she offered.

"Okay—the park it is." Stephen turned left out of Abuelita's property and continued up Highway 142 for just a few miles until they reached Romeo, where they turned onto 285. As they drove through town, the only sign of life was at Abe's, where the lights were already on and the music was loud. People milled about the sidewalk in front of the bar.

Claire laughed to herself at the memory of Abuelita—"meeting her friends there for *corridos* and country."

"What is it?" Stephen asked her.

"Oh, nothing, just a little joke." Then, sensing that he really wanted to hear, she told him, "You'd have to know my grandmother. She'd never be caught dead in a bar—she's sort of a teetotaler when it comes to alcohol—but the other day she told me she was going to Abe's with some friends. Eighty-year-old friends, no less. She said they were going for *corridos* and country."

Stephen laughed. "That's hilarious. She must be quite a character."

"She is," Claire said. "She loves to get a rise out of me."

"Did she really go? To Abe's, I mean."

"Heavens, no! If they were having a ballroom dance there, she might. No—she went to her friends' house to play chicken feet. It's a Mexican domino game. That's where she is tonight, too." Claire took off her scarf and placed it in her lap.

When they came to the edge of town, Stephen continued on Highway 285, past the grain silo. Claire admired the mural depicting two sandhill cranes, which a local artist had painted on it. The field of alfalfa—which used to be grain back in the day—used to be a pit stop for migrating cranes. Claire could vaguely remember them.

Ahead of them, she thought again that the fence posts, sticking up out of the ground and stretching for miles on both sides of the highway, looked like a form of earth acupuncture. She shivered a bit as she looked at the sky—so high and vast above them and such a cold blue.

The sun was beginning its descent over the mountains to the west, and Stephen turned toward the sunset, down a neat dirt road. At the end of this road was what locals called "the park." Claire shot to the edge of her seat, searching, but not seeing what she remembered.

The park of her childhood had consisted of a few swings, a merry-go-round, and, in the middle, a huge pine tree. The tree had been framed with smooth rocks from the river, and there was a bench underneath it. The legend—and the reason for the park—was that Georgia O'Keefe had lain under that pine tree next to her friend D. H. Lawrence and looked up into its branches, becoming inspired to paint them from the bottom up.

Claire had seen the painting at a gallery in Santa Fe once, with Abuelita, and it had fascinated her. She remembered the perspective—the strong, wide trunk that grew narrower as it went up, and the proud branches jutting out from it, with their full, feather-like greenery. The top of the tree pointed like an arrow into a royal blue sky that was studded with white stars.

"What happened to the tree?" she wondered out loud, for she had almost forgotten that Stephen was with her.

"It died," he said simply and then turned off the engine.

Claire got out of the truck and walked over to the area where the tree had been. The rock border was still there as well as the old, iron bench. But, where the great pine tree had once stood, there was now a new, smaller one in its place. Its trunk was about two inches in diameter, and it stood about as tall as Claire. The branches, with their sparse green twigs, looked like skinny arms. They seemed to wring their hands in the breeze, apologizing for their insignificance. The whole thing reminded Claire of Charlie Brown's Christmas tree.

Stephen's voice was beside her.

"The story goes that the other pine tree died because it was alone out here. Apparently, they need other trees around them in order to survive. That's the reason all these others have been planted around this new one."

As Claire looked around, she saw that several pines of about the same size had been planted throughout the park. The playground had been rearranged to accommodate them, and everything was actually quite nice and well tended. There was even a new marker explaining the legend and providing the date that the tree had been replaced.

Claire sat down on the bench, pulled her scarf back around her, and crossed her arms over her chest. " 'Nothing gold can stay,' " she quoted softly.

There was a pensive silence.

"Robert Frost." Stephen sat down beside her on the bench. " 'So dawn goes down to day.' " He pointed at the sun, which was a big, golden ball sinking toward the mountains.

Claire looked at him.

"Sorry about your tree." He sounded like he meant it.

"Stephen." Claire put her hands in her lap. "I need to apologize to you."

He didn't say anything, but his eyes were curious.

"I feel like a complete idiot, but I made an assumption about you— that you were involved with someone else—and that's why I said 'no' when you asked me out."

Stephen blinked his eyes and cocked his head to one side.

"I know I should have been honest with you." Claire fiddled with her nail polish, scraping her left thumbnail nearly clean. She made herself look up at him. "I am so sorry."

"Who—what gave you the idea I was seeing someone?" Stephen's eyebrows were bent, but his mouth was trying to curve up into a smile.

Claire closed her eyes and sighed. "You—your sister—me, I guess. I was analyzing it too much."

Stephen tossed back his head with a deep laugh. Then he laughed again.

Claire pulled her scarf up over her face to hide her smile and her red cheeks. She peered cautiously at him from behind the scarf.

Stephen stopped laughing. Gently, he reached out and tugged the scarf downward. For a moment he looked at her lips and then back up to her eyes.

Claire explained, "You know the day you called me about the mole?"

"The day you turned me down flat?" Stephen teased.

"Yeah—that day. Well, that same day, Graeme had an appointment with your sister. My abuelita asked her if we should get a second opinion about my mole—and that's when we finally made the connection. Doctor Marquez said, 'Well, I'd trust *my brother* with my life' or something like that. I could have died." Claire smiled at him. "Abuelita scolded me all the way home, just like I was a child. She threatened to call you herself about the date, but I was too mortified. I figured you might hate me anyway."

Stephen looked at her so kindly that Claire almost had to look away. There was something so deep in his gaze, so honest. *Am I being too vulnerable—too open with this man?*

"I don't think there's any danger of that," he said, "though you did give my pride a pretty big hit. Some people would tell you that's not necessarily a bad thing, though." Stephen looked back at the sunset, and Claire thought he sounded wistful.

She shivered slightly.

"Are you getting cold?" he asked her.

"A little."

"You know, my place is not very far from here. Would you like to go there and get a cup of coffee?"

Claire considered.

He stood to his feet, waiting for her with one hand extended and the other in his back pocket.

"I grind my own beans," Stephen added. He looked so hopeful, and under the tender gaze of his eyes, Claire felt something in her loosen just a tiny bit.

"Sure. Why not?"

Chapter Fourteen

....

"Who was that staring out the window?" Claire asked Stephen as he drove past the Patricks' house and turned into his driveway.

"That would be Nell," he chuckled. "And I will have to give her a full account of who *you* are tomorrow."

She looked at him, wide-eyed.

"Oh, don't worry about it. She and her husband are two of my best friends. They sort of adopted me when I moved here several years ago. They're wonderful people."

"Why does she stare out the window?" Claire asked. "Doesn't it bother you?"

"It did at first. But then I realized it's kind of nice to have someone looking out for me."

They pulled up to his house and Stephen turned off the truck's engine.

Claire looked at him and laughed thoughtfully. "Looking out for you—literally. That's a good one."

"No pun intended." Stephen grinned and got out of his truck.

He hurried over to her side to open the passenger door, but Claire beat him to it. She slid out of her seat, sort of bouncing down, and he couldn't help but notice the curves of her body. She'd wanted to change, but he liked her worn brown cords and the rust sweater. They looked comfortable, like the brown leather Mary Janes on her feet. She wasn't wearing socks.

Her face was just as pretty—maybe more so—without makeup. The crocheted hat only accentuated the tawny glow of her skin and subtle arch of her eyebrows. The natural flow of her dark hair past her shoulders was alluring to Stephen. He'd never seen it so "unfixed." Wisps of it kicked up in the breeze, and Stephen detected the scent of jasmine.

"Stephen?" Claire said. "Are you okay?"

He was glad it was dusk, so she couldn't tell he was blushing. "Uh, sure," he croaked. "Let's go in."

The door was unlocked, and as soon as Stephen opened it, Duchess and Regina bounded out into the yard. They jumped up on him, licking his face, and he scratched them both behind the ears and rubbed their heads. One at a time, they turned their attention on Claire, who was standing beside him with her arms crossed. Stephen couldn't tell whether she was offended or afraid.

Duchess pranced around her, tail wagging profusely. It thumped like a bass drum against Claire's legs. When Claire reached down to pet her, Regina jumped up and pawed her, licking her face with a flourish and nearly knocking her down.

"Girls! Girls!" Stephen grabbed them both by the collars to hold them still. "Make a run for it!" he told Claire, and she skipped up the steps and into the house.

A few minutes later, Stephen followed.

"I apologize for them," he said. "They're a little excited."

"That's okay. I'm not really used to dogs, but they seem friendly."

Stephen smiled at her. "That's an understatement—and a kind one." He took off his jacket and cowboy boots in the mudroom, crossed the dining room, and turned on the light in the kitchen. Claire followed suit with her shoes and scarf.

"Wow! That's warm," she exclaimed as she stepped into the dining room. She was looking down at her bare feet. "I wasn't expecting that!"

Stephen noticed the red-wine shade of her toenails. They matched her fingernails—all but the left thumbnail, which was bare. "Oh, you don't have to take off your shoes. This isn't a temple or anything. I just do it out of habit."

"Your floor is so warm—how is that?" Claire asked him, walking across it and taking a seat in one of the high, swiveling stools at his bar.

"It has a geo-thermal warming system. It's supposed to save money on the heating bill and be good for the environment."

"Does it? Save money, I mean?"

"Yeah, I think so. Of course, I've had it since I built the house, so I don't have a lot to compare it to."

Stephen took out a stainless steel bean grinder from a corner cabinet. He filled it with dark coffee beans that he poured out of a paper bag from the freezer. Next, he replaced the lid on the grinder and pressed down, crushing them to a coarse powder. He poured this powder into a small canister that said *Café* and repeated the action. Then he measured out eight scoops from the canister and filled his coffee pot with water. While it was brewing, he took out cream and milk from the fridge and set them on the counter along with two mugs of Native-American pottery.

Claire watched from her stool across the room. "You've got this down to a science."

Stephen walked over to where she was sitting. He stood beside her and casually rested his elbow on the granite bar. Her tan feet were alluring to him as she curled her toes around the black iron leg of his barstool. He'd never seen feet so elegant.

"How's your leg?" Stephen asked.

"It's good, but I'll admit I'm a little scared to remove my own stitches," she told him, raising up her pant leg and resting her heel on the stool next to her.

Her calf muscle flexed briefly as she did this and Stephen noticed that it was perfectly formed.

"Why would you take them out yourself? Why haven't you just come by—" Stephen stopped himself when he remembered what she had presumed about him and Maria. This woman was pretty stubborn.

"You know, I thought I was going to have to find a new doctor." She looked at him apologetically. "But I'll come by this week."

He moved over to examine her leg closely and tugged slightly at the skin around the stitches. "Well, I could just take those out right now."

"Really?"

"Yes, they're ready—if you are."

"That would be great."

Stephen took the pocket knife out of his jeans and snipped the threads before she even knew what happened.

"Excellent," she said, rubbing her leg. "That feels better. Thanks."

Stephen smiled at her. "No problem." He folded the knife and slipped it back into his pocket.

Claire pulled down her pant leg and resettled herself on the stool. "That coffee smells really good."

"How do you like yours?" he asked, walking over toward the coffee station he'd assembled.

Claire plopped down from the stool. "I'll make it."

He watched as she measured a spoonful of sugar and poured her cup half full of milk.

"Now?" he asked, holding the carafe of hot coffee.

She nodded, stopping him a half inch before the rim. She stirred it and took a sip. "Wow—that's good. What is it?"

"It's Colombian. My brother-in-law sent it to me."

"Actually from Colombia?" Claire looked surprised over the mug she was holding up to her lips.

"Yeah. He's over there on an extended mission trip."

"I think you mentioned that to me. Is he Maria's husband?"

Stephen nodded his head as he poured his own mug full of the steaming, black liquid.

"You like yours black? How can you stand it that strong?"

"That's the way I got through med school." He grinned, taking up his cup. Then he motioned to a wide doorway. "Do you want to sit out here?"

Stephen led her into the sunroom just off the kitchen. In it were two espresso-colored leather recliners and a matching couch, but Claire chose the floor. Sitting down Indian-style on the shaggy, cream-colored rug that covered a large section of the room's neutral tile, she leaned over to grab a coaster, placing her mug on the coffee table beside her.

"This chair is my throne, but I'd be happy to share it with you," Stephen offered, pointing to the recliner nearest the television.

"I like the floor just fine," Claire said, looking like she meant it.

Suddenly the rug looked softer and more inviting to Stephen than it ever had before. He eased down onto the floor a few feet away from Claire and placed his mug on the opposite end of the rectangular table. Leaning against it, he stretched out his long legs and crossed his feet, still clad with white socks. There was a low rustling of denim, then silence.

"I can't believe you're sitting in my living room," he finally said.

Claire laughed. "You know, I had that same thought when you were helping me unload groceries." She took another sip of her coffee.

Who are you, Claire Caspian? Stephen wanted to ask. Instead, he said, "How's Graeme doing?"

Claire glanced quickly at her cell phone, which she'd brought in by itself, separate from her purse.

"He's good," she said. "He's at a birthday party tonight. I'm a little weird about it—we're never apart except for school and work."

"So, the asthma is better?"

"Yes, it is. Thanks to you and Doctor—your sister." Claire smiled and bit her lip.

He'd seen women pay lots of money for lips like that.

"Thank you for sending us there. I really like her." She looked into his eyes, arching her eyebrows. "I like her *now*, that is."

Stephen laughed. Feeling emboldened, he turned more directly toward her and asked gently, "Claire, what brought you to Romeo?"

Claire looked down into her cup. Her thumbs massaged the handle of it, where the potter's hands had shaped a delicate indigo camber. Then she turned away from Stephen, looking off into the distance through the glass wall of the sunroom. Her eyes stared out into the dark, as though focused on some unseen horizon.

A cloud seemed to descend on her, and Stephen wished he hadn't asked that question.

"You don't have to—"

Claire's head turned swiftly back to him. There was a look in her eyes—almost a fierceness.

"It's okay," she said. "I don't mind telling you."

Stephen turned his body completely toward her, focusing all of his energy in her direction. He felt he'd been invited to witness a sacred thing—to enter a holy place. His eyes, like his heart and mind, were concentrated and intense.

"My parents were missionaries in Ecuador. They were linguists. We lived in Quito after I was born, but they needed more contact with the tribe of people whose language they were translating—a faction of the Colorado Indians—in order to translate the whole Bible.

"The group we were with decided that my parents should move into the jungle for a year or so to study the dialect of that particular group of Indians. There were already a few missionaries living among them, and so we planned to join those guys and work beside them. The only problem was that there were no other missionary kids and no school."

Claire set down her cup on the coaster and folded her hands in her lap.

"I was six years old at the time and had learned Spanish in Catholic school in Quito, though we spoke English at home. My father was Anglo and Mamá Mexican, and both were big on my learning both languages. Mamá considered homeschooling me for the year in the jungle, but she was torn between that and her translation work. In the end it was decided that I would live with her mother—my abuelita—and go to school in the

States for that year so they could both focus on the translation."

Stephen nodded, trying not to pass judgment on her parents for their decision. Stories like this always raised his ire. *How could anyone doing God's work dump their kid?*

Claire continued, "The plan was that I would return to Quito when my parents did, a year later, but it never happened. They were killed."

Stephen's eyes widened.

"It was completely random. There was some tribal scuffle, and they were caught in the crossfire. That's what the other missionaries told Abuelita." Claire tilted her head to one side and peered straight into Stephen's eyes. "I never saw them—or even their bodies—again."

"Oh, my God," Stephen said, nonplussed. He wasn't a person who used this expression for anything else except prayer.

Claire's tone was matter-of-fact. "I guess it was logistically next to impossible. The other missionaries buried them in the village."

She continued, "Abuelita raised me. I graduated from the high school in Manassa. After that, I went to college at Adams State, where I met my husband. His name was Rob MacGregor, and he was there on a track scholarship. After finishing our degrees, we moved to Arkansas, where Rob was from, for graduate school. I got my PhD. and Rob became an international lawyer. We built a house outside of Fayetteville—where the university is—and Graeme was born there. I had a job teaching. We planned to stay there—his family is very close—but Rob got pancreatic cancer. He died when Graeme was three, almost four."

Stephen did the math. "So a little over a year ago."

"About a year and a half."

Stephen's brain felt like it was spinning as he connected all of the dots in Claire's narrative. He shook his head, exhaling slowly. As he processed what he just heard, he never took his eyes away from her.

Claire looked back at him, Stephen realized now, from a deep well of sorrow. Her eyes seemed wise, like an old traveler's. There was also the sadness, the distance, the ache he'd recognized on some level before but not accounted for. Not like this.

"Claire," he said, "I don't know what to say."

She glanced at him with an urgency in her eyes. It seemed as if there was something more she wanted to say—something she had to get out before the moment passed.

"To answer your question, I came back here to get away. I had to get away—from our house, that town, our life. I can't explain it, and I don't know if it was right. But Rob's cancer almost killed me, too. It's an evil, horrible disease. He fought so hard—we fought it together, but…" Her voice trailed off.

"I know, Claire. I know," Stephen said softly. He'd seen pancreatic cancer a few times and knew how it ravaged the body, rapidly making patients so thin and wasted. As a doctor he'd been limited—there was very little that medicine could do for it once it was big enough to be detected.

Claire looked back out the window into the night, and Stephen knew she was far away. He wanted to reach out and touch her, but he didn't dare.

"The only reason I had to live was Graeme. I *wanted* to live, for Graeme. But everywhere I looked in Arkansas, I saw death. Our home, our friends, his family, the university, all of the memories—instead of being good, like all of the books and counselors say—it was like death was sucking me in. It was a black hole. I knew I had to get away.

"Abuelita and Romeo seemed the only safe place for me and Graeme. But, you know, I don't really feel safe here either. I don't know if I ever will again."

She looked up.

"I can't believe I'm telling you all of this."

Stephen couldn't either.

Chapter Fifteen
....

Claire felt as if a huge weight had been lifted from her shoulders. It was the first time in a very long time that she'd told her story to anyone. Why Stephen, and why it had happened in this way, at this moment, was a mystery to her. Like the evening, it had been a gradual unfolding. She certainly hadn't gone looking for the opportunity. And she had no idea of the consequences. The weight of it all might be too heavy for him. He might be bored, or scared, or any number of things. In a sense, though, it didn't matter what effect the listening had on Stephen. The telling had been good for Claire.

But as she looked into Stephen's face—the square jaw, the chiseled features, and the eyes, so curious yet soulful—Claire became aware that he was utterly engaged with her. Not just kind or patient or politely sympathetic—and certainly not pitying—but ostensibly not bored or uncomfortable, either.

Stephen looked to Claire like he wanted to touch her.

She reached over and squeezed his hand.

"Thank you. For listening," she said.

Stephen put his other hand over hers and nodded, saying nothing. Claire could feel the tortuous veins of his bottom hand pulsing underneath her palm. The hand that covered hers had a workman's roughness, and it scratched a little as it rested on top of hers. In another room, a clock ticked.

Claire had a sudden impulse to jerk her hand away, even to start running—again—like she'd run away from death. But, strangely, as they sat together in the quiet, listening to nothing but the clock and the low sounds of each other's breathing, something in Claire relaxed ever so slightly.

* * * * *

"Stephen," she said, after several moments had passed, "I've used up my word quota for the decade. It's your turn. Tell me about you."

He tilted his head to one side and smiled at her mischievously, a half smile.

"First things first. Do you want some more coffee?"

They both got up off the floor, stretching like cats. While he poured more coffee, Claire found the bathroom. She brought back a framed picture she found of Stephen and Maria, who were considerably younger when the photograph was taken in front of the Eiffel Tower.

"When was this?"

"Maria and I are twins—fraternal, obviously—and so we graduated from high school in the same year. That following summer we backpacked across Europe. The trip was a gift from our parents."

"Oh my goodness! How wonderful!" Claire exclaimed, taking the cup he prepared for her.

"It was, especially looking back. I think they just wanted us out of their hair for the summer, but what an opportunity." Stephen looked at the picture and smiled at what he saw. "We had a great time."

He replaced the carafe and led them back into the sunroom, where they settled back into their places on the floor.

"Thanks for doctoring my coffee," she told him, inwardly pleased that he mixed it just right. "Where did you go besides Paris?"

Stephen laughed, "Where *didn't* we go is a better question. We did a whirlwind tour of all of the major sites from Greece, up and across the mainland, and even over to Great Britain." He ran his fingers through his dark hair. "We didn't really know what we were doing—staying in hostels and sleeping on trains—we lived like gypsies. Even though that was a fantastic trip, I'd love to go back someday and take my time. You know, really interact with the culture."

"You and Maria must be really close," Claire said.

Stephen's eyes were serious. "Yeah. We are," he said. Then he took a sip of his coffee and grinned. "She tries her best to keep me in line."

"You know, one of the things that sent me into a tailspin was a picture of you she has in her office."

"Really? How embarrassing."

"I think it's sweet—now," Claire smirked. "What about your parents? Are they still living?"

"They are—in Florida. Maria and I grew up in Tulsa, Oklahoma, where our dad was a surgeon. When he retired, they moved to a golfing community in Florida called Naples." Stephen held his cup between his two hands in his lap and stared at it for a moment before looking up at Claire. "We're not really all that close. I see them about once a year, usually at Christmas."

Claire thought she saw something like grief—or at least disappointment—in Stephen's eyes. In that moment it was easy to imagine him as a little boy, with his long, sweeping eyelashes and chipped front tooth.

"Well, how did *you* get here? Romeo's a long way from Tulsa, Oklahoma."

Stephen cocked his head to one side. "Do you want the long version or the short?"

"Whichever one you want to tell me."

"The short version is that I followed Maria." His eyes were playful, his mouth a corrupt half grin.

Claire stared him down.

"You want the long version, huh? Well, I'm afraid that, compared to your story, it reads like a cheap romance novel."

She grinned at him and said, "Page one."

Stephen stretched out his long legs and wriggled his toes a little within his socks. His knees popped when he extended them. Claire noticed that his feet were big, and on a whim she wondered if they had the beautiful veins, meandering so close to the surface, like he had in his hands.

"We both went to college in Oklahoma, but then she came out here to med school, in Colorado Springs. I stayed in Tulsa—did my residency there—and got married."

Claire swallowed her surprise with a sip of coffee.

Stephen continued, though it seemed to her that the story bored him.

"Basically, Claire, I was a workaholic. I worked eighty-hour weeks, making money and establishing a reputation, doing what my dad did. I stepped right into his shoes."

"What about your wife?"

"She had a baby."

Claire registered her shock this time. "You have a child—children?"

"No," Stephen said, and he looked weary when he said it. "She had a baby with another man."

"Oh my, Stephen," Claire covered her mouth. "I can't imagine."

"Yep." There was irony—pathos—in the offhand way he said it.

Claire didn't know what to say next, but she tried to urge him on with her eyes.

"It was a mess—a sordid mess. Trust me, you really don't want to know the details."

Claire took that to mean he really didn't want to talk about it.

"So how did you end up in Romeo?"

"The main constant in my life—besides God, I guess, although I was pretty out of tune with Him at the time—the main constant was Maria.

134

She had met Manuel in residency, and they were married and settled in Salida. She wanted me up here. Away from Tulsa. She's the one who found the opening at the clinic in La Jara."

Stephen took a drink of his coffee.

"I applied for it and ended up staying with them in Salida for awhile, kind of getting my life back together after I started at the clinic. It was a total paradigm shift for me—but one I needed.

"I found this place in Romeo about eight years ago, and well—I just knew it was where I wanted to be."

"It seems really peaceful," Claire observed.

"It is. I can't really imagine ever being back in the city. It doesn't even seem like that could have been me back then." Stephen shook his head and looked up at the ceiling. When his eyes came back to Claire's, she thought they held plenty of regret.

"What about your friend, the football coach? Have you known him long?"

"Well, that's the other really cool thing about being here. Joe's my best friend from college. We were roommates at OU—played football together. He stayed there awhile after we graduated, working with the team and getting his master's. Then he coached at a few different high schools in Oklahoma. We've always kept in touch.

"After I got here, he came to visit a few times and really liked it. I told him when the head football coach's position came open in Manassa, and he came up here and got the job!"

"That's great. He must be really good."

"He is a good coach—and a good man."

Claire glanced down at her phone and looked up at Stephen in shock when she realized the time.

"Stephen, did you know it's one in the morning?"

"No." His eyes showed a look of surprise.

"I can't believe Abuelita hasn't called me. I think I'd better go home."

"Okay." He rose to his feet.

The drive home was quiet, inside the truck and out, except for the hum of the truck's diesel motor. Stephen seemed pensive to Claire— pleasant, but more serious than before. While her senses were heightened by all of the coffee, she wondered if he was tired.

Stephen's dusty gravel road was dim and deserted. Even the Patricks' house looked completely dark. No TV was on, and the window where Nell had stood watching—to Claire it seemed days ago—had its curtains drawn like a veil. Even the slanted roof of the house looked like a hat pulled down tight over someone's eyes, to shut out light.

As they turned onto Highway 285, which led through town, Claire noted the grain elevator and its proximity to Stephen's road. She recorded it in her mind, should she need to remember where he lived. How many times had she driven right past that road, never imagining who—or what—could be down it?

Other than the gaudy fluorescent signs, which blinked, advertising different beers available at Abe's Bar, Romeo proper looked like a ghost town; there was nothing open and virtually no one else in sight.

It was surreal in some ways for Claire, going home to Abuelita's and back to the reality of her life. She felt as if she was emerging from a bubble she'd been in for the past several hours. They turned onto 142. Soon, the sight of Abuelita's house and its gates gave her clarity.

Like the great iron fence in front of the Casa, Claire had had to build fences around herself and Graeme for protection—protection from pain. Part of that process was getting away from memories and from people in Arkansas who knew their story too well.

Since moving back to Romeo, Claire had permitted few people to even come close to those fences, and certainly only a select group had been let inside. Martina, Oscar—even Abuelita were only allowed to come so far.

And yet, as Claire reached into her purse and pressed the button on the remote to unlock Abuelita's big iron gates, she knew she'd done exactly that same thing tonight with the gates of her heart. She'd opened up and bidden Stephen Reyes to come inside and see what was there. Not everything, of course—but enough. Enough to scare her to death that she'd made a mistake.

Chapter Sixteen

....

Even though he was bone-tired, Stephen couldn't sleep. The evening had been amazing—first seeing Claire at the grocery store, with her scattered oranges all over the floor; and then the confession she made about him and Maria at the park in Romeo, where she seemed so deeply connected to the plight of the lone pine tree. It made more sense to him now—the way the pine tree's loss affected her—after hearing her story.

Had she really sat on his sunroom floor and told him that story over coffee? This very night? That beautiful, private woman who had become such an enigma to him over the past weeks and who he thought was out of his reach—had she really let down her guard and trusted him?

She had. In one evening they'd become friends.

* * * * *

The next morning Stephen slept in until seven-thirty. After a breakfast of oats and fruit and an article in the Colorado Journal of Medicine, Stephen took out the brisket he'd prepared the day before and placed it in the oven. It had to bake at 275 degrees for five hours, then get cold again in the refrigerator before he served it to Nell and Gene for dinner.

Knowing that Joe would be at church, he decided to go for a run by himself with his dogs. He planned to do the seven-mile loop he'd once calculated from his driveway, to the right and all the way to the end of the gravel road, which was the Evanses' place, and back to his driveway.

It was a beautiful morning. The cedars, *piñons,* and junipers, which were scattered along the road, shone with the rays of the sun, while wisps of cirrus clouds decorated the bright blue sky. Regina and Duchess frolicked and danced beside Stephen as he jogged, seemingly happy to have him to themselves after the relative neglect of the night before.

He could hear the *tap-tap-tap* of an occasional woodpecker on a tree somewhere and spotted an indigo bunting in a rosehip, or *champe* bush, as the locals called them, right beside the road. The vibrant plumage of the bird was magnificent. A quick splash of color, like it was painted right into dense branches of the bush—it was there and then gone.

Only the sight of the Evanses' place at the end of the road hampered Stephen's mood. The nice ranch-style house seemed darker than it ever had before, even though the sun was dazzling. Weeds showed through the usually well kept lawn and flowerbeds, and a frayed ribbon hung from the mailbox, like a black flag waving in the breeze. Stephen shuddered as he turned back toward home.

* * * * *

The Patricks showed up at Stephen's house in the Gator at two o'clock sharp.

"No nap?" he asked them, skipping down his back steps in work clothes and muck boots.

"No rest for the weary," Gene said, turning off the Gator's motor but sitting still in the driver's seat. His long, lanky form relaxed behind the wheel and his legs were spread apart. He wore starched blue jeans, muck boots, and a flannel shirt that was open at the collar. His worn, straw hat nearly touched the ceiling.

"It's 'no rest for the wicked,' Gene," Nell admonished him as she stepped down from her seat in Big Smith overalls and a red cotton shirt. Turning to Stephen, she said, "I guess you're all rested up after your busy night last night?"

Stephen knew it would be coming. "Yes, I am."

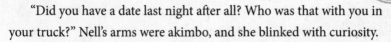

"Did you have a date last night after all? Who was that with you in your truck?" Nell's arms were akimbo, and she blinked with curiosity.

"Give the guy a break a minute, Nell," Gene slid out of the Gator. "We shore had us a fine date, thanks to your proddin', " he said to Stephen.

"That was mighty nice of you, son," Nell had to agree. "You shouldn't have done it, but I'm glad you did."

Stephen felt pleased. "Where did you two lovebirds go?" he wondered.

They all started walking together toward the west side of the barn where Stephen's corral was located.

"We went to that there Rumors up in Salida. Had a mighty fine steak."

Stephen thought, as he had many times before, that Gene could have come straight from an episode of *Gunsmoke*.

"I love that place. Did you sit outside by the river?" he asked Nell.

"No, it was too cold. But we sat inside by the fireplace, and that was real nice. Gene and me even split a dessert after our main meal was over."

Nell's eyes seemed to twinkle at the remembrance.

"No Frosty this time?" he teased her.

"We got this chocolate raspberry stuff with two forks."

When Nell smiled, Stephen thought he saw a glimpse of who she must have been when Gene first met her, fresh off the train in Romeo.

"Chocolate raspberry ganache? That's my favorite. I just shared one with my sister the last time I was there."

"The only bad part of the evenin' was when we got home," Nell shrugged. "Gene had to go down and fish Stan Evans out of Abe's Bar again."

"That's too bad." Stephen made a face. "How's Marsha handling… everything?"

"Better than Stan, I guess." Nell looked sad. "Least she's not drownin' her sorrows at Abe's."

He opened the first gate for them, where he already had their workstation set up, and Nell and Gene donned plastic aprons and assumed their positions. The little bull calves, separated from their mothers on the other side of the corral, were bawling loudly.

"You'd be bawling more if you knew about the surgery you're in for," Nell observed, nodding her head in sympathy toward the calves.

The whole operation went smoothly—like clockwork—for the entire afternoon. Stephen's nice, new corral, superior equipment, and skilled organization made everything noticeably easier than it had been at the Patricks' older place. Still, after several hours of work, they were beat.

"Why don't you guys come on in? Believe it or not, I've got dinner cooked."

Nell and Gene kicked their boots off by the back door; they wouldn't even bring them in the mudroom. Because of the plastic aprons Stephen had given them, however, their clothes were relatively clean. They followed his example of washing up in the deep utility sink just off the mudroom, in the spacious laundry.

"This laundry room seems like it was designed by a woman," Nell declared, rubbing her arms and hands with the towel Stephen provided.

"Why do you say that?" Stephen asked her, grinning. She never ceased to amaze him with her bluntness.

"Well, it's just perfect. Plenty of counter space to spread all of the clothes out and fold 'em—so they don't clutter up the kitchen table— places to hang them to dry like this rod here, and even your ironing board in a cabinet on the wall. That's a neat idea." She ran her fingers over the oak door that hid his ironing board.

"Thank you, Nell. And I have to admit you're right. My sister Maria designed it. You know I take most of my stuff to the cleaners'. It's just easier. But I guess the design *is* nice."

They walked into the kitchen and Nell said, "Let me help you with dinner."

She motioned for the fridge, but Stephen stopped her. "No way.

I've been working on this since yesterday, and I'm going to treat you."

Gene smiled at him, taking the bottle of water Stephen offered, and Nell finally relented, taking one, too. Stephen settled them into the sunroom—a recliner for each—and gave Gene the remote to the TV. "It will just be about thirty minutes."

Stephen could hear *Headline News*—and Gene's subsequent snoring—as he prepared the meal. He was intent on spoiling Nell, especially, with his cooking, and he couldn't wait to see her face when everything was ready. He preheated both of his ovens.

First, Stephen stirred together flour, brown sugar, baking soda, and salt in a big pottery bowl, and then he opened a warm beer and added it all at once. It bubbled and foamed. After mixing everything, he dumped the dough into a loaf pan, pouring melted butter over the top, and put it in his top oven at 375.

Next, he took the cooked brisket out of the refrigerator. After slicing it thinly with a butcher knife, he placed it back in its baking dish with the drippings and doused the whole thing with rich, thick barbecue sauce— the best money could buy—ordered from a place in Texas. Then he put the brisket back into the oven at 350, to reheat for thirty minutes.

While the brisket was warming, he took out the bag of shredded cabbage he'd picked up at the Market the day before and made slaw. Combining sugar, salt, buttermilk, mayonnaise, vinegar, and a little lemon juice, he poured it over the cabbage and tossed. Then he sprinkled it with celery seed and set it inside the fridge to chill.

Stephen took out his best dishes, a set of multicolored Fiestaware, and arranged three place settings on the table. He grabbed three linen napkins, which he rarely used, from the drawer where Maria had housed them, and anchored them down beside the plates with his heavy sterling silverware.

The kitchen started to smell like heaven. The brisket sizzled in the first oven, and the beer-battered bread looked golden brown through the glass window of the second. The coleslaw was waiting in the refrigerator. Stephen felt sure that Nell was probably dying to come in and be a part of the action, and so he called, "Nell? Want to come in and give me a quick hand?" He'd let her get ice and water in the glasses.

There was no answer from the sunroom, just the quiet droning of the television and Gene's snoring. Then Stephen heard another noise, a sort of whistling sound, and decided to investigate. Nell was reared back in the recliner, feet up and mouth open, snoring to beat the band.

* * * * *

When Nell woke, an hour later, Stephen was on the couch beside her chair in the sunroom. He was reading a book called *Neuroplasticity*, which a colleague in the clinic had recommended. Gene was still asleep.

"Turn that light on! You'll ruin your eyes!" Nell ordered. "What time is it?"

"It's seven thirty," Stephen answered. "Good evening, Sleeping Beauty."

"Did you eat?"

He could hear the wheels spinning in her head.

"No, not without you guys, but it's ready." Stephen put his book down on the coffee table.

"Gene! Wake up! It's nearly time for bed!"

Seated at Stephen's table, Nell and Gene felt like family. They were the kind of parents he wished he had—or, at least, the kind he wished his own parents could remotely resemble.

"How is Kelly?" he asked them, thinking he hadn't heard much lately about their only son.

Nell's eyes clouded. "Oh, you know, he's staying busy. We haven't heard from him in about a month."

"He's working on a big case, something with an oil and gas

company," Gene added. "I called him one day on his cell phone—he wasn't answerin' at home. Couldn't talk much, though. He was in the middle of a meeting."

Stephen understood Gene's apologetic tone all too well. He'd met Kelly Patrick twice in the past eight years, the two times the guy had been home. Stephen wasn't impressed with him, either. Kelly was a fast-talking, Rolex-wearing, big-city bachelor; a transplanted Texan who seemed at odds with his DNA.

"This brisket is some kind of good," Gene bragged, changing the subject.

"Thanks."

"And the slaw is, too—how'd you learn to make it?" Nell asked, helping herself to another serving of the stuff.

"Well, that's a good story. I had this teacher in grade school named Mrs. Law. She was a wonderful lady, very smart and full of life. Always doing unique things with her classes. Anyway, her husband was the preacher at the church we attended, and whenever there was a potluck, this is what she would bring." Stephen smiled at them both, enjoying sharing this little slice of his history.

"Over time, she became famous for it, and people started calling her "Miz Slaw." She even called herself that. When I got married, she gave me a handmade cookbook of favorite local recipes. This whole meal came from it." He waved his hand across the feast. "Obviously, I still have it."

Nell wanted to see the cookbook, so Stephen retrieved it for her from the kitchen. She ran her hand over the sewn gingham cover.

"This is really something," she said.

Turning to the first page, she saw a picture of a little boy with big brown eyes and a mop of brown hair standing by a piano. The woman beside him had horn-rimmed glasses and was grinning from ear to ear.

"Is that you and Miz Slaw?" Nell asked. "You haven't changed much!"

"That's us," Stephen answered. "She was my piano teacher for a while, too."

"You know, in all these years we've know you, you've never played the piano for us. Why don't you get over there and give us a tune?" Nell pointed to the grand piano that stood, like a stranger, in the living room to their left.

"Maybe some other time." Stephen grinned at them.

Gene snorted, pushing back from his empty plate. "That's what you always say."

"Well, I do want to tell you about my date."

Nell slammed the cookbook shut as though snapping to attention.

"Praise God for small miracles," she declared. "Gene done told me not to ask you about it."

"And I'd say it's a small miracle you decided to submit to me," Gene teased her. "But go on, son. We're both ready to hear."

"Well, I met this woman about a month ago in the ER. She came in with her son, who had had an asthma attack. I thought she was married at first, but later I found out she wasn't. Anyway, I kept seeing her around—first at a ballgame and then at a continuing education meeting over at Adams State."

He continued, "You guys know I haven't been interested in dating"—Gene grinned while Nell rolled her eyes and nodded—"but there was just something about her. I really wanted to ask her out."

"Let me guess what it was about her," Gene said, rubbing his chin. "Let's see. Her face? Eyes? Or was it some other of her wily ways?"

Nell kicked her husband under the table. "Don't pay him no mind," she said to Stephen.

"That's what got me, your wily ways," Gene chuckled, further rankling Nell by winking at her.

"Let the man talk!"

Stephen laughed wholeheartedly. "There's not much more to tell—"

"Yes, there is!" Nell spouted. "The last you told us, she turned you

down! We'd done decided we didn't like this girl! Now you spill the
beans! Was that her in your truck last night?"

"It was. I picked her up at the grocery store."

"Pretty romantic place," Gene commented, rocking back on two legs
in his chair.

Nell ignored him. "The *grocery* store?"

"She toppled the whole bin of oranges. I didn't know it was her when
I started helping pick them up, but there she was. It was actually quite
embarrassing for both of us."

"What happened then?"

"Well, like I said, it was a little awkward, and I tried to make it
easy for her to just walk away. At this point I thought she was just not
interested—but then she grabbed me by the arm and asked if we could
talk. She said she wanted to explain something."

Nell's eyes read Stephen like the pages of a murder mystery. She
couldn't seem to hear the story fast enough out of desperation for how it
would end.

"We went to the park—you know, with the pines—and she told me
why she turned me down."

Gene raised his eyebrows.

Nell leaned forward.

"She thought I was seeing my sister!"

Gene's face broke out into a smile. "No way!"

Nell gasped and then covered her wide-open mouth with one hand.
"Well, I'll be darned."

Stephen smiled at them both. He reflected, as he often did, on what a
blessing they were in his life. Who would have thought he'd ever find a home
with a simple farm couple in a village called Romeo? They really, truly cared.

"You know," Stephen told Nell, "you should get a gold medal for how
well you listen."

Chapter Seventeen

....

The house was a flurry of activity. Mickey, who had led the team in tackles the night before, was responsible for getting Gabbie over to Claire's abuelita's house by nine o'clock. His baby sister was currently packing a bag the size of Texas with high heels, baby dolls, gardening tools, and plastic cooking utensils. She was wearing a pink tutu with silver sparkles.

"Can I borrow your fishing pole?" she asked him, batting her long eyelashes.

"No, *hermanita*, not this time."

"Mommy!" Gabbie stomped her foot, scowling at her brother, and ran toward the kitchen.

Martina was on her third trip home from Art and Sol, the Mexican restaurant she and Jesús were opening today.

"Mickey!"

"Yes, Mom?"

Her dark hair was pulled back underneath a hairnet, and she wore a standard red cook's apron over her clothes. She was dumping what seemed to be the kitchen's utensil drawer into a big paper bag. She must have read the questioning look on her son's face, because she offered an explanation.

"I'm not making another trip to this house again until we close this evening."

Mickey grinned.

"Son, can you pick up ten heads of lettuce at the market after you drop Gabbie off? I need the green leaf kind—the ones I ordered from the supplier are too wilted already. And go ahead and pick up a bunch of cilantro."

"Sure, Mom."

Gabbie put her hands on her hips.

"Did you tell him, Mommy?"

"Tell him what, *niña*?"

"About the fishing pole!"

"Mickey does not have to give you his fishing pole. You have your own Barbie pole that is just your size." Martina replaced the drawer.

Gabbie crossed her arms and scowled at both of them, standing "big" as she called it.

"*Bastante*, Gabriela! That's enough."

"Let's go, *hermanita*," Mickey said, smiling sweetly as he followed his mother out of the kitchen.

* * * * *

The kitchen of Art and Sol was heating up. Jesús, clad in an apron like Martina's, was simmering separate pots of black and pinto beans, cooking chorizo, and sautéing peppers and onions on the gas stove top, while also manning the grill. The pork sausage for the chorizo was nearly brown—as brown as Jesús liked it—and he added in generous amounts of garlic and chili powder without draining the meat.

The look and smell of the chorizo, his grandmother's recipe, was soul-satisfying to Jesús as he stirred it. He put down the wooden spoon after a taste and then grabbed the handles of the two big skillets, running them back and forth across the burners to disturb the peppers and onions. This action stirred the small fires under the skillets, and they kicked out sparks. The onions, which were nearly caramelized, smelled like heaven. The peppers, too. He turned their burners off. Then he moved on down to the grill, which was covered with boneless, skinless chicken breasts. Turning them with meticulous care, Jesús poured on a little water. The grill sizzled and popped, blowing smoke in his face. He waved it away like a cloud of mosquitoes.

Dr. Banks, who had volunteered his services for the grand opening, was standing back-to-back with Jesús at a long, wooden table. His salt-and-pepper ponytail was covered by a hairnet and sweat dripped down his face. He wiped it with the shoulder of his shirt. He, too, wore a red apron and also surgical gloves. With a less-than-sharp knife, he was doing his best to dice fresh jalapeños, reserving the seeds. There was a mountain of white onions and a bucket of tomatoes in front of him, which were also to be diced and placed into stainless-steel containers.

Across the table from Dr. Banks, Frieda Franklin was grinding avocados with a mortar and pestle carved from lava rock. Her unruly hair was tamed somewhat by a hairnet, and her skin glowed under the fluorescent lights that shone from copper pendants running the length of the kitchen. She sat on a stool with crumbling gold paint, feet crossed, and leaned in with her shoulders to mash the ripe, green fruit. The texture had to be perfect. When she had a gigantic bowlful, she pressed fresh garlic, using both hands to grip the garlic press and force the cloves through. These she stirred together with sour cream and added to the bowl of avocado, just as Martina showed her when their home group had a potluck awhile back.

"This is good, if I do say so myself!" Frieda declared to the two men, crunching on a fried tortilla laden with the green stuff and smiling at the result.

Dr. Banks looked up, eyes bloodshot and burning from the fumes of the jalapeños. He wiped his chin with his shoulder. "Everything we're doing is making me hungry! What about you, Jesús?"

"I'm too nervous to be very hungry," Jesús replied, stirring the pots of beans.

Suddenly, the back door burst open and Martina stepped in, breathless.

"Hey, babe!" Jesús greeted her.

"The angel of mercy!" Dr. Banks cheered as she handed him a butcher knife from her paper sack.

"That one should be razor-sharp, Henry," Martina told him. Then, looking around the kitchen, she exclaimed, "Wow! You guys are amazing! This place smells fabulous!"

She handed Jesús some tongs for the peppers and onions and assembled the rest of the utensils in a large blue canister. Then she placed the canister on a shelf that stood against the wall.

"What do I need to do?"

Jesus pointed with the tongs. "All that's left to do is combining the *pico* and slicing up your famous cheesecake—until Mickey gets here with the lettuce."

"Sounds good. He should be here in a few minutes." Martina slid a huge sheet of lemon cheesecake out of the cooler and placed it on the table.

"I can do the *pico*, I think," Frieda offered. "Lime juice and vinegar?"

"Just enough to coat the veggies—and a little salt," Martina said. "Oh, and garlic. Mickey is bringing cilantro."

"I'm all over it!" Frieda hooted, hopping down from her perch on the stool and grabbing a big bowl from the shelf.

Just then, Sue poked her head into the kitchen through its front entrance, a swinging door with a porthole window.

"We're here!" She was wearing a white dress, which was covered to below the waist by a bright blue shawl. Her sandals were the color of the shawl, and she wore a necklace with many strands of colorful cut glass. Blond hair shining and brown eyes warm and inviting, she looked like quite the hostess.

Jerry came up behind her and opened the door wider so he could peer in at his friends.

"Are we ready to rumble?" he asked the group in the kitchen.

"As ready as we'll ever be!" Jesús answered.

"Well, I've got my running shoes on." Jerry held his foot through the door.

"Me, too." Martina took off her apron, tossing it into the bin in the corner, and removed her hairnet. "Let's get that drink station ready."

The drink station was a nook that Martina had designed between the two dining rooms. It was adorned by colorful painted tiles, randomly placed so that there was no apparent pattern to the whole. Some of the tiles were broken. Some were misshapen, rejects from the kiln that Martina chose for their character. The effect of all of these pieces thrown together was a wild mosaic of orange, cobalt, red, green, and gold.

As Jerry placed lemon slices on the rims of tall, clear glasses, Martina poured the freshly made tea into matching pitchers. Next, she poured several pitchers of water.

"I can't believe I've got a rocket scientist as my head waiter," she teased him. "If that's not a conversation starter, I don't know what is!"

"I just hope I won't ruin your grand opening," Jerry said. "I've never done anything like this before."

Martina patted his arm. "Just be yourself and look at it as a ministry. You've already blessed Jesús and me by being here to support us. It is our hope that many will be blessed today as they come through these doors."

As if on cue, Sue announced from the front that the first customers had arrived.

The heavy glass doors, set behind ornamental iron in the shape of a huge sun, opened wide. Claire and Abuelita walked in, with Gabbie and Graeme in tow.

"Mommy!" Gabbie squealed and ran into her mother's open arms. Gabbie had changed from the tutu into a wizard's outfit.

"Who are you?" Martina quizzed her.

"I'm Hermione and that's Harry," Gabbie said, pointing to Graeme with a plastic wand.

Martina scooped her up, holding her on her hip, and walked up to Claire and Abuelita. She gave them hugs with her other arm, kissed their cheeks, and ruffled Graeme's hair.

"Welcome to Art and Sol!"

"Let me take your picture." Sue stepped from behind the counter with her digital camera. "Say, *kay-so*!" she directed, her voice completely devoid of a Spanish accent.

This made them all laugh as they huddled together.

"*Queso!*" the group cried just before Sue snapped the picture.

"Let's get you seated," Martina said, as she noticed other people coming up the walk. Leaving them for Sue, she ushered Claire, Abuelita, and the kids into the dining area.

"Why don't you sit down here, and I'll get you some drinks. Would you like coffee, Abuelita?"

"*Sí, bueno,*" Abuelita nodded. She opened the menu, pulling her glasses out of her purse. "This looks good, *mi cara.*"

Abuelita was wearing a red silk scarf in her hair, which was smooth and pulled back tightly in a low bun at the nape of her neck. Her black silk blouse was tucked into a broomstick skirt—red and black silk—and trimmed at the waist by a wide, woven belt, which tied on one side. Red and black tassels hung down from where it tied.

Martina left the table but returned swiftly with a platter of three tall glasses and a mug. Graeme and Gabbie exchanged conspiratorial glances when they received theirs, both taking big gulps with their straws. Claire scolded Martina for indulging them.

"Oh, we only live once, *amiga!* They can have Sprite on our opening day!"

Abuelita agreed. "This coffee is delicious, Martina. Excellent choice."

"*Gracias*, Abuelita." Then, looking around the table, Martina asked, "Do you all know what you want to order?"

"I want a hamburger," said Gabbie, closing the menu she'd pretended to read.

"Me, too," said Graeme. "With fries."

Claire made a face in Martina's direction, but Martina was writing it down on her pad.

"Okay. What about you, Abuelita?"

"I'll have *tacos de carne asada*." Abuelita folded her menu and handed it to Martina.

"Claire?"

"I think I'm going to have this Speedy Gonzales."

"Speedy Gonzales?" Graeme laughed at her. "He's from Looney Tunes!"

"You're correct, Graeme. But it's also the name of a yummy Mexican dish that Tío Jesús makes. Do you want to change your order and try it?"

Graeme considered, looking back and forth between his mother and Gabbie. Then he made his decision.

"Nope, I'll stick with a hamburger."

* * * * *

By the time they finished their meal, the restaurant was filling up. Claire stopped Martina as she went by on a mad dash to the kitchen and asked her if she needed help.

"There was supposed to be a girl here at eleven o'clock—she came to training and everything. I don't know what's happened to her."

Claire shot a look at Abuelita, who completely understood.

"Well, Gabbie, Graeme, it looks like we're ready to go. How would you like me to take you to the park for a while, and then we'll come back and get your mommy, Graeme?"

"Awesome!"

"Double triple awesome!" Gabbie agreed.

* * * * *

Claire hadn't worked so hard—not physically, anyway—since she and
Martina were servers in high school. During the summers, they'd worked
together at José's, a café in Romeo that had since closed. But it was
amazing how it all came back to her now. After quick introductions to
Frieda and Dr. Banks, who recognized her from the seminar, she was
thrust into the controlled chaos of taking orders, filling drinks, and
delivering food to what must have been the whole of Conejos County. It
was wild, and Claire enjoyed the challenge.

When Abuelita came back an hour later, Claire said that there was no
way she could leave Martina, so Abuelita took the kids back to the Casa.

The pace didn't slow down until after two o'clock.

"Why don't you take a break now, Claire? I've got these last few
tables," Martina offered. "You can get a drink and go sit down in the
kitchen if you want to."

"Thanks, boss."

Martina stuck her tongue out at Claire.

Claire walked over to the drink station to fill a glass with ice and
water and then went into the kitchen. It wasn't until she sat down on a
stool in the back, by the open door, that she realized how tired her feet
were. It was a good thing she had chosen to wear her Birkenstocks, or
they'd be outright hurting. She looked down at her legs. Her faded jeans
were streaked with salsa and sour cream, and there was a guacamole
stain on the sleeve of her white poplin shirt. She blew a stray strand of
hair out of her eyes and took a long drink of her water. It tasted like rain.

"Mind if I join you?" It was Frieda, Martina's friend from the home group she was always talking about.

"Sure," Claire said, scooting over to make room for the stool Frieda was holding.

"Busy day," Frieda observed. "What a neat blessing for Martina and Jesús."

"Yes," Claire granted, though she hadn't thought of that until now.

"And I know it's been a blessing to others. This town was in need of a good gathering place."

Frieda plopped down on her stool and took a drink from her glass of water.

"Boy, that fresh air feels good."

"Yes, it does," Claire agreed. She wished she could think of something interesting to say.

"So, you're Martina's best friend from childhood?" Frieda's question was really a statement.

"Yes. We grew up together all the way through school."

"And then, let's see," Frieda said, thinking. "Martina says you went out into the world and made something of yourself while she stayed here and had a baby."

Claire was taken aback at the cognitive dissonance in Frieda's words.

"Well, yes, I suppose that's one way of putting it."

Is that how Martina described our different choices? The paths that ultimately led Martina to joy and me to sorrow?

Frieda laughed. "You know Martina. So straightforward and humble. She loves and admires you so much." Frieda's smile felt genuine.

"Excuse me, ladies!" Jerry called, swinging open the front door to the kitchen. "There's a two-top on the patio that's requesting you, Frieda."

There was mischief in his eyes.

"Me? I can't go out there; I smell like a garlic factory! Claire, you'll have to do it."

Claire looked at Jerry and then back at Frieda.

"It's somebody who wants to see you, Frieda," Jerry said. "They told me to get *you*." He smiled.

The door swung shut and he was gone.

Frieda turned to Claire. "It's probably one of my cheerleaders, but what if it's not? Martina didn't show me anything about serving. Would you mind going with me?"

Claire had rested long enough anyway. She stood to her feet with a smile.

When she saw who was sitting under the umbrella, Claire nearly dropped her tray of two ice waters. *Why did I tell him all of that stuff?* Her first instinct was to turn right back around, but the football coach and Stephen Reyes had already spotted her trailing behind Frieda with drinks that were obviously meant for them. There was no escape.

When Claire reached the table, the coach was standing up, giving Frieda a hug.

Stephen stood to his feet. "Claire, what a nice surprise!" He sounded like he meant it. His manner was easy, comfortable as an old denim jacket, and he was grinning from ear to ear. Claire could see the tiny chip in his front tooth and the look of obvious pleasure in his eyes.

Claire felt anything but pleased. She shakily set down the two glasses, spilling a little bit of water on Martina's woven Mexican table cloth. The pattern on this one was fish. In front of Stephen's seat, a spot spread out slightly over one of the fish, darkening the cloth. It quickly disappeared.

She looked up at him.

"Hi," she said weakly.

Stephen's eyes were steady. "Claire, this is Joe, my good friend that I told you about. And Joe, this is Claire Caspian. You already know Frieda?"

Claire nodded and took the hand that Joe offered her. It was big, and hers seemed to disappear when he covered it with his other hand.

"Nice to meet you, Claire," Joe said, pumping her hand heartily.

"It's nice to meet you, too, Joe."

Frieda put one hand on her hip and waved her other index finger back and forth between Stephen and Claire.

"How do you two know each other?"

"Well—" Stephen began.

"He's my doctor," Claire answered, before Stephen could finish.

"Oh," Frieda said.

Stephen sat back down. His jaw was tightening.

"So, do you ladies have time to join us?" Joe asked.

Frieda looked at Claire.

"Why don't you go ahead, Frieda," Claire told her. "We're not that busy right now. I'll let Jesús know in the kitchen."

"What about you?" she asked.

"I think I'd better stay available to Martina out here. But I'll wait on you guys. How's that?"

Stephen looked a little disappointed, and Claire hated herself for being so brusque. *What is wrong with me?*

"Could you come out with us later for dessert?" Stephen's eyes were imploring.

"Yeah, babe," Joe turned to Frieda. "We've got a little surprise cooked up for you two."

"That sounds great to me." Frieda settled into the seat next to Joe and smiled.

They all looked up at Claire, waiting for her to answer.

"Uh, I'm sorry, but I can't." Claire's words hit the ground with a thud. Taking up her order pad, she quickly changed the subject.

"Are you ready to order or do you need a few more minutes?"

"I think I need a few more minutes," Joe said.

Stephen didn't look up from his menu.

159

Chapter Eighteen

....

When Claire arrived back at the Casa, she found Abuelita, Graeme, and Gabbie sitting on the floor in the den. They were intently studying Graeme's oversized checkerboard, but it was not set with its regular black and red checkers. Instead, the squares were covered with an assortment of Graeme's dinosaur figurines.

Graeme and Gabbie were bent over one side of the board, advancing what appeared to be an army of meat-eaters, while Abuelita strategized from the other, setting a trap for their green T. rex with her purple triceratops.

"Oh, man!" Graeme exclaimed to Gabbie. "She's going to wipe out our T. rex!"

"*Hola* everybody! I'm home!"

Graeme jumped up to hug Claire, keeping one eye fastened on the board.

"Mommy! We're playing Dino-checkers!"

"Cool." She sat down beside them with Graeme in her lap.

"*Buenas tardes, hija.* I was just jumping Graeme and Gabbie's lizard king." Abuelita raised her triceratops dramatically and crashed it down onto the T. rex, knocking it over.

"Good-bye, tiny lizard," she said sweetly. "It has been nice knowing you."

She replaced the T. rex by standing her triceratops proudly on the empty square.

"We still have our allosaurus and velociraptor," Gabbie said, glaring down her nose.

At seven o'clock Martina called. Claire could hear a cacophony of voices in the background.

"Claire, I should have planned ahead better than this. I had no idea—Yes, Rosa, that goes to table five."

"Martina, do you want Gabbie to spend the night with us?"

"Can she? Would it be too much trouble? Alberto! Over here. This table needs bussing. There are fifteen people waiting!"

"It's fine—great. Graeme and Gabbie will be thrilled. Don't worry about a thing."

"I'll call you in the morning! *Muchas gracias!*"

"*De nada.*"

Claire hung up the phone and continued to peel the orange in her hand. Then she peeled a second one and pulled it apart, arranging the slices on saucers in the shape of two pinwheels. She poured Graeme and Gabbie each a cup of warm milk and herself and Abuelita cups of hot water, dropping a bag of chai in Abuelita's and Ginger Peach in her own. Arranging this all on a silver tray—one of Abuelita's many—Claire carried it out to the patio, where Abuelita was sitting in a lounge chair beside a big terra-cotta pot filled with colorful cacti. She looked very relaxed. Maybe even asleep. Graeme and Gabbie were squatted by the goldfish pond a few yards away.

"Are you two *fishing*?" Claire gasped when she saw their poles.

She set down the tray on the table by Abuelita and ran over to them just in time to see Gabbie's cork go under.

"You've got one, Gab! Reel him in!"

Gabbie jerked her pole and reeled as fast as she could. One of Abuelita's fantail goldfish, a calico about four inches long, appeared at the end of her line.

"Way to go, Gabbie!" Graeme jumped up and down, patting his friend on the back as if she'd just caught a prize Dolly Varden trout.

"Boy, that's a nice one!"

Gabbie held the fish right up in front of Claire's face. It wriggled on the hook, splashing her with tiny drops of water. Claire blinked and sputtered, appalled.

"Can you get him off for me? Graeme and I are going to cook him."

"*Cook* him? Abuelita, did you tell these children they could fish for your pets?"

Abuelita raised up her head and opened her eyes. "Oh, what's it hurt? As long as they put them back."

"Aw, we wanted to have fish for a snack," Graeme complained. "You could filet him up like Aunt Moira does."

"I am not Aunt Moira, and I do not filet fish," Claire reprimanded him. "Besides, those were catfish. No one is going to eat Abuelita's goldfish. They are her pets!"

She grabbed hold of Gabbie's line and eased the hook out of the fish's mouth, relieved to see that it slipped out without doing much damage.

"Let's put you back where you belong," she said, lowering the fish into the water's edge and gently letting it go. There was a *plop* and a flash of white tailfin, and the goldfish disappeared to safety.

While they were eating their snacks on the patio, Claire made an announcement.

"Gabbie, your mother called and asked if you wanted to spend the night with Graeme tonight. Would you like to do that?"

The children squealed in response.

"As soon as we finish our snacks, you each need to get into the bathtub. I'll let you sleep in the guest room where you can watch a movie."

"Can we take a bath in Abuelita's Jacuzzi?"

"Sure you can, Graemesy," said Abuelita. "You can fill it up with bubbles."

"Let's go, Gabbie!" Graeme said, setting down his cup.

They raced each other in the house and rambled up the stairs to grab some toys out of Graeme's room. Claire finished her tea and met them on the way down the hall to the master suite.

* * * * *

That night, when *Beauty and the Beast* was over and Graeme and Gabbie were both fast asleep, Claire knocked on Abuelita's bedroom door.

"Abuelita? Are you awake?"

"*Sí, hija.* Come in."

Abuelita was sitting up in her bed with piles of down pillows propped up behind her. She was wearing a peach-colored gauze gown trimmed in white Battenberg lace. Her dark hair, streaked with gray, fell in long, graceful curves below her shoulders. A Tiffany lamp cast soft light over the weathered pages of her Bible, which she held like a treasure in her thin-skinned, velvety soft, manicured hands.

Claire sat down on the edge of the bed. She suddenly felt like she was five years old.

"What is it, child?"

"I just wanted to talk to you a little bit."

Abuelita smiled. "Those kids are pretty sweet, aren't they? It reminds me of you and Martina when you were that age."

"Yeah. They really *get* each other."

"They do. So much is understood between them. That's a good way of saying it." Abuelita fingered an embroidered bookmark that was yellow with age. "Do you remember this?"

Claire leaned over to look at it. In crude purple stitches, the bookmark read, "Trust in the Lord with all your heart."

"I can't believe you still have that!"

"Of course I do. You made it for me in Bible school when you were seven. It is one of my dearest treasures."

Abuelita looked from Claire back to the bookmark, as though imagining her granddaughter as a little child.

"Abuelita, how have you kept your faith in God all these years? I don't mean just belief—I mean this daily, connected faith you've always had. How do you do it?"

Claire's eyes were as direct as her question.

Abuelita studied them as though she was trying to figure out a riddle written there. Then she spoke.

"I don't do it—He does."

Claire sighed and looked away. Abuelita could be really frustrating sometimes. "I don't understand what you're talking about."

Abuelita straightened her shoulders against the pillows. "Claire, I believe the Christian life is the best life to live. But I have found that it is impossible for me to live it."

"I think that's how I feel, too." It surprised Claire to find this common ground, for Abuelita to put into words what she herself had been feeling lately. "I mean, I still believe the things you and Mamá and Daddy taught me as a girl—most of them. I want Graeme to learn to be kind, to share, and to forgive. I even believe, at least I think I do, that God created us and that Jesus came to show us how to live. I try, but as far as experiencing any sense of daily connection with my faith, I just don't anymore. It's like this faraway thing—this set of old rules that don't apply to the game I'm playing."

"What game is that, *hija*?"

Claire drew her legs underneath her and gazed soulfully at Abuelita. She could feel her neck tingling and knew it was probably breaking out into a hundred red hives.

"It's life. A game where people get massacred doing the will of God and never come home. A game that kills a little boy's daddy with pancreatic cancer. A game where there's war and hunger and abuse and a million other things I don't understand."

Claire didn't intend to challenge Abuelita when she started talking, but she realized now that it came out that way.

Her grandmother didn't take the challenge. In fact, she didn't say anything for a long time. Claire's words hung between them in the air like mushroom clouds.

Finally, Abuelita spoke up. "I don't understand those things either, *hija*. And I am so very sorry for how you have suffered."

"It's not about me—not really. I know you have suffered, too, Abuelita."

Abuelita nodded, her gaze steady.

"But you keep going," Claire continued. "You keep reading the Bible; you keep praying; you keep living this impossible life. I admire you, and it seems to bring you peace, but I just don't get how you do it."

Abuelita chuckled a little. "I know it aggravates you for me to say this, but *I* don't do it. I couldn't do it, for the same reasons you can't. But He can."

Claire furrowed her brows, and Abuelita reached over to smooth them out with the pads of her fingers.

"He can, *hija*. Stop thinking so hard. It's not something that comes from the head, but His work within the heart."

"You know that everything in me rails against such an idea, Abuelita." Claire smiled at her grandmother, but her words were serious.

They sat in silence for a few minutes.

Then Abuelita cocked her head to one side and grinned impishly. "So, did you enjoy your time at Art and Sol? You seemed a little flushed when you got home. I guess Martina worked you pretty hard, eh?"

Does nothing get past her? "Well, actually, I was ready to get out of there. I felt like I was suffocating by the time I left."

"Suffocating? How on earth do you mean?"

Claire sighed. She might as well come out with it; sooner or later, Abuelita would fish it out of her. "Dr. Reyes came in there with his friend. They wanted to take me—and his friend's girlfriend—out for dessert."

"Oh! *Buena idea*! What a nice idea. Why didn't you go?"

"I didn't want to."

"What do you mean you didn't want to?" Abuelita looked at Claire like she'd just grown horns.

"I just didn't feel like it." Claire rose to go. "You're right that waiting tables wore me out; I'm tired. I think I'm going to go to bed." She bent over to kiss Abuelita on the cheek. "*Buenas noches*."

Abuelita kissed her back. "*Buenas noches* yourself. But before you go, I have one observation to make." Abuelita squinted her coal-black eyes at Claire.

"What is it?" Claire smiled at her from the doorway.

"You're not tired from waiting tables. You're tired from running away."

Chapter Nineteen

....

Stephen didn't stop in Romeo after climbing into his truck at Joe's. He
passed the iron gates of Claire's abuelita's mansion just outside Romeo, went
through Romeo proper, and kept going when he came to the turn onto
County Road 7. Highway 285 led him past the grain elevator in Romeo and
through the towns of La Jara, Estrella, and Alamosa.

It never ceased to amaze Stephen how the villages were laid out.
When the train came to the area in 1880, it had to stop for water every
seven miles. So, just like that, these dusty little towns were born along its
tracks at seven-mile intervals.

At least some of them had kept their original names, or at least been
named for appropriate things, Stephen thought. Like *la jara*, the willow,
or *estrella*, star. Poor Romeo, which outsiders incorrectly associated
with Shakespeare, was instead a corruption of the common surname
"Romero." Some railroad worker, keeping official records and obviously
off on his Spanish, converted it.

Stephen shook his head at the thought. He was nursing wounded
pride himself and suddenly stirred by the injustice of it all.

Unlike the train, Stephen didn't stop for water or anything else.
At Poncha Springs, he turned onto Highway 50 toward Salida and
called Maria.

"Steve?"

He could hear loud techno music in the background.

"Where in the world are you?"

"I'm at the gym. In an aerobics class. Where are you?"

"They let you take your cell phone into the class?"

"I'm a doctor, remember?"

The music abated, and he assumed she'd stepped outside of the class.

"When's your class over?"

"In about fifteen minutes."

"Do you want to meet at Rumors?"

"Where are you?" she asked him.

"I'm just driving into town. I can almost see S Mountain."

"Well, I'm sweaty. I can't be ready for Rumors very soon. Why don't you just go to my house and I'll meet you there? Do you still have your key?"

"Yeah."

"Go in and make yourself at home. Do the laundry or something."

"Ha ha."

"I'll be there in about half an hour."

"Okay."

* * * * *

The exterior of his sister's house was so *Maria*, just like the interior was. It was a large pueblo-style adobe, with solar panels for heat and light. The flower beds were full of useful cacti, like Aloe Vera, and blended with herbs and peppers and other plants Maria used for cooking. Rocks she'd collected from various expeditions in the mountains, or on drives along back roads, complimented the landscaping. Stephen recognized several from his own ranch.

Turning toward the porch, he saw her latest acquisition: Old Betsy, one of his elderly cows who had not made it through the last winter. He'd cringed when Maria hauled the cow's skull home in the trunk of her hybrid Beamer. But he couldn't argue with the result. Old Betsy's skull, bleached and cured in the sun, hung from a leather strap by the front door. Stephen imagined it would be distasteful anywhere else, but here it was totally natural, even beautiful. Artistic along the lines of Georgia O'Keefe.

Wiping his feet on the mat, he turned the key and went inside. As if company was expected, there were soft lights everywhere and music playing. Stephen recognized Beethoven's Ninth symphony. He set his keys on the table by the door, picking up a picture of Manuel and Maria on their honeymoon in Hawaii. They were wearing leis, and Maria was more flamboyant than any of the flowers, shimmering in her white linen dress beside the dark-tanned Manuel.

You are one lucky man, Stephen thought as he looked at his brother-in-law's image.

He set the picture down and walked straight ahead into the living room, where he sat down on the couch and popped a chocolate from Maria's candy dish into his mouth. He picked up the remote. Directly in front of Stephen was a red wall, which was mostly taken up by a stone fireplace that ran from the floor to ceiling. A huge oil painting in reds and golds on a background of gray blue was the focal point of the fireplace above the mantle, its violent distortions of shape reminiscent of Picasso's *Guernica*.

Stephen pressed a button on the remote and the painting disappeared, revealing a fifty-two-inch, flat-screen TV. He turned the channel to *Headline News*. He wasn't in the mood for silence.

As the "news from around the globe" droned on, Stephen decided to surprise his sister. He walked to the laundry room, which was just off the kitchen, and put in a load of laundry. Maria washed her own scrubs, and as he picked through the light ones for a load of whites, he noticed Bugs Bunny, Tweety Bird, characters from *The Incredibles* and *Nemo*, and a dinosaur he didn't recognize—presumably a cartoon for each day of the week. Stephen chuckled to himself as he dumped in a scoop of Cheer.

Grabbing a bottle of water from the fridge as he walked back through the kitchen, he spotted a note on the refrigerator door that was held there by a magnet. It was from Maria's husband, who was still in Colombia.

My dearest Maria,

The days here are long and the need great—but God's grace is sufficient for all things. I trust you are finding His grace sufficient at home.

Everywhere I go I see you in front of me then reaching out find it is only a mirage. I keep myself going with thoughts of your beautiful face and the sound of your laughter.

Only three more weeks until we are together again.

Pray for the people of Colombia.

Te amo,

Manuel

Okay, so maybe she was lucky, too.

A few moments later, Stephen heard the sound of the automatic garage door opening.

"Stephen?" his sister called through the back door.

"I'm just in here—doing your laundry!"

She rounded the corner of the kitchen and smiled at him. She was wearing a white terry-cloth jogging suit and had a bright bag emblazoned with the British flag slung over her shoulder.

"You do beat all!" she said, reaching out to give him a hug.

Stephen squeezed her tightly, inhaling the smell of lavender soap.

"To what do I owe this honor?" Maria deposited her gym bag in the laundry room and shut the door. She grabbed her own bottle of water from the fridge and sat down on a bar stool in the kitchen, staring at her brother.

"Oh, you know, I was just in the neighborhood and thought I'd stop by." He joined her on the nearest bar stool.

"Whatever! What's going on? I thought you had another date tonight with that cute little professor, Princess Caspian."

Stephen's eyes darkened.

"I'm not so sure she is a princess after all."

"What do you mean? What did she do to you?"

Maria set down her water, looking like she was suddenly ready for a fight. Her show of protectiveness lightened the mood for Stephen. He had to laugh.

"She didn't do anything to me. That's kind of the problem."

"What do you mean?"

"Well, you know, Joe and I went to that new Mexican restaurant in Romeo this afternoon. Some people he knows just opened it. Frieda—that's Joe's girlfriend—was working there for them and we thought Claire might be there, too, because the woman running it is her best friend. This was the grand opening so everybody was pitching in, helping them out."

Stephen took a sip of water.

"Okay," Maria said, "I think I followed all of that."

"Anyway, we were going to see about taking them out for dessert, maybe roasting some s'mores or something at the ranch. But when Claire saw me she would hardly say a word. Turned us down flat about dessert. It was more than a little awkward. She said she'd wait on us, but once she brought our food, we never saw her again. Martina—she's the owner—came and told us Claire had to go home."

"She was waiting tables?" Maria looked shocked.

"Yeah, they were really busy. She was doing it to help her friend out."

"That's kind of cool."

"I thought so, too, until she lit out of there." Stephen shrugged his shoulders.

"So what did you do?"

"We ate, and then Joe took me to his house to get my truck. He was going over to Frieda's. I was headed toward home, but I decided to drive up here and see my therapist instead."

Maria smiled. "So, you want my professional opinion?"

"That's why I pay you the big bucks."

Maria looked directly into Stephen's eyes. "You better run like your hair's on fire," she said. "This woman's not worth your time."

Chapter Twenty
························

"Are you serious?" Stephen nearly fell off his bar stool.

"What do you mean?" Maria asked him.

"I mean, just like that, you think I should forget about Claire?"

"Why not?"

"What about all of those conversations we've had about my marriage to Janet and how I should forgive her for what she did—how insensitive I'd been—how selfish. You and Manuel have both preached to me about how relationships are hard work, and they take two people. What about all of that?"

Maria rubbed her lips together, trying not to smile.

"What about it?" she asked him.

Stephen got down from his stool and walked over to the couch, sinking into it. He held his head in his hands, fighting off anger.

Maria turned on her stool to face him.

"Why are you so angry, Steve?"

He looked up at her.

"I'm confused and, frankly, surprised at you. After all of the times you've told me the whole thing with Janet was partly my fault—because I wasn't there for her—and now you think I should just walk away from Claire? She's the one woman I've cared about since then. I don't get it, Maria."

Maria got down from her stool at the bar and walked over to where Stephen was sitting on the couch. She sat down beside him and touched his knee.

"Are you listening to yourself?" she asked gently.

"No, I feel crazy."

"Well, that's why you're here for therapy."

They both laughed, diffusing the tension that had been there a moment before.

"Steve, I broke the first rule of counseling awhile ago when I told you what I thought you should do. But I didn't really do it to give you my opinion."

His eyes were unsteady, questioning her.

"I did it to help you find out what's in your own heart." Maria touched him gently on his chest, and the light of realization began to dawn on Stephen. But now he wasn't sure he wanted to go there.

Maria pressed him. "What have you heard yourself say? I think there's a lot you've said that's important here."

"I don't know."

"Well, first, you've said you care about Claire. She's the one woman you've cared about since Janet. That's pretty significant." Maria's eyes were blue crystals, boring holes through him.

"Okay, that's true. I do care about her—a lot." Stephen took a deep breath.

"The other things you said were about Janet. Do you believe you were at fault in your divorce?"

"I know that it wasn't all her. I am partly to blame because I wasn't there for her. I was caught up in myself—my career. I know that."

Stephen felt like a cork had popped off his soul and the contents were spewing forth at a rate he couldn't control. He was also aware—and thankful—that it was safe to be with Maria. That's why he'd come here.

"But Janet didn't have to have an affair and play me for the fool— that was wrong of her. And I was wrong in how I dealt with things, both before and after. I was a prideful jerk. I was horrible to her, really."

Several years of remorse washed over Stephen like a melting glacier. And though the cleansing felt good, Maria stopped him from drowning in it.

"Well, let's don't go too far. Janet's no saint."

Stephen straightened his back. "What about Claire?"

"Who knows?" Maria wagered. "One difference here is that you *aren't* married to her. You really could walk away and may need to. She may not yet be ready for another relationship. I certainly don't know her well enough to say."

Stephen searched a spot on the wall for the answers.

"What do you truly believe in your heart, Steve? What do you believe about this woman? *Is* she worth your time? Does she have the character you are looking for in a woman? Or is she a flake?"

"I thought when we had that incredible time together that she was amazing—like a mine full of diamonds. There was so much more I wanted to learn about her. I didn't think she was flaky at all."

Stephen blew out a loud sigh and clapped his hands on his knees. "But she really seemed to push me away today. That was hard to take."

"Do you think she could be scared of you? Scared of getting closer?"

"Maybe. But I thought from what she said that she was ready to try, or at least open to trying."

Maria looked him straight in the eyes. "Well, it seems like you have a decision to make. Get out with this minimal investment, or take a chance on her and risk your own heart—without knowing whether she'll give you hers. This could be a test for you to see how well you can swallow your pride."

"I'm not real good at that." Stephen allowed.

"How well I know."

They both grinned.

"I really do think she's worth it, Maria. I could be wrong, but I believe she is. At any rate, I guess I have to find out."

"Well, you've answered your own question, then."

They sat in silence for awhile, watching the headlines run across a TV that had long since been muted.

Finally, Stephen spoke up. "Thank you—for listening."

Maria stood to her feet. "You're welcome, but it's going to cost you."

"Huh?"

"Dinner at Rumors. You're buying."

* * * * *

Maria changed into a cashmere sweater and jeans, and soon they were sitting at their favorite table watching the Arkansas River roll by.

Maria ordered grilled mahi mahi with garlic mashed potatoes, and Stephen had a salad.

"I had a late lunch, remember?" he explained when she looked at him crossways.

"Oh, yeah. That elucidates it." Maria flashed her eyebrows up and down at him, challenging his vocabulary. It was a little game they'd always played, to try to find a word the other didn't know.

"You're irascible."

"Quick-tempered? How? I don't think that's really fair." She crossed her arms and frowned at him.

Stephen corrected himself. "That's not the word I meant. I meant incorrigible."

She brightened. "Oh, like inveterate."

"What's that?"

"It's the same as incorrigible. I think I got you that time!" Maria gloated.

"Have you been sitting around reading the thesaurus?"

"Well, I have been pretty lonely."

For the first time that night, Stephen thought he saw clouds skim across her sky-blue eyes. It could have been the lighting, but he didn't think so.

Just then a waiter with multiple piercings came to the table with their food.

"Mmm." Maria cut into the flaky meat of the fish with her fork and dipped it into a buttery-looking sauce.

Stephen took a bite of raw spinach that was covered with a Korean red sauce and sprinkled with bacon. *Delicious.*

"How's Manuel?" he asked her.

"He's doing great. I mean, I think he's pretty lonesome, too, but it's a good work they're doing."

"What kind of stuff is he seeing over there?"

"Everything. He says he's seen it all. But the most amazing thing that's happened is supernatural healing. He says many of the people they deal with have childlike faith—they're very open and trusting. He says when they pray they really believe."

"What a novel idea," Stephen remarked.

"I want to go sometime. Wouldn't it be amazing to be in that setting—where people recognize the Lord as their only hope? I mean— He's our only hope here or anywhere, but sometimes our wealth and sophistication keep us from seeing that."

"I hope Manuel doesn't get a wild hair and try to carry you off over some shark-infested waters to live. It's bad enough him being over there all of these weeks."

"Oh, Steve, honestly. It's been the trip of a lifetime. He wrote that the other day he rode in a boat down the Amazon River to another village. On the way they saw pink dolphins!"

Stephen was thinking about Claire's parents, who were murdered on the mission field, but he decided not to mention that to Maria.

"That's cool. Did he get pictures?"

"He says he got some good ones."

"Well, how are *you* surviving? When did you start reading the thesaurus?"

Maria shrugged. "It's just sort of hit me lately. We're halfway through, and I guess it's just started seeming a little long."

Suddenly a thought came to Stephen, a way he could treat his sister to something unusual.

"Do you still like s'mores?" he asked her.

"Who doesn't like s'mores?"

"Well, Claire's loss is your gain. I'm going to take you on a little adventure after we get done here."

* * * * *

High above Salida on S Mountain, Stephen built a little fire in the moonlight with some sticks he and Maria gathered. They were facing southeast, down toward the twinkling lights of the town. The rivulets of farmland and forest beyond that inched upward, away from Salida, and peaked at the snowy mountains. The night air was chilly, and the friendly firelight flickered and breathed out the earthy smell of wood smoke.

Stephen grabbed the Mexican blanket, which he kept under the backseat of his truck, and spread it out next to the fire. Then he used his pocket knife to carve two skewers out of the limbs of a young juniper.

Maria, for her part, assembled chocolate bars and graham crackers on a paper plate. Stephen toasted several marshmallows, and she captured them between graham crackers as they came off the fire. The melted chocolate oozed off the sides of the s'mores and tasted delectably sweet.

They sat there on the Mexican blanket, two kids from Oklahoma. Two medical doctors who looked as different as any two people could look on the outside. They listened to the sounds of a Colorado nightfall, eating s'mores and not saying a word until most of the lights of Salida had gone out. Then, like the twins that they were, they gathered their things in silent agreement and drove back down the mountain toward Maria's home.

Chapter Twenty-one
....

When Claire arrived at her office Monday morning at eight thirty, she had fifty-six e-mail messages. Scanning through her inbox for a place to start deleting, she spotted one from Martina and one from Moira. She clicked on Martina's message, which was posted late Sunday night.

Claire Claire,

Thank you again for helping me yesterday. It was fun having you at the grand opening (till you left), and Jesús and I have laughed many times at the idea that we had a professor and a rocket scientist on our wait staff. Quite impressive for a first day! In all seriousness, it meant the world to me that you were there. And also that you took care of my baby for me. Please thank Abuelita again for her part in that.

I have had a good day of rest, which I desperately needed. I hope this schedule will work out well, being off Sunday and Monday.

I won't write about it here (I still don't fully trust computers), but remind me to tell you something important about Mickey. Something very upsetting happened on Saturday night, which I am still processing.

XXOO

Martina

Claire smiled at her friend's use of the old childhood nickname "Claire Claire." Martina had called her that starting in first grade, when they met another boy in their class whose parents called him "John John."

The second e-mail of interest was from Moira, Rob's sister in Arkansas. It had been sent Friday night at ten o'clock from her e-mail address at Arkansas Tech University, where Moira taught biology.

Claire imagined her sister-in-law—wire-bespectacled green eyes, wavy, russet hair going every direction, no makeup, wearing a faded jean skirt with a Grateful Dead T-shirt—sitting in her lab typing on a laptop with dry, cracked fingers fresh out of some chemical solution and scrubbed with antibacterial soap, while she timed an experiment.

Claire.

> *How are you? Any dreams lately?*
>
> *Your in my prayers.*
>
> *I have two things to tell you: One is that I would like to have Graeme come and stay with me sometime in the summer if you (and he) are up to it. You could come to, of course, or could consider it a little break for yourself and be kid-free for a couple of weeks. The other is that I feel a new sense of joy as I pray for you. A new hope. I believe that the Lord is doing a new thing in your life, and I want to encourage you to expect it, even embrace it!*
>
> *Must get back to work. We're doing fruit flies in Genetics lab on Monday.*

Moira

Claire's inner editor cringed at Moira's use of "Your" where it should have been "You're," and "to" when she meant "too." How could a scientific genius, which Moira certainly was, use such abominable grammar? It must be a left-brained thing, which Claire would never understand.

Claire reread the email, this time ignoring its mistakes.

No way will I be up to letting Graeme go to Arkansas alone, she thought, even though she knew he needed to see his father's family. Maybe they could both go. There were few people she loved and trusted more than Moira.

And what was this "new thing" Moira wrote about? Her sister-in-law could be a little "out there" in her ideas sometimes. But Claire had to admit that Moira was a spiritual rock for her, the only other person she really confided in besides Abuelita.

Suddenly it struck Claire. *Surely she isn't talking about Stephen Reyes?*

* * * * *

On the drive home that afternoon, Claire called Martina.

She answered after the first ring. Claire could hear the sound of cars going by in the background and imagined her friend in the backyard.

"So tell me about Mickey," she said. "That was so mean of you to e-mail it like that and have me wonder about him all day."

"I'm sorry."

"Is he okay? Are you? Can you talk about it? I mean, is he around?"

"No, but there are little ears. I'm in the backyard pushing Gabbie on the swing."

"Well, do you want to tell me later?"

"Let me see if I can go over here and water the plants. Can you pump awhile, sweetie?" Martina called.

Claire couldn't hear Gabbie's answer, but it didn't sound very favorable. She also heard the sound of running water.

"Okay, can you hear me? I'm watering my plants on the patio." Martina spoke very softly.

"I can hear you."

"Well, it's awful."

"What happened?"

Martina's voice was barely above a whisper. "Mickey went to a party Saturday night and was drinking!"

"Saturday night? I thought he was at the restaurant!" Claire exclaimed.

"He was. He washed dishes for us until ten o'clock, and then we let him go. He said he had plans with his friend Juan. They were going to spend the night over at Juan's house."

"Martina, are you crying?"

"Yes, but I can't let Gabbie see. Just a second."

There was the sound of a nose blowing and then Martina returned. "Okay. I have to stop that. It's doing no good."

"Oh, Martina, I'm so sorry. I know you are very hurt. But is Mickey okay?"

"Yes, he is okay. He's in lots of trouble, but he's okay."

"How did you find out?"

"Juan's mother called me Sunday. Oh, Claire, this is the worst part."

Claire waited on the other end of the line.

"I didn't know it, but Juan's parents are separated. Apparently the boys spent the night with his father and there was a party over there. *He* bought the alcohol."

"Oh, Lord."

"I've been so absorbed with getting this business going that I haven't kept short accounts with Mickey like I usually do. I trusted him so much. Too much for a teenager, I guess."

"He has been so trustworthy."

"I know, but they still need guidance." Maria sniffed. "Mickey came home the next day—he was supposed to meet us at church but he missed. He was home when we got here, just said he was too tired to make it. But he was acting so strange all day and then she called, and he finally told us about it."

Claire sighed. "I'm shocked, and I know you are very disappointed, so I don't want to make light of it, Martina. It *is* a big deal. But Mickey is a good boy."

"I know he's a good boy. I just can't believe he did this!"

"How are you handling it? I mean, what are you and Jesús doing for consequences?" Claire, who couldn't help but sympathize with Mickey a little, waited for the bomb to fall.

"He's grounded forever. And he had to tell his coach—we took him over there on Sunday. He broke a team rule. The coach is making him run."

There was a pause, and Claire could hear Gabbie calling her mother.

"Martina?"

"What?"

"Everybody makes mistakes. You're a good mom and Mickey's still a great kid. We all have lessons to learn."

We all have lessons to learn, Claire thought a minute later as she pressed the END key on her cell phone. Her own words troubled her a little. Just a few days ago, Abuelita had all but told Claire she did too much thinking and not enough believing. Not enough trusting. Now Moira wanted to keep Graeme in Arkansas for two weeks, by himself. She also wanted Claire to embrace a "new thing" in her life, which could mean only one thing: *Stephen.* But Claire didn't trust her own heart, and she was afraid to trust God's love. Trusting had taken her to some painful places in the past. What kind of lessons did she still have to learn?

On a whim, she flipped through the numbers on her cell phone. "REG FAM CARE" came up on the tiny screen, still there in the phone's memory from the time she called about her mole. Claire selected the number and pressed SEND. Her heart pounded as it rang.

"Regional Family Care, this is Irene. How may I direct your call?"

"Is Dr. Stephen Reyes available?" Claire had no idea what she'd say if he was.

"Excuse me?"

"I said, is Dr. Reyes available?"

"Do you mean for an appointment?" The voice on the other end sounded annoyed.

"Oh, uh, no. I was wondering if he was available to talk for a moment."

"Who is this?"

"This is—Dr. Claire Caspian." Claire figured the fractious receptionist wouldn't remember her, and she apparently didn't.

"I'll give you his consultation line. He or his nurse may pick up if he's available. Please hold."

There was acoustic guitar music while Claire held. She never used her title when introducing herself and realized it had been a little sneaky. Irene likely assumed Claire was calling for professional reasons.

Finally, someone picked up.

"This is Stephen Reyes."

Claire's face turned red as a beet, she saw, as she glanced into her rearview mirror. "Hello?" he asked again.

"Dr. Reyes?" Claire croaked. Ideas flashed across her mind like lightening bolts as she tried to think of something to say that would not be completely ridiculous.

"Yes?"

"Uh, I was wondering if you might know a cure for someone with very cold feet?"

"Is this Claire Caspian? *Doctor* Claire Caspian?"

It seemed to Claire that she could hear him smiling. The tone of his voice had completely changed, and she imagined his long eyelashes and the crinkles around his eyes. The image of him smiling warmed her.

"I'm afraid it is. Thank you for speaking with me, Doctor."

"What seems to be the problem with your feet?"

"They're just—cold. And it's causing me to take wrong steps—and perhaps give others the impression that the rest of me is cold." Claire surprised herself with the accuracy of her chosen metaphor.

"*Are* you cold, Doctor Caspian? How about in your heart?" Stephen played along, and Claire was very glad he hadn't hung up.

She admitted, "I don't want to be. No, I'm not."

"Well, perhaps we could work on a cure for those feet together."

It was Claire's turn to smile. She pressed forward. "Would you like to have lunch with me tomorrow? In Alamosa?"

"Let me look on the schedule."

There was clicking sound and Claire presumed he was pulling up his schedule on the computer.

"Claire, I'm booked tomorrow—unless you could do an early dinner."

She hated to be away from Graeme in the evenings but knew Abuelita wouldn't mind. "I could do that," she ventured. "What time were you thinking?"

"It would be about four thirty before I could get there," Stephen said.

"That's okay. I have plenty of work I can do. Why don't you come on up and I'll show you my office?"

Claire felt she was being extremely forward. It was like an out-of-body experience, this phone call, but she went with it. After all, she reasoned, she owed this man a measure of goodwill after how badly she had behaved on Saturday night.

Stephen said, "That would be great."

"It's in the building just across from the one where we had the seminar—it's called Irby."

"Irby. Okay. Let me write that down."

Claire could hear Stephen scribbling.

"My office is in the English department, of course, on the third floor. Room 318."

"Room 318. Got it. Okay, that sounds great!" He sounded genuinely pleased, and Claire started to feel entirely embarrassed.

"Claire?" Stephen said.

"Yes?"

"You do realize you just asked me out, don't you?"

Claire took a deep breath. "Don't rub it in."

"Did you mean to?" he asked her.

"I think—I believe—I did."

"Don't stand me up."

He had a right to worry about that, and Claire knew it.

"I won't, Stephen. I won't. I promise."

Chapter Twenty-two

....

At 4:45 there was a slight knock on the open door of Claire's office. Christina, whose eyes were as big as a deer's already, ogled them at Claire as she stood up from her desk.

"Someone's here to see you," Christina said. "A man."

"Thank you," she smiled sweetly at Christina, faking a confidence she didn't feel as she stepped past the girl and out of the safety of her office.

Stephen was sitting in one of the chairs by the front desk. He was wearing scrubs, and his face looked a bit drawn. Claire noticed, for the first time, something that glinted in the light—a bit of silver in the hair near his temples. He swept it back with his hands before folding them in his lap and crossing his long legs.

"Hi, Stephen," Claire said simply. Seeing him sitting there in the English office made her happy somehow, and she reached out her hand.

He stood and took it in his own, giving her hand a friendly squeeze.

"Hey, I'm sorry I'm late. And I'm sorry for how I'm dressed. It's been a crazy afternoon."

"That's okay. I'm glad you made it."

Christina hovered around, watching them like a chaperone until Claire introduced her.

"This is Christina, one of our student assistants here in the English department."

"Nice to meet you," Stephen said courteously.

"Hi, nice to meet you too," Christina bowed her head.

"Would you like to see my office?"

Stephen nodded, and Claire motioned down the short hall. He followed her.

Stephen walked slowly around room 318 as if he was taking everything in. He noted her diplomas on the wall, then stood at the bookshelf and pointed to the little hog figurine.

"The Razorbacks?" he said.

"*Pig sooie.*" Claire smiled and explained, "Where I got my PhD."

"I remember you telling me that."

Stephen pointed to a picture of Graeme. "And this is our little asthma patient?"

"Yeah. That's Graeme when he was three."

"Wow. He's cute. He looks just like you," Stephen said, then he blushed.

"Everyone says that. His father—" Claire started before she cut herself off.

"It's okay; go on. What about his father?"

"His father used to joke that Graeme belonged to the milkman, since he looks nothing like Rob."

"Rob—that was your husband?"

"Yes. I met him here at school."

"I remember you telling me that, too."

Stephen picked up a worn Spanish Bible that sat next to Graeme's picture on the shelf.

"What's this?"

"It was my mother's Bible. I don't usually keep it here, but I used it the other day in a class."

"Really, what for?"

"Oh, just an illustration."

Stephen's eyes, tired as they seemed before, were bright and earnest now. "Tell me about it."

"Oh, I started with one of Benjamin Franklin's sayings from *Poor*

Richard's Almanack. You know, he's famous for many of the clichés we all use today, such as 'Don't judge a book by its cover.' "

Claire walked over to Stephen and took the Bible in her hands. She touched the cracked binding gingerly with the ends of her fingers.

She explained casually, "I just showed this to the class and we talked about what it looks like on the outside. The students gave input about that, how old and ragged it is, and ugly. Some said how they would never pick it up or buy it in a store."

Claire looked from the Bible to Stephen, who listened with rapt attention.

"And then I just opened it and talked about what treasure there is inside because the Bible is so valuable. If nothing else, it's an important literary and historical document. Christianity gets such a bad rap sometimes from intellectuals, and many students don't get that, don't respect it."

Stephen nodded. "Hmm."

"Then I told them that this one is also priceless to me on a personal level because it was my mother's and it represents her faith and my own."

"You told them that?"

"Yes."

"That's neat that you could share that with your students."

"I didn't really go any further."

Claire's voice trailed off as she said those words. She wasn't sure she wanted to go any further with Stephen about issues of faith, either.

His eyes held hers for a long time as though he was holding on to the subject, but finally he said, "I like your office. Now I can picture you here."

"I like yours, too—the clinic, I mean."

Stephen smiled. "It's nothing compared to my sister's. A bit bland, I think, but I've never been as—colorful—as Maria." He looked down as though to inspect himself. "I apologize again for how I'm dressed. I got held up, and I didn't want to be any later so I didn't change."

"You look fine to me." Claire admitted to herself, though not to Stephen, that she'd call that an understatement.

"Are you hungry?" he asked.

"Yes, I am. There's a great little bistro here downtown. Would you like to go there?"

"Sure. Sounds great."

"Well, I'm not taking any work home, which is a first, so all I need is my purse." She grabbed it from the bottom drawer of her desk and snatched her scarf from the hook behind her door. Stephen shut it behind them, and Claire locked it.

The front desk area was empty. Claire turned off the lights and locked that door behind them, too. She couldn't help but think, as she led Stephen out of the building, that the English department in Irby was sealed up like a fortress. It was as tight as her heart—or as tight as it had been, before she met Stephen.

"Where are you parked?" As they stepped out of Irby, Claire scanned the parking lot that seemed all but deserted

"Just there." Stephen pointed to his truck, which was not only in a red zone but also up over the curb.

Claire winced when she saw it. "Oh my! Well, I was going to drive, but we better get you out of here before you get a ticket, if you haven't already."

"I guess that is pretty bad, isn't it? I was in a hurry."

"The campus police wouldn't care about that. The students call them 'Parking Nazis.' I'm surprised they haven't already nailed you."

Stephen opened the door to the passenger's side, and Claire climbed in. He shut the door carefully behind her. While he was walking around to his side, Claire buckled her seat belt and again recognized the scent of wood smoke. She marveled at how clean and neat it was inside Stephen's truck, which she knew he used for farm work, as well. There was evidence of that in the backseat, where she saw a rope, gloves, and a sack of feed cubes.

"I guess you're going for a ride in the redneck-mobile," Stephen joked, pulling away from the curb with a bump.

Claire smiled at him. "It feels like quite an adventure."

"Well, you direct me to this little bistro of yours and I'll try to park more appropriately."

They pulled in front of a downtown strip that housed the place in question. The sign above the door read SPUTNIK.

"What kind of name is Sputnik?" Stephen inquired. "Do they serve apricot blini?"

"I don't know," Claire answered. "I think it's a sort of Zen name. You know, a bit random, to draw you in."

"That's interesting. It could be a political statement."

"Yeah, it could be, but I don't think so. I've gotten to know the manager." Claire jumped out before Stephen could get there to open her door.

"And what about you? Are you trying to make some kind of political statement?" he teased.

"What do you mean?"

"By not letting me open your door. You're going to have to quit doing that!" he scolded.

"Why? I can open my own door. I'm not helpless."

Stephen looked hurt. "I know you're not helpless—believe me. And I'm not much of a gentleman. But I'd like to be, if you'd let me."

Claire hadn't thought about it that way. When they reached the door of the restaurant, she stood and waited for him instead of blazing her own way through.

"That's better!" He laughed as he opened the door and held it for her.

Claire felt conspicuous, like she was in some honored position, and she told him so.

"I think that's the idea." Stephen smiled as he held out her chair.

The lighting in Sputnik was dim and the décor simple. The bistro was contained in an old building in downtown Alamosa, and the owner had chosen to expose the antique brick walls and the copper pipes and electrical work in the ceilings. The floor was grey concrete.

There were candles on each table, assorted colored tapers stuck in empty wine bottles that had melted—layer upon layer—into their own unique designs over time. Batik tablecloths covered the tables. A variety of music was served via the owner's CD collection, which was as eclectic as his menu. Pearl Jam was the band du jour.

"What's good here?" Stephen asked.

"Well, I like the halibut, and their soups are always good."

The waiter arrived with stemmed goblets of water. "Ready to order?" Stephen nodded toward Claire.

"I'll have the lobster bisque and a dinner salad—house dressing on the side."

"And for you, sir?"

"I'll have this shrimp skewer with steamed fresh vegetables."

"We'll have that right out for you." The waiter smiled as he took their menus.

"That's like Abuelita," Claire observed, squeezing lemon into her water.

"What?" Stephen asked.

"She asks me what to wear and then completely ignores my suggestions."

"Oh—the halibut." Stephen made a face. "I'm sorry, but I just don't like halibut."

"That's okay."

They both laughed.

"How is your abuelita doing?"

"She's as feisty as ever. Her latest thing is beating Graeme at Dino-checkers."

"What's Dino-checkers?"

"Oh, it's a game he invented where you play checkers with several species of plastic dinosaurs."

"I see."

"When I walked in the other evening, Abuelita was gobbling up his apatosaurus, I believe, with her T. rex."

"Sounds vicious."

"She's very Darwinian when it comes to Dino-checkers. 'Survival of the fittest' and all that."

The waiter appeared, setting Claire's soup in front of her and a basket of hot, buttered sourdough bread between them.

"Mmm." Stephen sniffed appreciatively. "Could I have a cup of that?" he asked the waiter.

"No problem, sir. I'll be right back."

Stephen cleared his throat. "So," he began cautiously. "Do you feel like talking about what happened the other night at Art and Sol? Can you tell me why you left?"

He seemed to be treading lightly, but Claire knew she should account for her flighty performance.

"My goal for our next date—I mean, if there is one—" Claire colored slightly, swallowing the lump that was rising in her throat. "My goal would be to not begin with a need to apologize to you for stupid behavior."

Stephen grinned at her.

"You don't have to apologize."

"Yes, I do. Again. I behaved badly. There's no way around it."

The waiter returned with Stephen's cup of lobster bisque, and they both dug in.

"That's good," Stephen commented.

"Told you so." She grinned.

"Claire, what I would like to know is whether I did something to scare you away. Was it presumptive to come there, hoping to see you and asking you to join me and my friends for dessert? Did I put you on the spot? Am I rushing you? I don't want to do that." He seemed wholly sincere.

"I don't think so, Stephen. In my right mind I am happy—flattered— that you came to see me. But, as much as I hate to admit it, I'm not always in my right mind. Just like the other day—I get frozen by fear."

Stephen's eyes were warm and sympathetic.

"Well, let's treat those cold feet. What exactly are you afraid of?"

"Abuelita says I'm running away."

Stephen squinted his eyes, like he was trying hard to read her, like he wanted to understand. "From me?"

Claire looked into the cup of soup as though practicing some form of seafood divination. She felt like she did once as a kid, the first time she jumped off a diving board at the public pool in Manassa. Now an older and supposedly wiser Claire Caspian was standing at the edge, staring down at nothing but deep water. *What is there to lose at this point?* She decided to take the plunge.

"From the love of God."

The waiter came to the table, bringing the rest of their food and refilling their water glasses. He seemed to sense that the air was charged, because he left their ticket on the table.

"If you need anything else, just ask," he said as he quietly stepped away.

Claire noticed tiny lines come into Stephen's face and then vanish, as if an invisible hand had drawn them, thought better of it, and quickly erased.

"I understand that," he said. "I've been there myself."

"Tell me about it," Claire urged.

"I'd rather talk about you, if you don't mind."

Claire did mind, but she wasn't about to push him away again. Not now. "I've done some thinking about it since the other night, when Abuelita and I talked."

"What did she say?"

"She says I think too much—I need to trust more. But I don't know how to do that."

"Well, let's break this apart into pieces we can manage."

Claire could see Stephen's scientific mind working, and it excited her, even if what they were talking about was scary.

"It seems there are two things going on, really. You get cold feet with me so you try to put distance between us, but you're also having problems trusting God. Is that right?"

"I'd say that's probably right, Doctor." Claire's tone was playful, but her words were serious. "Do you have any recommendations?"

"Well, in all seriousness, Claire, I understand why it's hard for you to trust. You've lost a lot, and none of the bad things that have happened to you in your life make sense."

"That's true. But I know Abuelita thinks I should give up trying to make sense of everything and just live. Or what she actually says is, 'Let the Spirit of God live His life in me.' "

"She sounds like a pretty wise old woman."

"I get exasperated by how simply she puts things that seem impossible for me, but in the end I can't argue with her. She has suffered too—she knows a lifetime of loss—and yet there is this presence of God with her, not just as a metaphysical concept, but as a daily existence. It's an experience that is very real to her and, I have to admit, real to me as I look at her life."

"That sounds like a very pure gospel. Especially from someone who has lived with her."

"It is. But I think the question is how to make it my own? I haven't been able to find that answer."

Stephen looked at Claire for a long time, studying her. When he spoke again, his words seemed to come from a raw place.

"I think I'm learning the answer, at least for me—or I hope I am."

"What do you mean?"

"Well, after everything that happened with my ex-wife, I had a bit of a death experience. I died to a lot of things that had been very important to me."

Claire knew all about death experiences. "Like what?"

"Dreams. Goals. Most specifically, my pride. I won't say that it's never a struggle for me anymore, because it is. But when your wife cheats on you, you truly realize what it means to be humiliated."

Stephen stirred the soup he hadn't yet finished.

"I didn't tell you this before, Claire, but another bad part of that whole thing for me was church. My wife and I went to a big church in Tulsa. We were pretty involved, at least on the surface. Gave lots of money. But when all of that happened, I was excommunicated."

"No way!" Claire gasped.

"Well, not literally, not like you're thinking." Stephen smiled at her. "It was subtle, more like I wore a scarlet "D" for Divorce from there on out. Of course, there were other divorced people in the church—tons of them—but I guess this was sort of high-profile. I embarrassed the church. And in my Sunday school class, the group we hung out with, well, I found out I didn't really have many friends."

"That's horrible!" Claire felt sick.

"It was horrible. But looking back after eight years now, I can understand it somewhat."

"How? That's ridiculous!" The thought of it raised Claire's ire.

"Well, you're right. The response of many people was poor. But my response was worse."

"How did you respond?"

"Well, I responded to my wife's affair by throwing her out of the house."

"That was justified, if all you've told me is true."

Stephen's eyes grew darker—and flat. "It was all true, but you know, Claire, I wasn't much of a husband. I see that more and more all the time. What I needed was someone to help me—straighten me out—but I wasn't ready to be helped. At least most of them didn't coddle me just for the money. I have to give them that. You see that happen some places, where sin is just overlooked if the money is big enough."

"Yes, but what about 'judge not'? What about brotherly love?" Claire was utterly stricken by Stephen's experience.

"Well, there was some instance of kicking a guy when he was down— that's true. But I'm sure many of them didn't see it that way. Janet made it pretty clear what a crummy husband I'd been. Many of their sympathies were with her, and probably justifiably so. But I got out of there pretty soon, anyway."

Claire's sigh carried bit of a groan. "Well, what is it you've learned? How has this translated into your learning the answer to how to live the Christian life—to knowing God experientially?"

"Well, my world came crashing down—and with it, my sense of self. I could no longer scientifically manage and control it all—"

"I have to admit that sounds sort of familiar." Claire dipped her fork into the dressing and then stabbed a bite of salad.

"At first I didn't think I had anything left. But then I realized I still did have a little bit of faith."

"Like a mustard seed?"

"About that much." Stephen's boyish smile showed itself again, for the first time since much earlier that evening.

Chapter Twenty-three

....

"Dare I ask if you want dessert?"

Claire narrowed her eyes at Stephen and grinned. "Not here," she said. "They have great desserts, but I'm ready for something a little lighter."

"As in fewer calories?" Stephen asked.

"As in lighter atmosphere. And lighter conversation."

"I see." Stephen nodded, grinning at her. "Well, that sounds good to me." He stood up, stretched his long legs, and grabbed the ticket.

"I think I'll go to the ladies' room."

Stephen paid for their dinner, leaving a handsome tip. Good service was sometimes about leaving people alone, which their waiter seemed to understand. When Claire emerged from the ladies' room and walked across the restaurant toward him, he could hardly believe she was with him.

"You know, you're really beautiful," he told her. "Is it okay to tell you that?"

"Nothing offensive in that statement," she answered, flashing him a resplendent smile.

He opened the door, followed her outside, and offered her his arm, which she took as they crossed the road.

"Where would you like to get dessert?" he asked her.

"You know, I don't think I want any dessert, if that's okay with you. Why don't we just take a walk here along the water? Then I really must be getting home to Graeme. I haven't seen him since this morning."

"That sounds great." Stephen was glad she didn't let go of his arm.

The road in front of Sputnik was bordered on the other side by public parking and a sidewalk that encompassed Alamosa City Park.

The sidewalk, parallel for a quarter mile with the road, also ran parallel with the Rio Grande, which ran through the edge of the park. Two bridges leading from the sidewalk traversed the river and led pedestrians over it and into the grassy section of the park, where there were ball fields, playground equipment, and picnic tables.

Stephen and Claire walked along the river, which at this time of day—sunset—was a greenish-brown hue. The oaks across the way, with just a hint of autumn color, soared high above and were reflected in the water as in a mirror image. Frogs sang an off-key chorus in the cattails down by the river's edge.

"This was a fun idea," Stephen told Claire. "I've never been here before—not walking like this."

"Me, neither," she admitted. "But every time I eat lunch at the bistro it always seems so inviting."

Stephen wanted to ask her who she ate lunch with, but instead he asked, "Why haven't you ever done it?"

"Oh, too busy I guess. I'm usually with a colleague who needs to get back to campus, or I need to grade papers or prepare for a class."

She patted his arm with her free hand and then clasped it, forming a circle around his arm with both of hers.

"I'm afraid I'm not much good at having fun, Stephen," Claire admitted. "I used to be—I mean, I think I was—but it's part of my problem now. I know it is. Abuelita says I'm always thinking too hard to have fun. 'Let go, relax, and enjoy yourself,' she always tells me. She has fun all the time."

"Well, are you having fun now?"

"I am."

"Congratulations!" Stephen smiled at her.

She smiled back thoughtfully, not showing any teeth.

"I'm glad to be a source of mindless fun for you," he teased.

"You're hardly that."

They came to the end of the sidewalk where there was a bridge.

"Do you have time to go across?" Stephen asked her.

"I'd really like to, but I don't think I should."

He was disappointed but didn't let it show. He understood how important it was for her to be home with Graeme, and he respected that.

In the truck on the way back to campus, it seemed to Stephen that Claire sat a little closer. She put her arm on the armrest between them so that her hand was close to his instead of in her lap.

"Can I play a quick song for you?" he asked her.

"Sure, that would be lovely."

Joe had lent him one of Frieda's CDs. It featured old hymns—really old ones that were largely out of fashion—set to new arrangements by a stellar pianist, one of the best accompanists Stephen had ever heard. The singer was a black woman whom Frieda admired, and her voice was powerful.

> "Be still my soul, the Lord is on your side;
> Bear patiently the cross of grief or pain;
> Leave to thy God to order and provide
> In every change He faithful will remain.
> Be still, my soul; thy best, thy heavenly Friend,
> Through thorny ways leads to a joyful end."

As the music played, Stephen reached out and took Claire's hand. They drove to the parking lot behind Irby immersed in the ethereal sound and the poignant words of all five verses of Jean Sibelius's hymn.

When it ended, they were parked in the empty space beside Claire's car. The silence seemed as loud—or louder—than the music had been just moments before. The only light was a street lamp some distance away; the parking lot was not well-lit by safety standards.

Claire did not let go of Stephen's hand but gripped it, which surprised him. He sat—trying not to think too hard himself—and enjoyed the moment. When she turned her face toward him, her eyes were shining with tears.

"That was beautiful," she said. She still didn't let go.

"Could I walk you to your car? I don't want this evening to be over, but I want to help you get back to Graeme."

Claire nodded, releasing his hand. "Thanks. Yes."

He got out. She sat in the truck and waited for him to come around and open her door. Then they walked the few feet it was to her driver's side door.

"I'll follow you and make sure you get home safely," Stephen offered.

Claire smiled at him. Her eyes lingered, and her smile, just long enough.

They were standing painfully close. Stephen hoped she couldn't hear his heart, as it beat like a big bass drum in his ears.

He reached up with his right hand and cupped her face gently, leaning forward and nudging only her face, her lips toward him. It required great restraint for Stephen not to take her in his arms. He kissed her softly but honestly.

When she opened her eyes, he saw no fear in them.

"Can I call you?" he asked, his voice husky, his world in a tenuous balance.

"You'd better," she said with a coy smile.

Chapter Twenty-four

....

Stephen honked the horn as Claire turned off the highway and into her driveway, pulling through the open gates of the Casa. She beeped back and paused a moment to watch his truck pass by. There was the faintest scent of wood smoke in the air around her—or in her hair and clothes, she supposed, from sitting next to Stephen in his truck, holding his hand, and kissing him.

It had been so long since she had kissed a man. As Stephen's truck disappeared, Claire was unnerved a little by the longing she felt. The hunger. She had never expected to feel this way about another man, never imagined herself kissing anyone else but Rob. He had been her husband; he had fully satisfied her on many different levels.

Of course he wasn't perfect—no relationship was—but Rob had been *the one* for Claire. The one who knew her and loved her; the one she thought would always be there. They had planned to grow old together. To take care of one another. He was the father of her child.

But Rob was gone. Like the vapor rising from the Rio Grande River, their life together had vanished, become a part of the atmosphere of memory. It was no longer a thing of here and now. Their story was over.

Stephen was here and now. And that thought—instead of making Claire want to run the other way, toward a past that was gone—in this moment at least, comforted her. The tenderness of his hands, the warmth of his lips, and the strong heart beating inside his chest awakened something in her. Something fragile as a bird's wing just before it takes flight. Something electric and quivering like a bowstring after its arrow is released. Something that felt like life.

"Hi, baby!" she hollered when she saw Graeme at the kitchen table eating a snack. He was wearing Batman pajamas complete with the black cape, and his hair hung in damp ringlets around his face. "I see you've already had your bath!"

She set her things down in the entryway and rushed up to him.

Graeme looked at her with dull eyes. "Yep." He looked away, taking a bite of cereal.

Abuelita, who was sitting beside him with a cup of tea, smiled weakly at Claire, raising her eyebrows just a touch to indicate trouble.

Claire bent down to Graeme's eye level and looked him in the eyes. "Can I have a hug?" she asked.

"Well, maybe when I finish my cereal." Graeme stirred his spoon around the bowl casually.

"Graeme, you give your mother a hug!" Abuelita chastened.

He shot Abuelita a scowl but reached his arms out limply.

"Gee, thanks," Claire said, embracing him. She sat down at the table on the other side of Graeme. "So, what have you guys been up to?"

"Oh, we've had such a good time," Abuelita said. "We went to Sonic after school for an early dinner."

"Ooh—you're spoiling him, Abuelita."

"Well, we thought that since you were having a date, we'd have one, too, didn't we, Graemesy?"

Graeme nodded his head curtly.

"Then we went to Dempsey Park and played a little while," Abuelita went on.

"What did you play?" Claire asked Graeme.

"I swung, and Abuelita pushed me."

"Ah, but I didn't have to push very much, because Graeme is such a good pumper!"

"Graeme, that's great!"

"Gabbie taught me how at recess, but now I can do it better than her."

Claire almost chided him for bragging but decided against it. "Did you play on the monkey bars?"

"Nah, just the swings and the merry-go-round."

"And the slide! Don't forget the slide!" Abuelita reminded him.

"Oh yeah, they got a new slide! It's supercool."

"What's it like?" Claire was so glad to have him look at her that she kept asking questions.

"Well, it's red and curvy, and—well, you'll just have to see it. Maybe tomorrow we can go there. If you're not too *busy*."

Graeme's tone told Claire what his gestures and words—or the lack of them—had all meant. She leaned her head on one side and scooted closer, trying to make eye contact.

"Graeme, you know how important you are to me. I love spending time with you, and I'm not away from you very much."

"Well, why did you come home so late tonight? And not eat dinner with me and Abuelita?"

Graeme's green eyes seemed to expand as Claire stared into them, searching for a way to help him understand.

"First of all, it is not late at night. It's seven thirty. And I came home early from my date specifically so I could be with you."

Graeme nodded his head slowly.

"Do you know Dr. Reyes? The one who took care of you in the emergency room that first time when you had to go from school?"

"When Nurse Bonita took me and you met us there?"

"Yes, that's right."

"Yeah, I remember him. He's Dr. Marquez's brother."

"You're right! He is! And he's just as nice as she is. He took Mommy on a special date for dinner this evening."

"Why?" Graeme asked. "Did you need some medicine?"

"No. It was because he likes me, and we wanted to talk to each other."

Graeme made a face like she had suddenly sprouted horns. "That's weird," he said.

"Why is that weird?"

"Because, it just is. Why did you have to go out on a date to talk to each other?"

"Well, it's kind of like you and Gabbie. She's your friend, and you like to spend time with her, don't you?"

"Yeah. But I don't see how that's like you and Dr. Reyes."

"Well, we want to be friends. So we're going to spend some time together to get to know each other."

Graeme looked unconvinced.

Claire decided to move on. "Have you practiced your violin?"

"No, Abuelita didn't make me."

Claire looked at Abuelita.

"I don't know how to practice that thing with him!" Abuelita threw her hands up in the air.

"Well, let's do it, then. Go get your violin and I'll meet you in the parlor."

"Oh, Mom, do I have to?"

"Yes, sir, you do."

Graeme took his bowl to the sink and then trudged up the stairs.

"Did you have fun?" Abuelita asked Claire with a sparkle in her eye.

"I did." Claire smiled wryly. "But it looks like it's going to cost me."

* * * * *

After they'd been through Graeme's repertoire, which consisted of the first six songs in *The Suzuki Violin Method, Volume One* and included several variations of "Twinkle, Twinkle, Little Star," Claire asked him to show her his bow positions. Graeme held the bow straight up, thumb on the frog and fingertips peeping over the bow "like snakes on a log." He motioned as he recited: "Up like a rocket, down like the rain. Side to side like a choo-choo train. Round and round like the great big sun, pointing my fingers, curving my thumb."

Then he bowed low from the waist, keeping his knees straight, tucking the violin under his arm and holding the bow straight down. "Now it's time to take a bow, *ichi, ni* and *son* is how." He counted to three in Japanese, bowing three times to the sides and center.

Claire clapped her hands approvingly. "Bravo! Bravo!"

Graeme fastened his violin and bow back into their case and zipped it up. "Can we watch my movie of Daddy before bed?" he asked.

Claire put on her pink cotton pajamas, got the DVD ready, and curled up with Graeme in her bed. She pushed PLAY, and Rob's face—still healthy-looking and robust to the undiscerning eye—appeared on the flat screen of the TV Abuelita had installed in their room.

"Hey, buddy," Rob's voice said.

Graeme grinned, mesmerized as usual by his "movie."

"I'm making this DVD because there are some things I want you to always know. One day I won't be able to tell you, but you can watch me on this and it will remind you, okay?"

"Okay," Graeme whispered.

"Daddy is sick, and pretty soon I'm going to go to heaven. When you don't see me anymore I want you to remember that I am in heaven, but I am also in your heart."

Graeme looked at Claire and snuggled closer. She stroked his back and played with his curly raven hair.

"I've made you some other movies for when you're bigger. They're about some of the things I wanted to teach you and do with you. But this one is the most important. In this one I want to tell you the three most important things to remember for your whole life."

Rob's eyes were steady, unwavering. Claire remembered how meticulous he'd been about recording these sessions to leave for Graeme—how crucial it was for him. She took a deep breath and held Graeme closer.

"The first thing is that Jesus loves you. No matter what happens, you must always remember that. Jesus loves you. He thinks you're awesome. He loves you more than anyone else ever can or will. And He will never stop, no matter what. Okay? So that's the first thing I want you to always remember. Jesus loves you."

Graeme looked up at Claire and smiled peacefully. He was getting sleepy. This film was exactly what Rob had intended it to be—a mode of connection, a safe place, a security net for his son.

"The second thing is that I love you. You and Mommy are the best things that have ever happened to me, and I wouldn't trade you for anyone else. I thank God every day that I get to be your daddy. Always remember that I love you and that even if you can't see me, I still love you, because love is forever."

Claire knew, by the slight break in the movie, and also because Rob had told her about it later, that he had had to stop for a few moments after that segment. He had filmed it by himself while she and Graeme were out running errands.

They had always taken lots of pictures—both still and video—but after the terminal diagnosis, Rob went on a filming spree, building Graeme a video library for the future. There was a demonstration of shaving and one of how to tie a tie. There was a talk about puberty and even how to ask a girl for a date. Rob also filmed himself telling Graeme stories about his life. Claire assisted him with all of it, capturing moments of them playing or reading together, even napping. It was important to Rob that Graeme have those concrete images to refer to—to help him remember, and to be able to see how much he was loved.

They always had a special relationship, but when Rob learned he was dying, he spent even more time—every moment he could—with Graeme. They packed lots of fun into a few months. Before the palliative chemo stopped working and the cancer spread. Before Rob was emaciated, jaundiced, and incoherent much of the time. Before he couldn't get out of bed.

Claire emerged from her thoughts to see that Graeme's movie was concluding.

"The third thing is this: We can see each other again someday. If you believe in Jesus and trust Him with your life, we will be together in heaven. I hope you live to be an old, old man, even older than Grandpa. But when your life is over, I'll be looking for you in heaven. Be there!"

Rob smiled, and Claire knew he was holding back tears. The DVD clicked off. She looked down at Graeme, saw he was asleep, and gingerly shifted him over onto a pillow.

Not ready to go to bed herself, Claire padded down the stairs in pink slippers and walked into the kitchen. She made herself a china cupful of chai tea and then moved into the living room, where Abuelita was crocheting squares for an afghan and listening to the news on TV.

"Can I get you a cup of tea?" Claire asked her.

"No, *hija*, thank you. I will wet the bed if I drink any more."

Claire laughed, and it felt good. Abuelita had a knack for bringing her back from the brink.

Abuelita looked up from the orange square she was working on and smiled.

"I am so glad you came down. I have been waiting to hear all about your date with the handsome doctor."

"Oh, Abuelita, I am a bit of a mess. Graeme and I just finished watching his 'Daddy Movie.' "

Abuelita sighed and clicked her tongue.

"It is a beautiful thing Rob did for Graeme, and I am not surprised he wanted to watch it tonight."

"I know. I just wish it was easier for me to watch." Claire took a sip of her tea. "Do you think Graeme is okay?"

"I think Graeme is flourishing. You are a wonderful mother, and he is a strong, smart boy."

Claire smiled appreciatively.

"It will be easier for you both someday. And though Dr. Reyes may stir up a little trouble at first, perhaps he'll help with that."

Abuelita looked Claire square in the face before she continued. "You will always love Rob, and he will always be a part of your life's story. But you must keep moving forward. I am very pleased that you went on a date with Dr. Reyes. Now tell me all about it."

Though Claire was tempted to wallow in the "mess" that Graeme's movie evoked, she forced herself to move forward as Abuelita instructed. She settled in and told all about Stephen, their dinner, the walk, and even the kiss, feeling something like she had the night she returned home from her high school prom to find Abuelita waiting in the same chair, presumably with the same crochet needle. Just different thread.

"Ooh la la!" Abuelita exclaimed, covering a giggle with her hand after Claire described the kiss. "*Muy bueno!*"

Claire found herself giggling, too, but then she felt guilty. "I never thought I'd kiss another man," she confessed.

"I know," Abuelita said. "We never know what direction our lives will take. Only God knows our story from beginning to end. But it's best to follow wherever the Spirit leads. I am proud of you, Claire, for opening your heart."

"Stephen *is* a special person," Claire admitted. "I've seen that. There is depth to him and humility. I want to believe that God has brought him into my life."

"Then why don't you believe it?" Abuelita asked.

"I don't know—I guess I'm afraid."

Abuelita put down her needle and thread. "What are you afraid of, *hija*? The Lord loves to give us good gifts."

"It's not the giving I have a problem with, but the taking away."

Abuelita's eyes were tender when she looked at Claire. "The Bible says not to fear, for He is with us."

Claire's heart started to race, and she wished she could suppress her exasperation out of respect for Abuelita. "I *know* that, but anything can still happen. You've lost a husband and two children. I've lost my parents. And Graeme and I lost Rob to a hideous disease."

Abuelita's expression was unmoved and her voice patient. She didn't answer right away. "But He is with us through it all, *hija*. And while He may not be all we would choose, if we are honest, He is enough."

* * * * *

They watched an episode of *I Love Lucy*, which was on after the news. Then Abuelita put away her crocheting and they kissed each other good night on both cheeks. Abuelita ambled down the hall to her room, and Claire returned to the kitchen to put her teacup in the sink before going up to bed.

Back up in her room, she opened her Bible. Turning through its pages, she found what she was looking for—a letter Rob had given her a few weeks before he died. It was written on a piece of yellow paper that had been torn out of a legal pad and was already somewhat fragile from being handled so many times. Claire smiled wistfully at the sight of the black ink and Rob's small, distinct handwriting.

Dearest Claire,

You know the medicine I take for pain makes me crazy half the time. I think of things I need to do and say and then my thoughts get lost in the fog before I can carry them out. That's why I'm writing this down in a moment of clarity.

I've tried to buy as much emotional insurance for you and Graeme as I could with the time we've had. I know it won't be long now until I'm gone, and I feel there's still something left undone. It bothers me.

We haven't been in denial since getting the terminal diagnosis. You and I have talked about everything we could and tried to plan for yours and Graeme's future without me as much as possible. As for Graeme, I've made all of those videos so he can see how much I loved him, and hopefully he'll be able to remember me enough to know something of me and where he came from. I have total faith in your ability to raise him. I trust that my family and your abuelita will help you as much as they can.

I believe you are holding up amazingly well considering how tough this time has been. You are such a strong and beautiful woman, and I have complete confidence in you to manage—even thrive—after I am gone. There is one thing you've refused to discuss, however, and that is the subject of loving another man or even marrying again.

I know you are trying to protect me because of how difficult it is to think about this possibility or talk about it. I suppose it's the lawyer in me that has to consider every option, and I know I've angered you about it. But from a practical standpoint I believe it is best for you that we address it.

I have told you that I want you to be happy—whatever that means— when I am gone. As hard as it is for me to imagine it, I know that our life together is coming to an end. I also know that you are young, and I pray you have a lot of living left to do. I cannot bring myself to believe that you will be alone all of those years. In my best and strongest moments, which I admit are few, I even pray that God will give you someone who will love you as much as I do and who will love Graeme after I am gone.

We don't have to talk about it anymore if you don't want to. But I hope at some point this letter will be a comfort to you—and a release. I want you always to have complete freedom to go wherever the Spirit leads you in life and in love. I find in my heart that this is the last gift I can give you, the last way I can love you—and that God can love you through me. (It is strangely empowering to have something left to give, even though at this point you will not receive it!)

You and Graeme are my dreams come true. Thank you for lavishing your faithful love upon me. I have no regrets.

Love you forever,
Rob

Claire brushed away her tears before they could smudge the page. She ran her fingertips over the words Rob had written—some of his last—with his own hand. She stopped when she came to the signature, "Love you forever, Rob." The smooth pad of her index finger hovered over his name like a butterfly near the center of a flower. She closed her eyes, inhaling deeply, as though she could draw up through the ink Rob's goodness and the magic that had gone with him out of her life.

Chapter Twenty-five

. . . .

"Well, that was quite a sight, Stan Evans walking down the aisle at church this morning," Gene said over sirloin tips and a baked potato, which was his favorite meal at his favorite restaurant, Western Sizzlin'. His small blue eyes sparkled with joy.

Stephen, who wasn't crazy about Western Sizzlin', treasured Gene and Nell's company anywhere. He had offered to drive, so the three of them piled into his truck and headed down to Antonito, seven miles south of Romeo, for lunch.

"The Lord is happy today," Nell commented, squeezing lemon into her tea. "Stan Evans was saved and Stephen came to church!"

His friends were obviously soul-satisfied, and well they should be. The investment they'd made in the Evanses' lives since Sydney's death was a literal testament to loving one's neighbor, and Stephen was blessed by it. He'd been excited, along with the rest of the church, to see Stan show up at the Patricks' church today. No doubt it was a better place for him than Abe's Bar.

"Yep, I could get used to that!" Nell smiled across the table at him like a beauty queen.

Stephen grinned at her sheepishly. Seeing the look on Nell's face when he had walked in—and witnessing Stan's response to the Spirit— had definitely been worth going to church today, but he wasn't sure he felt led to become a regular there.

"I wish Stan had come with us," Stephen mused. "I get the feeling he's not comfortable around me."

"Well now, I tell you what. I don't think that was the reason he didn't come," Gene observed.

"Me neither," Nell agreed, taking a bite of a tired-looking potato that was doused in margarine and sour cream. "He's worried about Marsha."

"How is she doing?"

"Stan said she didn't feel well today, but I think there's more to it." Nell's blue eyes darted back and forth. "I've tried to call her on several days when I know she's home, but there hasn't been any answer. I'm getting pretty worried myself."

"I thought it was *him* doin' awful," Gene declared. "She's always been the strong one."

"I know! And he *was* doin' awful, drinkin' and stuff, but now it seems like he's getting himself on track and she's the one who might be fallin' apart."

Stephen finished a bite of his salad. The darker greens had been hard to come by on the food bar, but he had dug them out of the big clear bowl that was sitting in ice. "You know, I think that's fairly common for people who are grieving—this swinging back and forth like a pendulum."

"What do you mean?"

"Well, Marsha may have been strong, as you say, because she felt like she had to be for Stan. Because of that she may have put off some of her own grief process, trying to hold it together for him. Now that he is stabilizing, more of her own issues may come to the surface."

"I'm no doctor, but that makes sense," Gene acknowledged with a wrinkle of his forehead. He cut a bite of steak.

Nell sighed. "Poor woman. I can't even imagine what she's going through."

"She needs support," Stephen cautioned. "And possibly medicine."

"What do you mean?"

"I mean, if this keeps up very long, I hope you'll bring her into my office."

"Well," Nell said, "I'm sure she'll be okay. She's a wonderful Christian lady. The Lord will help her through this." She tore off a piece of her Texas toast and dipped it in a sort of *au jus*.

"I have no doubt of that. And she may not need anything—I hope she won't." Stephen looked at Nell with unflinching eyes, making sure he had her attention before he continued. "But you have to remember that this is an extreme situation. It doesn't get any worse than losing a child, and a person never fully gets over something like that." He put down his fork. "If Marsha needs help, you bring her to me. There's no such thing as a magic pill, but I've seen the Lord help more than one person regain their footing through the temporary use of antidepressants."

Stephen gently pushed back his chair and left them to think about that while he went to the salad bar to hunt for some fruit. When he returned with a plateful of watermelon, shipped in from who knows where, Nell crossed her hands under her chin and watched him sit down.

"So, tell us about your big date."

"What big date? Did somebody have a big date?" He took a bite. "Good watermelon," he said to Gene.

Gene chuckled, but Nell chided him.

"You are a wicked man. I don't know why I put up with you."

Gene hooted.

"You either!" There was practically steam coming out of Nell's ears.

"Oh, you know I'm just playing," Stephen said. "I know how lucky I am to have somebody keeping tabs on me."

"Me, too," Gene concurred.

Nell raised her eyebrows as if to say, "So?"

"It was really good. I mean, I hope it was as nice for her as it was for me."

"What did you do?"

"We went out for dinner—an early dinner—and then we went for a short walk there in Alamosa by the river."

"That sounds good."

"It was. We talked quite a bit, just getting to know each other better, and then I took her back to the college where her car was. She was very conscious of getting back home to her son."

"I like that," Nell observed.

"Me, too, even if it did put a bit of a time constraint on things."

"You may as well get used to it if you plan to take this any further."

"I know. You're right."

"What did you talk about? Do you want to tell us?" Nell probed.

"We talked about lots of stuff," Stephen said, biting into another slice of watermelon. He never bothered to take out the seeds but swallowed them whole.

"Isn't that something how he eats the seeds?" Gene remarked, motioning to Nell.

"It's probably good roughage." She waved Gene away like a housefly. Turning to Stephen, she urged, "Go on."

Stephen laughed at them before he continued. "Well, you'll be happy to know we talked about spiritual things, how we both need to trust God more, and just different things that have happened in our lives."

"Did you tell her about Janet?"

"Yes. I'd already told her some, but we talked about it a little more."

"And what was her reaction?"

"She seemed to understand. You know, she's been through so much that I get the feeling that nothing surprises her."

"Hmm."

"Did she apologize?"

"For what?"

"For being so fickle and kind of pulling you up and down like a yo-yo?" Stephen had to grin at Nell's candor.

"Yes, as a matter-of-fact she did."

"Good," Nell said. "She needs to quit that."

"I really believe she will this time. I think she's just afraid."

"Well, I'd be more afraid of missing my chance at you—" Nell stopped herself and broke out into a demure little smile. It was a rare sight.

"You've got yourself a good woman," Stephen told Gene, winking at him.

"Ain't that the truth, and don't I know it!"

* * * * *

After dropping off the Patricks at their Buick in the church parking lot, Stephen turned in the opposite direction from home. He hadn't seen Claire since their date on the previous Tuesday and had only talked to her very briefly one day on the phone. He hoped it would not be too forward of him to stop by her house. *It's a perfectly normal thing for a friend to do,* he told himself on the way.

Turning into Abuelita's drive, he saw quickly that the iron gates were closed as tight as a mussel shell. He pressed the button on the intercom and then pressed it again when no one answered.

"*Sí?*" said a voice that sounded old but not unpleasant.

"Uh, hi. This is Stephen Reyes."

There was a crackle in the intercom line.

"*Sí?*"

Was it an automated system?

"I was wondering if Claire Caspian is available? I was just in the neighborhood and thought I'd stop by."

"*Sí, señor.* Let me get her for you."

Several moments elapsed, and Stephen wondered whether he should have come. Then, finally, there was another crackle and Claire's voice.

"Stephen?"

"Hi. I hope I'm not intruding, I was just out and about and thought I'd stop by to see you, but the gate is locked."

"Oh. So it is."

"Is this a bad time?"

"No, no, it's fine. I mean, it's good. Here, let me open the gates and you can come on up."

"Okay."

The iron gates creaked open.

"Stephen?" There was a bit of noise coming through the line. "Abuelita is here—and Graeme."

"Great," he said, meaning it.

Stephen pulled his truck into the same spot as the first time he'd been to Abuelita's, when he had followed Claire from the grocery store. It had been evening then, and in the lower light he hadn't noticed how much the lawn looked like a golf course. Zoysia grass flourished on the several-acre plot around the Casa, which was encased in black iron fencing, and as Stephen stepped out of his truck, he noted the perfectly manicured flower beds on both sides of the garage.

The grass next to the sidewalk, which he followed around the house and up to the front doors, had been cut painfully to the quick. Between the cobbled bricks that Stephen stepped on, not a blade was out of place. More elaborate beds, featuring desert roses, jasmine, poppies, irises, lilies, and cedars trimmed in perfect swirls, bordered the front of the house. He imagined that Abuelita kept several Romeo citizens employed by her landscaping alone.

Claire met him at the double doors, which were made of wood and hung behind glass ones with iron bars. He noticed that her hair was wet, and she wore a long, black, gauze dress that doubled as a cover-up. It had a deep V-neck, with a tie at the top that was open, and Stephen could see the damp outline of her swimsuit, which was also black, underneath.

"Hi," she said. "This is a nice surprise."

She stepped back for him to enter, and they stood together in a grand foyer on big terra-cotta tiles. Her shoes were squeaky.

"I hope I'm not intruding—"

"Oh, no. Graeme and I were just having a swim in the back."

Stephen ran a hand through his hair.

"I'm sorry! I didn't hear you—I would have just walked around."

"That's okay," Claire told him. "It's indoor. Too cold for an outdoor pool here in the fall."

She smiled facetiously and Stephen blushed. "Right."

"Come through here and meet Abuelita."

Stephen followed her through the foyer and across the great room, past the sweeping staircase he had seen before from the kitchen. The back wall of the room was all glass, and Claire opened a huge glass door, stepping through it. Stephen followed suit, closing the door behind him.

Walking out onto the patio, which seemed to be pulled from the pages of *Better Homes and Gardens*, he saw what must be the pool house to the left across the patio and catty-cornered behind the garage. It was beige stucco, like the big house, with a terra-cotta tiled roof that matched the house as well as the brick of the sidewalks and patio. Crank windows, presumably for opening in summer months, were shut. A glass and iron door at the entry swung open, and Graeme ran out to meet them.

He was wrapped in a brightly colored towel that covered his body from shoulders to feet. Dragging a few inches of the towel like a train, he scampered over to Claire, who put her hands on his shoulders and held him there in front of her, rubbing his arms up and down.

"Can you say hi to Dr. Reyes?"

"Hi," Graeme obeyed.

Stephen smiled and bent down to Graeme's eye level, putting out his hand.

"Hello, Mr. MacGregor."

"Hey, that's like in *Peter Rabbit*," Graeme observed.

"So it is. I was wondering if you have a garden around here," Stephen improvised.

Graeme's wet, curly hair framed his face like a black halo. His long eyelashes were fused together by water in sections, making the size of his green eyes seem even more pronounced as he stared at Stephen, sizing him up. He blinked drops of water away, not smiling but not frowning, either.

"*Hola,* Graeme! Come get your shoes!"

A voice called from the door of the pool house, and Stephen spotted a blur of red and black material before it banged shut. When it opened again, a pair of blue rubber Crocs flew out, landing in their direction, and Abuelita appeared in a floor-length, tropical-print gown. Her hair was swept up in a loose French twist, secured with colorful cloisonné combs, and she wore her big, black sunglasses with gold interlocking C's—for Chanel—on the sides. A woven straw basket was slung over one of her arms, and the other hand closed the door gently behind her to prevent its banging. She came toward them in black beaded flip-flops, and Stephen noticed that her toenails were red, like the hibiscus on her silk caftan.

"Abuelita, this is Stephen Reyes," Claire introduced him. "And this is my abuelita."

Stephen smiled and reached out his hand.

Abuelita allowed him to take hers, bowing her head regally.

"It is nice to meet you, Dr. Reyes," she said.

Suddenly all of the stories he had heard about this interesting character—from Claire and others—converged, made sense. Stephen suppressed a nervous laugh.

"Nice to meet you, too," he said soberly. "Claire has told me so much about you."

"Well, she's not told me much about you," Abuelita said. "But I can see she was right about your being handsome."

Stephen, rarely at a loss for words, was taken completely aback by this older woman. He didn't know what to say next, but the nervous laughter found its way out.

Abuelita threw back her head then and laughed, too.

Claire just shook her head, turning a light shade of pink underneath her darkened skin, which Stephen found enchanting.

"Graeme, come help me get a tray of snacks." Abuelita raised her eyebrows significantly before turning to Claire and Stephen. "Why don't you two just sit down out here? Graeme and I will be back."

They obeyed like two teenagers who were not yet allowed to formally date, pulling up ornate iron chairs with green cushions to a matching ironwork table. They plopped down in the chairs. Each had lots to say, but neither said a word.

Claire fiddled with the nail polish on her left thumb while Stephen looked around, taking in more of the surroundings.

"Is that a goldfish pond?" he finally asked her, pointing across the patio.

"It is," she answered.

"Does it have fish in it?"

"It does. Graeme and his friend caught one just the other day."

"Caught one? They went fishing for goldfish?" Stephen was amused.

"Yes, I'm afraid so. And were very disappointed when I made them throw it back."

"That's funny," Stephen said.

"Not so funny for the goldfish."

"I suppose not."

There was an awkward silence, a stillness interrupted only by Claire's leg vibrating under the table.

Stephen reached over to stop it, and she jumped like a frog in the air. He instantly removed his hand from her knee.

"I'm sorry. I didn't mean to scare you."

"That's okay. It's a bad habit."

He thought he saw the tremor of a smile at the corners of her mouth.

"Scaring you?" He grinned.

"No, shaking my leg."

"I've noticed you do something else when you're nervous," Stephen ventured.

"What's that?" she asked, rubbing the place she'd just peeled on her thumb.

"You scratch off your fingernail polish, and you always start with that thumb."

Claire, self-conscious, dropped her hands into her lap. "Wow, I didn't even realize I did that. Okay, Mr. Observant. What else have you noticed about me?"

"Well, sometimes you twist sections of your hair. But not when you're nervous—usually when you're just thinking."

"I see. What is this, 'Claire's Quirks 101'?"

"No, just 'Claire 101.' I'm learning lots of things about you. I'm a scientist, remember?"

"That's kind of scary." She leaned back against the back of the chair and put her feet up on its base.

"The goal is not to scare you. It's to know you. You said that was okay, remember?"

Claire folded her hands and smiled mischievously at him. "Well, I've noticed a few things about you, too."

"Like what?" He ran his fingers through his hair.

"Like that. You put your fingers through your hair when you're on the spot."

"I do?"

"Yep. And you've got a chipped front tooth, and when you smile you get these little crinkles around the edges of your eyes."

Stephen couldn't help but laugh at that. When he did, he reached up to feel the crinkles. "I think that's what women call crow's feet."

"Well, whatever they are, I like them."

It was Stephen's opportunity to turn pink.

"And I like it when you blush."

He had looked away toward the goldfish pond, but now he looked right at her. "Good, because it seems like I do it a lot around you."

They were interrupted by the sound of the glass door sliding open.

"Snacks are served!" Graeme called.

He was carrying lemonade in a pitcher of glass with a cobalt-blue rim, the kind that can be found in any Mexican border town. Stephen hoped he wouldn't drop it. Abuelita followed behind Graeme with a tray. When Stephen stood to close the door behind her, she nodded her thanks, proceeding onward.

"I got these for you," Graeme declared, heaping a handful of bright orange baby carrots on Stephen's plate.

"Ah. Thank you, Mr. MacGregor." Stephen played along. He took a bite of one. "Delectably sweet."

"You know, lettuces are soporific," Graeme informed him. "At least the ones from Mr. MacGregor's garden."

"I did not know that. But perhaps that's why I am feeling sleepy. I had salad for lunch."

Graeme looked at him shrewdly.

Abuelita, who had poured four tumblers full of fresh lemonade, said, "Graeme helped me make this. He's very good at squeezing the lemons."

"See my muscle?" Graeme flexed his skinny arm for Stephen to feel.

"Wow. That's impressive. Where'd you get biceps like that?"

"My dad had big muscles," Graeme explained.

Abuelita and Claire exchanged a look that was not lost on Stephen.

"He must have been really strong."

"He was," said Graeme. "Superstrong."

"Thank you for the tapas, Mrs.—" Stephen realized he didn't know Abuelita's last name.

"It's Romero. And you are very welcome," Abuelita said. "I am glad you could come here and join us, Dr. Reyes."

"Please, call me Stephen—or Steve."

"Okay, Steve." Abuelita flashed him the smile of an old beauty queen, and Stephen recognized where Claire got some of her looks.

"This is a fascinating place. I've admired it from the road for years."

"Thank you. My father built it. It is the only home I have known here in the States."

"I see. Well, it—and you—have quite a reputation for hospitality. I have heard from many people about your family's generosity in this community. I am glad to finally be meeting the legend."

Abuelita acknowledged the compliment with the least bit of a nod. Then she changed the subject. "I also have friends who think very highly of you. They have said so."

"Really? Who is that?" Stephen was genuinely surprised and curious.

"Louisa and Pablo Ortíz."

That eccentric old couple who were patients of his. Of course. "Well, they are too kind. I enjoy their stories."

"They have many stories to tell, many that are lost to this generation. I have tried to get Claire to write some of them down."

"I plan on it—in fact, I plan on making it a project for a class next semester. The comparative lit seminar." Claire interjected.

"Oh! You hadn't told me. I am so glad!" Abuelita beamed at her granddaughter.

"I submitted a proposal this week to the administration, asking permission to create the class."

"That's wonderful!"

Claire explained to Abuelita and Stephen, "If it works out, I'll partner with a professor in the history department, and we'll team-teach it next semester. If it goes well, we may be able to add it to the regular curriculum."

"Wow," Stephen said. "That really sounds cool."

Graeme, in his mother's lap, was clearly bored with the conversation. "Do you take naps?" he asked Stephen, hearkening back to their earlier exchange.

Stephen grinned at him, switching gears. "Whenever I get the chance, which is not very often."

"You're lucky, then. I hate naps."

Stephen noted that Graeme's eyelids were getting heavy. "Oh— I bet you'll like them one day."

"I bet I won't!"

Claire patted Graeme's back. "Speaking of naps, it's almost time for yours," she reminded him.

"And mine," Abuelita said, rising. "Why don't you read me the book about the flopsy bunnies?"

Graeme started to whine but must have thought better of it when Claire looked at him sternly. She gave him a big kiss and hug before he slid out of her lap. Abuelita took Graeme by the hand, and he followed her reluctantly, looking back at Stephen with a wave and the expression of one who might have been on his way to the guillotine.

When they were out of earshot, Stephen raised his eyebrows. "Do all five-year-olds know what 'soporific' means?"

She smiled. "He loves Beatrix Potter."

"Well, that boy is sure cute—and smart."

"Thank you. I'm sure I'm just like any other mother, but I'm crazy about him. The sun rises and sets by Graeme as far as I'm concerned."

Claire looked toward the house and then added, "He's the best thing that ever happened to me."

"I don't think all mothers are like that," Stephen remarked. "At least mine isn't."

Claire looked back toward him, surprised. "What about when you were a little kid?"

"When I was a kid, my mother worked even though she didn't have to. And when she wasn't working, she was playing golf. My sister and I had a nanny who was good to us—genuinely loved us—but I don't think we were much fun for my mom. She had other fish to fry."

Claire crossed her arms in front of her somewhat defensively. "Well, maybe she needed to work for herself. Women—mothers—are not one-dimensional, no matter how much they love their kids."

Stephen saw he'd been misunderstood.

"I know that, Claire, and I'm not judging her for working or anything else. In many ways I'm sure she did the best she could. But I'd be lying if I said my mother was crazy about me—never in my recollection has that been true. She's crazier about her dogs and golf and going on trips. That's just who she is. Dad, too. They really didn't have the emotional space in their lives—and still don't—for me and Maria."

"I can't imagine that. Why have kids?"

Stephen laughed. "I don't know. I think it was just the thing to do. Or maybe we were an accident."

"Well, lucky for me and for lots of other people," Claire said, settling back down in her chair.

Stephen grinned at her.

"I'm glad I'm not flunking 'Claire 101'—at least not yet."

"Sorry I got my fur up at you. I guess I'm just touchy sometimes about women and work and, probably more so, even, about motherhood. It's the toughest job I've ever done. And I want so badly to get it right—

for Graeme to see someday how hard I tried. If he ever felt like you do, well, I don't know what I'd do. It would break my heart."

"That's not going to happen," Stephen said softly. "Anybody can see what your priorities are."

"Is that okay, I mean, with you? Because if it's not, well—"

"It's more than okay. It's what attracted me to you in the first place."

"Really?" Claire asked.

Stephen had to be honest. "Well, that and your big green eyes."

She batted her eyelashes at him, and Stephen remembered the first time he met her in the ER. He had been so glad when he saw that she wasn't wearing a ring. He couldn't say that, though, not now that he knew her story. So he just smiled at her and reached for her hand. Tracing the small veins that rippled across the top of it, he whispered, "And other things."

Chapter Twenty-six
....

Joe didn't like to use the expression, but there was really no other way to describe it. At least not in his current mental state. This had been the week from hell.

This Friday would be the biggest game of the football season so far. They were playing the La Jara Falcons—the school that had threatened to annex Manassa High, should the lawmakers choose consolidation for the smaller districts. No Manassa Grizzly wanted to become a Falcon, and it was well-known that some wealthier Falcons considered themselves superior to the "farm boys" of Manassa. The result was a bitter rivalry. Joe's house had been egged the night before, and all of the local newspapers were predicting an upset for his team, which was positioned for the play-offs, unless they lost on Friday. The game would be played at La Jara.

To make matters worse, Frieda was still mad at him for what she called his "abuse of power" as a coach. She didn't get the whole thing with Mickey Rodriguez—how important it was to discipline him for drinking—even though she said she did. She claimed she just disagreed with Joe's choice of consequences, or at least the length of them.

Joe was still pretty sure his choices were right on, but even if he had his doubts, he could never turn back now. He had pushed Mickey every day like a slave driver, and he had to hand it to the kid. He had taken it. He was almost finished serving his punishment; it was day eight of the ten days Mickey had to run sleds.

It was also Tuesday. Home group night. Martina and Jesús probably wouldn't be there since they had the restaurant to run—the group was going to need to talk about changing nights to accommodate them. Joe didn't know what other night he could do it with his crazy schedule. He'd have to figure out something.

As he sat at his desk, fiddling with the playbook before practice, Joe kind of wished he could just miss the group tonight. He dreaded seeing Frieda there. But he had already invited Stephen. He knew Stephen might not come, but what if he showed up and Joe wasn't there? No, he had to go. He was committed to it. At least tonight he didn't have to prepare anything. Jerry and Sue were hosting.

* * * * *

After the end-of-practice huddle and the customary "Go Grizzlies!" chant, the team trooped into the locker room. Joe noticed Mickey's shoulders sagging as he walked toward the end zone to pick up the sled.

"Hustle up, Rodriguez!" he hollered.

Mickey picked up the pace, running the rest of the way, and then he grabbed a hold of the sled, fitting his shoulders in front of the red vinyl pad like a harness. Joe met him on the forty and jumped on, using the sound of his whistle like a whip cracking. Up and down the field Mickey ran, with Joe riding the sled. He whistled whenever Mickey slowed down and also to signal each turn.

From where he stood on the painted metal bar, Joe could see the bulging muscles across Mickey's back, taut with the strain of pushing. Sweat beads glistened on his arms and ran in rivulets through the deep outlines around his biceps and triceps. His dark hair was matted to the sides of his face and the back of his neck. More sweat shook off, like rain, with every pounding footfall.

About halfway through the seventh round, Mickey just stopped. He dropped the sled. Then he wiped the sweat from his brow with a hooked finger and slung it to the ground.

"I quit, Coach," he said. Simply, impossibly.

"What did you say?" Joe demanded from his perch atop the sled. He thought his ears had failed him.

"I just can't do it anymore."

Mickey's eyes were not defiant; they were very matter-of-fact. The kid was done. He stood there with one hand on his hip, catching enough breath to be able to walk away.

Joe stared at him. His brain was searching every nook and cranny for an answer. In a matter of those few seconds, Joe's mind ran down every play he'd ever studied, every drill he'd ever run, and even thought of every coach he'd ever known. But he came up empty. There was nothing in the vault of his experience to prepare him for how to handle this moment.

Mickey took his first step toward the field house.

Joe closed his eyes. *God, help. This can't be how this ends.*

Suddenly, Joe got a message. But it wasn't from his mind—it came from deep within his heart.

"Mickey."

The kid turned and saw Joe strapping on the sled. He blinked his eyes like someone in the desert, trying to discern if he was seeing a mirage.

Joe felt more vulnerable than he ever had as a coach. Scary as that feeling was, Joe knew in his gut that it was something good. Something right. He said softly, "Will you run it beside me?"

Mickey hesitated. Then he nodded and Joe saw a flicker of fire come into his eyes for the first time in days. He climbed back into the harness, this time with Joe beside him. They finished the appointed ten together.

* * * * *

That night at the home group, Joe shared the story of his day as a prayer of thanksgiving. Frieda looked at him from across the room, and the warm glow in her eyes and in her smile felt like a hug.

"It's interesting how that happened today, Joe," Jerry said, "because it goes right along with what I wanted to talk about tonight."

Jerry stood to his feet beside the small marker board he had set up in his living room.

"As Sue and I were preparing to have you guys over here, I felt led to talk about what it means to us that Jesus is our Good Shepherd." He opened his Bible, taking out his notes, and said, "I have a few verses here; Sue, will you read John chapter ten, verses eleven and fourteen? And Stephen, will you read verse twenty-seven? Dr. Banks, will you read Psalm Twenty-three, verses one through three? That will be good to start us off."

Sue opened her Bible and read reverently, " 'I am the good shepherd. The good shepherd lays down his life for the sheep…I am the good shepherd; I know my sheep and my sheep know me.' " She smiled sweetly, savoring the words.

Stephen, who was next, read from the King James Version, "My sheep hear my voice, and I know them, and they follow me."

Dr. Banks followed, and Joe noticed that he scarcely looked at the page in his lap as his voice resonated: "The Lord is my shepherd, I shall not be in want. He makes me lie down in green pastures, he leads me beside quiet waters, he restores my soul. He guides me in paths of righteousness for his name's sake."

Dr. Banks paused tentatively, as though he could barely keep himself from going on.

Jerry smiled at him. "Okay, that's great. I know Psalm Twenty-three in its entirety is precious to many of us, but I just want to focus on one aspect of it tonight."

He wrote several phrases on the board:

Good Shepherd.
I know them.
Hear My voice.
Know Me and follow Me.

"I was thinking earlier about what it means that Jesus is our Good Shepherd. There are many, many things we receive because He is our Shepherd, but in these verses, I want to focus on His guidance."

Jerry went on in his quiet, methodical way, drawing out the relationship between a sheep and a shepherd. He explained how, as the Bible says, they *know* one another. The shepherd knows all about his sheep and their needs, and the sheep know and rely on their shepherd. His voice is the one they listen to for guidance.

"Joe, when you didn't know what to do today, the voice of the Holy Spirit spoke to your heart."

"That's true, man. It was as clear as a bell. One moment I had no idea where to turn—I thought everything I'd tried to do with Mickey was lost—and then the guidance came in the nick of time. And look at Mickey's response—it's amazing. I know it was the Holy Spirit working in both of our lives to bring us to that point."

"We've been praying for you both," Martina said. She had left the restaurant early to come to the home group, while Jesús stayed behind and cooked.

Frieda spoke up next. "It reminds me of another verse, here in Isaiah chapter thirty, verse twenty-one, which says, "Whether you turn to the right or to the left, your ears will hear a voice behind you, saying, 'This is the way; walk in it.' "

Stephen elbowed Joe and whispered, "Sounds like the coach got some coaching today."

"Yeah, and I needed it."

Jerry turned back to the marker board to write, *Feed My sheep*.

"One last thing I wanted to touch upon has to do with a command Jesus gave to his disciples. In John twenty-one, verse seventeen, He told them—and us, too—to feed His sheep. What do you guys think that means?"

"I've heard lots of preachers say they feed people by preaching," Dr. Banks remarked.

"Okay, yeah. What else?" Jerry asked.

"Probably teaching, witnessing, those types of things," Martina added.

Stephen surprised Joe by clearing his throat.

"Well, I suppose this is not very sophisticated, but I have a couple of sheep, and when I feed them I'm just meeting their basic needs."

Everyone in the room focused their attention on Stephen, who spoke more like a simple farmer than an MD. "I've got one penned up in the barn with a broken leg right now, and if I don't bring her food, she can't get it any other way. It's not always convenient, but she would die if I didn't feed her."

Joe noticed Frieda smiling and Dr. Banks nodding his head.

Jerry clasped his hands together. "That's an interesting perspective, Stephen, and I sense a good one to end on. Gives us all something to think about. How can we witness to people if we're not meeting their basic needs? Thanks, man, for that."

The meeting concluded with a hymn that Sue played on the piano and Frieda, in her great soulful alto, led.

"Savior, like a shepherd lead us,
Much we need Thy tender care;
In Thy pleasant pastures feed us,
For our use Thy folds prepare:

Blessed Jesus, Blessed Jesus,
Thou hast bought us, Thine we are;
Blessed Jesus, Blessed Jesus,
Thou hast bought us, Thine we are."

After football practice the next day, Joe was prepared to run the sleds with Mickey, even looking forward to it. But he didn't have to. A group of seniors on the team lined up across the field and took turns with Mickey until all ten sets were done. Then they repeated this action the next day—which was the last.

If he had tried to plan it on his own, Joe could not have come up with a better exercise to build teamwork. The seniors were unified and leading, the rest of the team was fired up and following, and Mickey was stronger than ever. By game time on Friday, the Manassa Grizzlies would hit an all-time physical and emotional high.

Chapter Twenty-seven

....

"Mom! We have to go to the football game tonight! Billy Sanford says the Manassa Mauler is going to break the school record for tackles." Graeme brimmed with excitement as he opened the car door in front of Manassa Elementary. Climbing into the backseat, he buckled himself loosely in the center so he could lean in and talk to Claire better. "I'm so glad you let me get out of that booster seat. It was a little humiliating!"

Claire grinned at his use of such a big word. Before pulling out of the school's driveway, she leaned back and kissed him on the cheek.

"You know I just want you to be safe. But I agree with you that it was time."

"Yeah, I mean Billy Sanford and even Gabbie don't have to sit in boosters anymore. You're not supposed to in kindergarten!"

"I know, I know. And while we don't set our standards for safety— or anything else—by other people, you are legally big enough," Claire explained, feeling like a square. "Did you have a good day?"

"Yeah, I did. We got to play with modeling clay in art, and I made this one-eyed monster with snakes coming out of his head."

"Sounds...cool."

"Billy Sanford and I were sitting together at the table and we had a war with our monsters."

Graeme's face was very animated, and he spoke with the conviction of Muhammad Ali.

"His was wimpy, though. It looked like a spider. Mine was round and could take its eyeball out and roll right over his, smashing it flat like a pancake." Graeme clapped his hands together and squeezed, to

241

emphasize his monster's flattening prowess.

Claire laughed. "Sounds like that monster was a Manassa Mauler in art today."

Graeme admonished her. "No, Mom, it was a Medusa monster. That's what I named it because of the snakes."

Claire was impressed, as usual, by her son's intellectual process. "Oh, I see. Well, what did you make the snakes out of?"

"Pipe cleaners. They were all different colors. And I twisted them around all spirally."

"Sounds like my hair when I get out of the shower."

"Yeah, it is kind of like that," Graeme said thoughtfully. "But you have two eyes."

Claire was chuckling silently to herself when her cell phone rang. She flipped it open. "Hello?"

"Hi, Claire."

It was Stephen! Claire's heart skipped a beat.

"May I speak to Graeme?"

What's he up to? "Uh, sure. He's right here."

Claire handed the phone, a little warily, back to Graeme.

"It's Dr. Reyes," she told him.

"Hi," Graeme said cheerfully into the receiver. He loved engaging in such a grown-up activity as talking on the phone.

Claire could hear Stephen's voice, but it sounded to her like an adult figure on a Peanuts movie. She could not make out the words.

Graeme spoke up excitedly. "Yeah, I know! Billy Sanford says it's the biggest game of the year!"

Claire negotiated a turn, leaving Manassa for Romeo, while Graeme and Stephen continued their conversation.

"Uh huh," Graeme was saying. "Yeah. That sounds really cool."

There were more unintelligible sounds, and then Graeme said,

"Okay. I'll ask her. Hold on a second."

He held the phone out from his ear, covering the mouthpiece with one hand. "Mom, would you go on a date with me and Dr. Reyes tonight?"

"You and Dr. Reyes?" Claire was incredulous.

"Yeah. We really want to go to the football game, and we'd like you to go with us."

"I see."

Graeme grinned conspiratorially from ear to ear. He was unbelievably cute, even if he was her kid.

"What time would we be going?" Claire asked him.

"What time would we be going?" Graeme repeated verbatim into the phone and then listened carefully for Stephen's answer.

Whatever Stephen said, Graeme made a face. "But I wanted to pick."

Claire could hear silence from the other end as Graeme seemed to be considering his options.

Finally he sighed, covering the mouthpiece again with his hand, and said, "He could come get us about five thirty, and you get to pick where we eat. That's because we're gentlemen." Her son looked less than convinced about the value of the last part.

Claire smiled at him. "Do you want to go?" she whispered.

"Yeah," he said.

"Okay. Then tell him I accept. We'll see him at five thirty."

"We'll see you at five thirty!" Graeme called into the phone. " 'Bye!" And he flipped the phone closed before he handed it back to Claire.

* * * * *

Stephen pulled up to the Casa at five thirty sharp. Graeme, who watched the road from Claire's bedroom window while she got ready, announced his arrival with a "Whoop!" and rushed down the stairs to meet him.

Claire's heart was touched at the sight of Graeme so happy and excited. She thought it was ingenious of Stephen to arrange the date as he did. A month ago, she might have been offended at the short notice, even angered by Stephen's presumption and her lack of control in the matter. But at this point, she felt only joy. How nice it was to be this comfortable with someone, to feel she'd made a real friend.

Claire turned around in front of the mirror, lingering just a moment over her appearance in her black pants and turtleneck. She'd tried a new, copper-colored eye shadow and was pleased with how it enhanced the color of her eyes. As she pulled on her green wool blazer and sprayed just a whisper of perfume, she congratulated herself on her outfit—and her newfound ability to let go and live a little. Only maybe it wasn't newfound, she corrected herself. *Maybe it's just being resurrected.*

Claire walked down the stairs into the great room, measuring her steps so as not to seem too eager. Graeme and Stephen were not at the door, as she expected them to be; she could hear by their voices that they had moved to the living room. As she approached, she saw Stephen closest to her on the slip-covered couch next to Graeme, who was setting up Dino-checkers. Abuelita was sitting across from them in her rocking chair. They hadn't noticed her yet. Claire stopped just short of the arched stucco doorway.

"Graeme, I don't believe you have time for Dino-checkers," Abuelita was saying. "At least not if you are going out to eat before the ball game."

Graeme looked back and forth from Abuelita to Stephen, contemplating whether to push it.

"How about a quick Dino-battle instead?" Stephen picked up one of the plastic dinosaurs from the checkerboard and held it in attack position.

"I get the T. rex!" Graeme yelled, grabbing it off a square.

"Roar!" Stephen snarled as he sprinted his brown stegosaur forward on the couch like a charging bull.

Graeme growled back, baring his little teeth and gnashing them together, sending a shower of saliva into Stephen's face. He plunged the tyrannosaur's mouth onto the stego's front leg and wiggled it wildly, dramatizing what would have been the loss of that dinosaur's leg had Stephen not fought it loose.

Stephen then turned his dinosaur around and butted Graeme's green T. rex with the stegosaur's rubber bony plates. "Take that, and that, and that!" he said with emphasis as he slashed the stego's tail back and forth.

"Did you know those spikes on the stego's tail were probably three feet long?" Graeme asked him.

Stephen paused in his action and looked at Graeme sideways. "Really?"

"Really!" Graeme confirmed. Then, seizing his opportunity, Graeme grabbed the stegosaur again with the T. rex's teeth, wrenching it free from Stephen's grip. "But they are no match for the T. rex's giant razor-sharp teeth!" He shook the smaller dinosaur like a dog would a piece of meat and then tossed it across the room, where it landed on Abuelita's stockinged foot.

"Watch it!" she warned.

"Man!" Stephen exclaimed. "You got me."

"I guess my T. rex outsmarted your walnut-sized brain," Graeme remarked, raising his eyebrows and nodding his head coolly while Stephen laughed.

"Graeme!" Abuelita chided. "Watch your mouth."

"I didn't mean *he* had a walnut-sized brain, Abuelita, just the stegosaur."

Abuelita shot him a look that was clearly skeptical.

Claire walked into the room then and clasped her hands together. "Is everybody ready?"

"Wow—you look pretty," Stephen praised her, rising.

"I just defeated Stephen in a Dino-battle," Graeme said proudly. Her son's face was lit up in a full-wattage smile.

"I see. Well, congratulations. But don't you mean 'Dr. Reyes'?"

Graeme looked back and forth from his mother to Stephen. Then he gave Stephen a slight punch on the arm, like they were old comrades.

"Actually, I mean *Stephen*. He said I could call him that, didn't you, Stephen?"

Claire searched Stephen's face for any hint of uncertainty. She found none. "You did?"

"I did," he admitted, suddenly looking like a kid caught with his hand in the cookie jar. "I mean—if that's okay with you," he added sheepishly.

Claire and Abuelita exchanged a look. Then Claire punched Stephen lightly on the arm. "Well, that's okay with me," she conceded.

He grabbed her hand and squeezed it before letting it go.

"Why don't you come with us?" Stephen offered to Abuelita, who had also risen from her seat.

"I can't, but thank you for the invitation," Abuelita said.

"What are you doing tonight, Abuelita?" Claire asked.

"I am hosting a meeting of the OFS," Abuelita told her. "In fact, I need to get my *tapas* together before everyone arrives."

"Hmm." Stephen seemed to be considering the acronym. Claire widened her eyes at him and shook her head, but he didn't seem to get the message. "What is the OFS?" he finally asked.

"It is a pillar of this community," Abuelita answered. "A very old and prestigious institution."

"Really," Stephen said. "Sounds interesting. I'm surprised I've never heard of it. What does OFS stand for?"

Abuelita's smile was so sweet it might as well have been dripping with honey. "OFS—the Old Farts' Society."

Chapter Twenty-eight

The Manassa Grizzlies rode in a caravan to La Jara, which was only
about fifteen minutes away. The team buses led, the band followed, a
pep bus full of students came next, and the cheerleaders, in the school's
minibus, brought up the rear. Of course, trailing them like a string of
colorful beads were cars full of parents and other fans, headed by Jesús
and Martina Rodriguez. They had closed Art and Sol for the occasion,
and it was just as well, because from the looks of things, Romeo would be
a ghost town tonight. Most of the town's population, including Stephen,
Claire, and Graham, were on their way to the game.

All along the twelve-mile stretch from Manassa to La Jara there were
signs on butcher paper taped to the fences near the highway. Some of
them, compliments of Frieda's Grizzly cheer squad, sent encouraging
messages. *Go Grizzlies,* one read. And another, *Bears are #1.*

But the closer they got to La Jara, the more ominous the signs
became. *Falcons Rule the Roost* and *Bears, Go Back to Your Den*, they
taunted. The worst one of all was on the gate leading into La Jara High
School. It said, *Welcome to Your Worst Nightmare.*

Stephen loved football. After all, he was a high school standout and
a college quarterback. For football in southern Colorado, it didn't get
any better than La Jara versus Manassa, and this particular game was an
important one.

Plus, Stephen's best friend was the coach, so he had a personal stake
in what was happening on the field. The record-number crowd was going
crazy. Any other time, he would have been glued to a game like this. But
tonight Stephen couldn't take his eyes off Claire Caspian.

Graeme had found his friend Billy Sanford in the nosebleed section, thanks to Billy's carrot-red hair. That was where the only remaining seats could be found by the time they arrived during pregame warm-ups. Claire and Stephen had followed Graeme's lead up the cold metal bleachers to the fourth row from the top. There, Graeme plopped down by Billy, Claire beside Graeme, and Stephen next to her. A family of four filed in behind them, squeezing everyone together on the row like sardines. But Stephen didn't mind.

He could smell the scent of jasmine in Claire's hair. The wool of her green jacket scratched against the sleeve of his leather one every time she moved. Their legs touched, and once in a while she rested her small, lovely hand on his knee. Graeme appeared happy; Claire seemed happy; Stephen was happy. It was a winning combination.

"Do you want to go to Taos with me tomorrow?" he whispered loudly in her ear, trying to make sure she heard above the cheering Grizzly fans.

"Yes," she said simply.

Stephen hoped she had heard him correctly. He wasn't used to her answering him with such little reserve.

"What's in Taos?" Exuberance spread over her face like a sunrise.

"A cool art gallery, an excellent restaurant, and you, if you'll go with me," he grinned. She had heard him.

"Sounds good to me. I'll check with Abuelita about Graeme, but I know it will be okay."

Stephen imagined Abuelita at her meeting of the OFS. "Your abuelita is very naughty," he commented.

"I know. And you walked right into that one. I tried my best to warn you."

"I'm going to have to think of a way to get her back."

"Good luck with that. She's pretty quick for an eighty-five-year-old."

"She's pretty quick for any age, I'd say."

"She's always been that way."

The crowd, including Graeme and Billy Sanford, stood to its feet and applauded, screaming madly.

"What happened?" Claire asked Graeme as she and Stephen rose, too. He strained to hear what Graeme would answer.

Graeme rolled his eyes at Claire. "Mom! Mickey just broke the record for tackles! Aren't you paying attention?"

"Not quite enough to the game, I guess." She smiled back at him and then at Stephen. "But you can keep us posted."

Two hours later, they were on the field with the rest of the Grizzly fans, surrounding the tired but euphoric players as they knelt in a huddle. Bowing their heads for the Lord's Prayer, many people mouthed the words led by Mickey. At "Amen" there was a loud roar, and the crowd pressed in as helmets rose high in the air. Everyone wanted to congratulate his or her favorite player.

Graeme, from atop Stephen's shoulders, shouted, "There he is! And there's Gabbie and Aunt Martina!"

Stephen and Claire followed Graeme's points and yells through the labyrinth of people until they approached the members of the Rodriguez family, who were cheering and chatting with a bruised but exuberant Mickey.

"Way to go, Manassa Mauler!" Graeme hollered. "You taught those Falcons a lesson!"

Mickey turned a lopsided grin up at Graeme and roughed one of his knees, which shook Stephen's shoulder.

Claire hugged a frazzled Martina, who was completely hoarse, while Jesús, with Gabbie on his shoulders in full Grizzly cheerleader attire, shook Stephen's hand.

Not far away stood Joe with Frieda at his side. He was talking into a microphone, answering a news reporter's questions about the game.

When he finished, he waved at Stephen, who trotted over with Graeme still on his shoulders.

"Way to go, bro!" Stephen said, slapping him on the back.

"Who's this little fella?"

"This is Graeme MacGregor, a future Grizzly."

"Nice to meet you, Graeme," Joe said, looking up at the boy.

"Nice to meet you, too," Graeme said politely. Then, turning to Frieda, he said, "You're pretty."

Frieda laughed at this, a deep belly laugh. "Thank you!"

"He's a smart kid, I see," Joe said to Stephen.

Stephen nodded. "That was an awesome game, man. I'm really happy for you."

"Yeah, me, too. I'm really proud of those guys. They worked hard."

Mickey and a couple of other players filed past, and Joe clapped one of them on the backside with his clipboard.

"Hey, don't let me keep you; I know you need to get into the locker room."

"Thanks for coming, man. I appreciate it."

"No problem. I enjoyed it. Let's try to get a run in next week."

Stephen and Graeme sauntered back over to where Claire was standing with Martina, Jesús, and Gabbie. Together, they all walked off the field, which was clear now except for a few other stragglers and some litter from the concession stand.

On the way through the parking lot, Stephen could see that Gabbie was making some mysterious hand motions from her perch on her father's shoulders, but he couldn't see Graeme's response. He could only feel him bouncing up and down at whatever question she had posed. They stopped at the Rodriguezes' car.

"Mommy, can Graeme spend the night?"

"What, Gabriella?"

"I said, can Graeme spend the night with us? It's his turn. Last time I spent the night with him at his abuelita's, and we went fishing for goldfish and took a bubble bath and watched *Beauty and the Beast.*"

"Well, I don't know. We need to see what Aunt Claire Claire thinks."

Claire looked at Graeme, who was nodding his head fiercely and bugging out his eyes from the top of Stephen's shoulders. Then she looked at Martina and Jesús. "What about the restaurant?"

"Oh, it'll be fine. I've had more time at home since we've gotten our people up front trained. And Jesús does most of the cooking and bossing at Art and Sol, don't you babe?"

"Especially on weekends and in the evenings. She's the *art* of the home and I'm the *sol* provider," he joked.

"Well, okay," Claire said. "Martina, I may be gone all day."

"She will," Stephen interjected, "if I have anything to say about it."

Martina and Jesús exchanged a knowing look.

"That's no problem. Graeme can stay all day if he wants. But if he gets tired of us, we'll take him to Abuelita's."

Graeme swung down from Stephen's shoulders and hugged his mother.

"I'm sorry I can't go with you guys wherever you're going," he said to Stephen. "But I need to spend some time with my friend Gabbie."

"I understand, Graeme," Stephen assured him. "We'll catch you next time."

* * * * *

The ride back to Romeo was short and sweet. They drove through the Wendy's near the exit in La Jara and ordered Frosties on Gene's recommendation, which Claire said she thought was cute. They ate them on the way home. Stephen learned that she preferred chocolate to vanilla.

When they arrived back at the Casa, Abuelita's party appeared to still be in full swing. There were several cars in the driveway, and the place was lit up like a Christmas tree.

At the door, Claire turned to him.

"Would you like to come in?"

Fully charged by her presence and excited about the prospects of tomorrow, Stephen was in no hurry for the night to end. However, he was going to have to get up early in the morning to get everything done. Did he have another hour or so to spare?

He quickly went over the events of his morning in his head: Woolworth, his wounded lamb, had to be sheared and fed, and the dressing on his leg changed. Oreo's pen was a pigsty—in the worst sense—and he couldn't in good conscience leave her in it that way another day. Regina and Duchess needed attention, the cows all demanded to be checked, and he had to make a run into La Jara to check on a patient he was treating in the hospital. If he was going to make it to Claire's house by ten, he needed to start by five thirty.

"Claire, I would, but I have a few things to do before we go to Taos tomorrow. I don't want to ruin our trip by falling asleep on you. I think I'd better call it a night."

She looked at him, pensive. Had he offended her?

"That's fine. It will be good for me to turn in a little early. Thanks for the fun evening—and especially for how you treated Graeme."

Her eyes concentrated on his face for a long moment, and then she reached up, tentatively. She ran the pads of her fingers over one of his eyebrows and then his cheekbone and jaw, just to the boundary of his hairline.

Stephen raised his hand and caught hers in it as she brushed his chin. Then he lifted her fingers to his lips and kissed them, one by one, on their velvety tips. *So soft and delicate,* he thought. *And yet she's as strong as steel.* He really, really didn't need to stay any longer.

"Good night, Claire," he said, backing away and smiling at her but still holding onto her hand.

The light from the black iron chandelier on the porch danced in her eyes like moonlight on water. Something in their depths seemed to beckon to Stephen, but she blinked it away. It took a great deal of effort for him to let go.

"See you in the morning, Stephen."

Chapter Twenty-nine
....

Claire was standing on the edge of a cliff. At least it seemed to be a cliff. She could hear the sound of moving water below her but was afraid to look over the edge—afraid she'd fall. In spite of the cool breeze blowing up from the water, sweat poured down her brow, stinging her eyes. Or were those tears?

Claire didn't know how she had gotten to that spot, only that she was dreadfully exhausted and her feet hurt. She looked down at them and saw raw gashes and cuts that oozed blood. Behind her, leading into the woods, was a grown-up path strewn with jagged rocks. No wonder her feet hurt. Is that where she'd been? Where were her shoes?

Claire's pants, rolled up at the ankles, were splotched all over with mud. Cockleburs wedged themselves through the fabric and prodded her tired legs like little pitchforks. She reached down to pick one off. That's when she realized that her arms felt heavy, hanging from her shoulders like dead weights.

Claire rubbed them up and down with the palms of her hands, hugging herself and trying to bring her muscles back to life. She found that the sleeves of her linen shirt had been ripped open in places by thorns. Some of the thorns were stuck in her hands. As she tried to pull them out, she noticed that her fingernails were dirty and broken.

"Where am I?" Claire wondered aloud.

At the sound of her voice a pair of doves took flight, and their sudden movement scared Claire. She wobbled on her sore feet for a moment by the edge, flinging out her arms and trying desperately to keep from falling.

"Just jump," a man's voice said. "I'll catch you."

"Who said that?" Claire asked, straining to see the water, where she thought the voice came from.

In just that moment the alarm clock by her bed went off with several loud beeps. Seven o'clock. The alarm was loud and disorienting, but Claire was relieved to wake up. Peeling off covers like layers of consciousness, she slowly became aware that she was safe in her bed, her feet and fingernails intact. As frightening as it had been to stand on that cliff, when she fully realized it was only a dream, a part of Claire longed to go back to sleep and hear that voice again.

"Claire? *Hija*?"

There was a soft knock on her bedroom door. Claire rolled over in bed and saw Abuelita entering with a silver tray. She was fully dressed in black pants and a colorful silk poncho, and her hair was pulled back in an elegant chignon. Tucked into the chignon was a large, red flower, reminiscent of Evita Perón.

"Good morning, Abuelita," Claire said, sitting up and rubbing her eyes. "Wow—what is this?"

Abuelita set the tray down by Claire on the bedside table. "Here are tea and oats, the paper, and there is the honey. I am leaving. I have to take Mrs. Jones to the hospital today. She is having tests run and cannot drive herself."

"Oh."

"I will be back in time to pick Graeme up at Martina's. I want you to have a wonderful day and not worry about anything."

Claire rose up on her elbows. "You didn't tell me last night about Mrs. Jones. If you're too busy today—"

"Of course not!"

"I don't ever want to put you out, you know."

Abuelita reached down and squeezed Claire's hand. "You're my

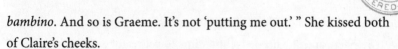

bambino. And so is Graeme. It's not 'putting me out.' " She kissed both of Claire's cheeks.

"Thank you," Claire said sincerely. "You spoil me."

"*De nada*." Abuelita turned to exit the room.

Claire called after her. "Abuelita, do you think it's okay for me to leave him all day like this?"

"I think it's more than okay. I think he needs it—and so do you."

Listening to her grandmother's shoes clicking down the hallway and then down the stairs, Claire felt pleasantly alone. After a quick trip to the bathroom, she settled back in bed with her tea and *The New York Times*. She'd enjoy just a few moments to herself, and then she needed to do some schoolwork before getting ready for her trip with Stephen. If she was going to spend a whole day away, she wanted to devote all of Sunday to Graeme without having to grade papers or prepare for class.

As she sipped the tea Abuelita had prepared for her, one of the headlines in the *Times* caught Claire's interest. The subject of the article was the fence built along the border of the United States and Mexico to keep illegal immigrants out. As she read, Claire was struck by an idea. She rummaged through the drawer of the bedside table to find a pen and paper and started taking notes. This would be a great launchpad for the discussion she planned to lead in one of her classes on Immigration Literature.

Berlin Wall. Great Wall of China, Claire scrawled across the paper. Then, going a step further in her mind, she wrote, *Why do people build walls? What are we keeping inside? What—and whom—do we want to keep out?* She looked out the window and gazed for a few moments at the gates of the Casa. *Walls can keep us safe*, she wrote. *But they can also close us off from life. Bringing them down may be necessary for our growth as a nation and as individuals.*

Claire shrugged as her writing turned to doodling. She'd have to develop this idea later. She had a section of essays to grade before she left with Stephen, and she needed a little time to get ready. Setting the tea back on the tray, she got up and walked over to her desk, paper-clipping her notes from the *Times* to the inside cover of her grade book to think about another day. Then she dug into the pile of essays on her desk.

After all of the essays were graded, Claire hastily made her bed, showered, and dressed. She had chosen to be comfortable today in khaki jeans and a thin ivory sweater. Over the sweater she would wear a jacket she bought at an artsy, southwest-style boutique in Alamosa; it was a woven mixture of turquoise, hot pink, yellow, burnt orange, and green.

Standing in front of her full-length mirror, Claire fastened her brown leather belt. Then she hurried into the bathroom to put on a little makeup. It was almost ten. Feeling like a teenager, she decided to wear just a hint of dark-green eye shadow along with her smoky black eyeliner. Her lipstick was the color of red wine.

Makeup done, Claire pulled her hair back on the sides, plucked a few stray grays, and secured it with a tortoise-shell barrette. Gold highlights, from days on the patio, shimmered through the darkness of her widow's peak, and Claire was satisfied with the face she saw in the mirror.

She jumped almost a foot in the air, however, when she heard something hit her window. *Was it a rock?* There it was again. Claire darted into her room and pulled back the heavy Italian curtains.

When she recovered from her shock, Claire laughed out loud at what she saw. Stephen Reyes was standing beneath her window. He was dressed in jeans and a starched Polo shirt the color of his eyes, with a white t-shirt underneath. A vibrant cluster of flowers, wrapped in tissue paper, was in his hand.

But that was not the funny part. As soon as he saw her, he went down on one knee, holding the bouquet of flowers across his heart and grinning like a cat. She undid the latches to open the window.

"What are you doing?" she asked, leaning out the window over an iron window box that had recently been winterized.

" 'But soft! What light through yonder window breaks? It is the east, and *Claire* is the sun.' "

Claire stared at him in disbelief for a moment before she completely cracked up. Stephen looked so silly down there—so goofy. It was a side of him she hadn't seen before.

"What's this?" he asked, feigning offense. "You're laughing at me? I'm on my knee quoting Shakespeare to you and you're laughing?"

Claire laughed more, really cackling. She couldn't help herself.

"What's a guy got to do to court an English professor?" He stood to his feet and held out his arms in mock confusion.

"Sing!" she suggested.

"I think I've got a better idea." Stephen tossed the flowers up to her and then disappeared. It was a lovely arrangement of red gladiolus, fuchsia daisies, Asian lilies, and yellow roses. Claire removed the tissue and was arranging them in a vase on her desk when she heard him back at the window. *Could he be climbing up the house?*

"Stephen?" she asked, looking out again and seeing him climbing a ladder toward her. "Where did you get that?"

"From the toolshed." He made it to the top and stood there, facing her through the window.

"Hi." Stephen's face was beaming.

Standing face-to-face over the window box, Claire found nothing in his eyes but boyish excitement, and yes—trust. Vulnerability. Instead of second-guessing it all, she did an instinctive, spontaneous thing.

She kissed him on the lips.

Then, whispering softly in his ear, Claire quoted, " 'All my fortunes at thy foot I'll lay, and follow thee, my lord, throughout the world.' " She could feel the muscles in his jaw stretch into a smile, and when

259

she leaned back and looked him in the eyes, they were very wide. She grinned. "Or at least to Taos."

"That's cruel. Very cruel," Stephen said, but he didn't seem to mean it. He looked past her into her bedroom. "Shall I just climb in thy window, m'lady?"

Claire raised her eyebrows at him. "Why don't you put that ladder away, Romeo, and I'll meet you downstairs." She smiled primly, dusting one of her hairs off his shoulder. "Thank you for the flowers."

* * * * *

They turned left out of the iron gates onto Highway 142, which took them through downtown Romeo, and made a left onto Highway 285. In less than ten minutes they had crossed the border into New Mexico, and the ten-thousand-feet-high Ute Peak passed behind them like a distant memory.

"It must have been something to grow up in this area," Stephen commented, "with all of the wide open spaces and the mountains. I love it."

Claire reflected. "I think I took it for granted," she said. "I always liked it here, but I also liked the other places I've lived. I used to think I could be happy anywhere—and Arkansas is extremely beautiful. It wasn't until my husband died that I began to feel stifled there." She looked over at Stephen. "After that happened, I suddenly needed to come home to feel like I could breathe."

"Your home was with him," Stephen said carefully. "That's not something geographical."

"You're right." Claire nodded, appreciative of his understanding. "But the geography here is tied in with who I am—my culture and history—and my abuelita. It's been good to rediscover those roots and realize that they are strong. Strong enough to survive."

Stephen looked out at the landscape through which they were driving. With its pristine blue sky and long stretches of nothingness, it was similar to where they lived in the San Luis Valley. The San Juan Mountains bordered the road to the west, standing like silent guards, and after a stretch of desert, the Sangre de Cristo Range rose up around them in the east. Claire could tell by Stephen's brows and the set of his jaw that he was thinking about something.

"Claire?"

"Yes?"

"Do you believe that everything happens for a reason?"

"I do—but I hate it when people use that phrase."

Stephen laughed lightly. "What do you mean?"

"Well, it was ingrained in me early. I can still remember people telling me that when my parents were killed. Maybe they don't mean it this way, but when people use that expression, the implication is that whatever happened was worth it. You know? 'God killed my parents so that many people would be saved.' That didn't make sense to me then, and it still doesn't. It would never be worth it to a kid—or to anyone who has seen a loved one suffer. I have never wanted anyone to say that to Graeme."

"Have they?"

"A few times. It's a pretty typical response for some Christians, especially those who don't have a clue." Claire was instantly sorry for how bitter she sounded, and she said so.

Stephen assented. "What did you tell him?"

"I told him the same thing my abuelita told me. God loves us, and He loved Daddy. Sometimes things happen that nobody understands. Our job is to trust."

"Sounds good—and hard."

"I've said it so many times it's become like a mantra."

"Has it gotten any easier to believe...or to trust?"

"For a while it seemed to be impossible, but believe it or not, I think it is getting easier."

"That's interesting," Stephen said. "Did you know there's a scientific explanation for that?"

"No, I guess I was thinking of it as a spiritual thing."

"It's amazing to me how often the two coincide."

"What do you mean?"

"Well, for some of my continuing education, I've been studying up on the brain and how it can retrain itself after injury. I came across this concept called neuroplasticity, which refers to the way we can actually reshape our thought patterns—train our minds to think in different ways."

Stephen glanced over at Claire as though he was trying to gauge whether he was boring her, but she was totally hooked.

"One of the ways is by telling ourselves things over and over, or meditating. That probably sounds so Oprah—but if we meditate on truths from the Bible—well, that's where there's real Spirit and life. That's how we can really be transformed."

"Like, 'Pray without ceasing.' "

"Yeah, or 'Rejoice in the Lord always.' "

"Stephen, that's so cool!"

"I know, but I can't take any credit for it. There's this doctor in Arkansas—you may have heard of her—Bernadette Alberty—who put it all together. I've just read some of her stuff. She calls it common sense, but I think she's probably going to start a revolution in the medical community."

Claire hadn't heard of Dr. Alberty, but she was impressed. "Wow," she said, grinning. "You'll have to tell Carlos about her. He thinks only hicks come out of Arkansas."

Stephen turned left at Tres Piedras and onto Highway 64 toward Taos. "We kind of got off the subject," he said, "but I want to go back to something. You said that you *do* believe everything happens for a reason, even though you hate that phrase."

"Gosh, you should have been a lawyer."

"I'm not trying to interrogate you—I just want to learn about you, remember? 'Claire 101'?" Stephen reached over and patted her knee.

Claire took up his hand and played with it, tinkering with his long, surgeon-like fingers. "Well, Abuelita and I have talked about this a lot. Her take on it has always been that everything in the universe ultimately happens to bring glory to Jesus. He doesn't owe us any other explanation." She slid her fingers through his and rested their entwined hands on her knee. "Abuelita has two mantras: 'In acceptance is peace,' and 'In trust is joy.' "

"She must have been at those for a long time," Stephen said.

"As long as I can remember."

* * * * *

Just northwest of Taos on Highway 64, Stephen asked Claire if she wanted to stop at the Rio Grande Gorge Bridge. She did, and they pulled over along with a few other tourists and walked up to the gorge. The cold wind whipped Claire's hair, and she was grateful for the warmth of Stephen's arm around her.

The view from the bridge was magnificent. Six hundred and fifty feet below, a tiny yellow raft flowed by, carrying a group of adventurers down the Rio Grande River. Claire had done that before with her church youth group. As she stood there beside Stephen, random thoughts of people and experiences surfaced in her brain, and she wondered briefly what he was thinking about. The bridge reminded her of Thornton Wilder. It also reminded her a little bit of her dream. She was getting lost in a reverie when Stephen's voice broke through the silence.

"I wish I had my camera," he said, his breath warm beside her ear.

Claire turned to him. "We can buy a postcard, I'm sure."

"I didn't want a picture of the gorge."

Like a magnet, his smile pulled her forward.

"You know, you're a really good kisser," he told her when they were back in the truck.

Claire reddened. "So are you—a little too good."

When they reached Taos, Claire was stunned to see how much the village had changed. As a teenager and even a college student, she had been there several times to snow ski. She, Rob, and a group from the Honors College at Adams had done a service project once at the Taos Pueblo, to interact with the Native American village and tribe. That was their senior year. But she hadn't returned to Taos since she left college. Even though it was only an hour and a half from Romeo, she and Rob had never driven back there during their visits to Abuelita's.

"We can do whatever you want, but I was thinking we'd park downtown and then walk around. There's a restaurant my sister told me about, tucked into a little hole in the wall. It's on Kit Carson Road. She says it's the best in town."

"How is your sister doing?" Claire asked. "I sure appreciate how she takes care of Graeme. His asthma is well under control." Since the mystery of Maria's relationship to Stephen was solved, Claire had realized how much she liked the other woman.

"She's great. I just talked to her this morning; she was at the airport in Colorado Springs. Her husband finally made it home from Colombia, and she took this week off to be with him. I'm going up there Monday night to see them both." He pulled into a public parking space. "Is this okay with you?"

"This is great. I love to walk."

Claire waited while Stephen came around the truck to open her door, and she hopped out. It was not nearly as windy in Taos proper as it had been at the gorge, but she still needed her jacket. Stephen grabbed his from the backseat.

"Are you hungry? Do you want to eat now?" he asked her.

"Actually, I am. I didn't eat much breakfast."

Stephen glanced at his nickel-colored watch. "Well, it is almost noon. Why don't we head on over to find Roberto's?"

They crossed the street in front of them and started down Kit Carson Road. Forgetting her hunger, Claire was tempted to stop at several of the quaint shops and studios that lined the street. Sculptors, glass artists, metalworkers, and weavers sitting in their doorways drew her in.

She and Stephen reached the end of the street before she knew it. There, on the corner under a faded red awning, was a wooden door. Hand-painted letters, in peeling white, pronounced ROBERTO'S. But there was one problem. A sign written on notebook paper was taped to the door. In haphazard letters, it read, "Gone skiing. Be back at dinner."

"Oh, man!" Stephen looked really disappointed.

"That's pretty funny. I'll have to tell Martina and Jesús about that one."

"I'm sure there's other good food here, but that's the only place I know about." He looked at Claire hopefully. "Do you know of any others?"

"Well, there used to be a fun little place in the ski valley called Tim's Stray Dog Cantina, but we'd have to drive out there," Claire told him. "Then there's Lambert's—it's kind of fancy. They serve antelope and other stuff like that. We passed it on the way into town. But I don't know if they're open for lunch."

"Do you want to drive out to the ski valley?" Stephen asked her.

"Nah. Let's just find a place around here. Anything's fine with me."

When she said that, Stephen seemed to relax. It was cute to Claire that he felt so responsible, and she wanted him to know she was having a good time. A great time, actually. The best she'd had in years.

"Back up the street there's a place called Tapas," Claire offered. "I saw it when we passed. Want to try it?"

"Sure—okay."

The food at Tapas was nothing special, but that didn't keep Claire and Stephen from having fun.

"The best laid plans of mice and men—" he began as they exited the restaurant.

She finished his sentence, linking her arm through his. "—sometimes go awry." And as they walked across the Plaza, she added, under her breath, "And sometimes God has other plans."

"Your abuelita would be proud."

They browsed through the many art galleries, which featured oil paintings, watercolors, photographs, drawings, pottery, woodworks, and ceramics.

In one jewelry store Claire was particularly taken with a pendant made from old stained glass. It was a fragment in the rugged shape of a raindrop, and the color was a dazzling aqua blue. The artist said he gleaned the piece from a broken church window that had been thrown away. Some forgotten process, done to the original window, gave it a luminous quality. He didn't know what the piece of glass had been a part of, perhaps the sky or the sea, he suggested. It was set in a gleaming silver lining.

Claire turned it over and over, and it shimmered in her hand. She fingered the glass reverently, thinking about its story. *Is this what it means to be redeemed?*

While she was pondering that question, deep in her own thoughts, Stephen bought an eighteen-inch box chain and looped it through the pendant in her hand. Then, to her enchantment, he lifted her hair and fastened it around her neck. Claire didn't know what to say, so she just hugged him for a long time. He kissed her on the head and rubbed up and down her back with a strong hand. When they walked together out of the store, the necklace sparkled like a medal on her chest.

It was late in the evening when Stephen and Claire started back to Romeo. They had strolled the streets of Taos long enough to eat a world-class dinner at the famed Roberto's. Claire insisted on buying Stephen's meal. This seemed to nearly do him in, but in the end he relented. She couldn't let him pay for the whole trip *and* the necklace. It was just too much.

On the way home they chatted easily about Joe and Frieda, Graeme, the Patricks, the Rodriguez family, and their jobs. Claire couldn't remember the last time she'd felt so relaxed and comfortable in her own skin or with another person. She sighed contentedly. It had been a perfect day.

"What are you all doing for Thanksgiving?" Stephen asked her.

"Well, Abuelita has this idea in her head of hosting a Thanksgiving dinner for the community."

"Really? At the Casa?"

"No, she wants to have it at the community center. That's what the OFS was meeting about the other day."

"I see," Stephen said, laughing at the memory. Then he added, "That place looks pretty deserted."

"I know—that's what I told her—but she said there was an event there last spring. She thinks it mainly needs to be mowed and cleaned on the inside."

"Well, let me know, and maybe I can help with that. And I might be able to round up a few others."

"That would be great. I'll tell her."

"I'd like to score a few points with your abuelita," Stephen admitted.

Claire grinned. "I think you're doing all right in that department— with her and with Graeme." *And with me, too*, she thought but didn't say.

"What's coming up for you this week, Stephen?" she asked him as they turned onto Highway 285.

"Well, I'm doing a pro-bono clinic on Tuesday. Dr. Banks and I worked it out at the Wound Care Center."

"Really? Do you do that regularly?"

"No. This is the first time. But it may become a regular thing."

"That's interesting. What will it be like?"

"It's for people who can't afford to go to the doctor. Women who need breast exams and pap smears but don't get them, men who need prostate screening. Stuff like that."

Claire marveled at some of the subjects that so easily rolled off his tongue, but he took no notice. She supposed that to him it was all the same.

"Many of the people who need these services don't speak English, so I hope I can effectively communicate with them. I really need to find a good Spanish tutor." He grinned at her.

"What was the impetus for starting something like this? I mean, I think it's great. Some of my students probably need to know about it."

"Send them on," Stephen said. "Dr. Banks and I got the idea the other night after Bible study. It was really more his idea—but it was in response to something I shared."

"What's that?" Claire was curious.

"Well, the group leader talked a lot about Jesus being the Good Shepherd and us being sheep, and then we talked about that verse that says we're supposed to feed the sheep." Stephen ran his hand through his hair. "Different people shared what they thought that meant, and I just told them what it's like to do it literally. Because I have sheep, you know."

"So this is about feeding sheep? You lost me somewhere."

"Dr. Banks suggested we feed the Lord's sheep by meeting some basic needs for people. You know, as a way to minister."

"Oh! Now I get it. Abuelita's big on that."

Stephen grinned. "Well, you be sure to tell her I'm doing it, then."

Claire laughed and promised that she would.

When they pulled through the gates of the Casa, it was nearly nine thirty. Stephen cut the engine and walked around to open Claire's door. He was clearly planning to walk her to the front, but she stopped him at the garage.

"I'd invite you in, but I think I should go straight in to Graeme and give him some attention. I'm going to slip in through here. He's probably not asleep." She got out her garage-door opener from her purse.

"Thank you for a wonderful day," Stephen said simply.

Claire thought in that moment that she'd never seen more honest brown eyes.

"Thank *you*," she said.

Then he did something that surprised her. He reached out his hand for a handshake.

Intrigued, she offered hers in return.

"You're going to have to help me," he said as he gripped her hand tightly, still keeping a distance.

"Okay—uh—with what?"

"With purity." Stephen looked down. "I don't want to mess things up."

This was a new one for Claire. *Wow*. Even Rob, when they dated, had never said anything like that.

"You've got a deal," she said as she shook his hand to seal it.

Chapter Thirty

....

Stephen had been checking on patients in the hospital since seven o'clock, and he had just a few minutes to spend in his office before his first appointment. From the looks of his computer screen, he had a loaded schedule ahead of him, and he wasn't looking forward to it. To make matters worse, Desirae was out, having somehow managed to contract hepatitis, and he would have to go through the whole week— maybe longer—with Ashli as his substitute nurse.

"I didn't move to a small town to be this busy," he said to no one in particular.

"Dr. Reyes?" Irene's nasal voice came over the speaker in the hall. "Dr. Reyes, line one."

Stephen snatched up the phone on his desk and pressed the appropriate button.

"This is Dr. Reyes."

"I've got a Nell Patrick on the phone who says she has to talk to you. Says it's urgent. I told her you were booked solid today." The condescension in Irene's voice annoyed Stephen, and he could visualize her at her desk, looking down her nose through her horn-rimmed glasses.

"Put her on," he growled.

Irene said sweetly, "Mrs. Patrick, here's Doctor Reyes."

"Stephen?" Nell said, her voice sounding a little ragged around the edges.

"You can hang up, now, Irene. I've got it."

There was a click.

"Nell, is everything okay?"

"What rock did you find *her* under?"

Stephen was glad to hear that Nell's humor was intact. He laughed. "How's it going on the farm?"

"Oh, same as usual. Gene's fine; I'm fine. You workin' hard?"

"Hardly working."

"I know that's not true," Nell snorted. Then, in a softer tone, she said, "Hey, you know I'd never ask you this if I didn't think it was important. But I've a notion to get Marsha Evans in to see you today."

"Really? What's going on?"

"Well, Stan came by himself to church again yesterday. He was going to get baptized but said he'd better wait a week. Marsha didn't feel like coming with him to watch him. Now that's just not normal for her."

"Have you seen her?"

"I went down there last night—she looked awful. I bet she's lost twenty pounds. I thought about what you said about the medicine and all, and I told her we might better go to the doctor today."

"Did she agree to come?"

"She said if I could get her in to you, she would."

"Did you tell her I'd see her today?"

"Well, sorta. I told her I knew you would if there was any way you could."

"That's right. You bring her on. I'll tell Irene to work her in as soon as you get here."

"Thanks, son."

Stephen studied the schedule a moment longer and then took a deep breath as he exited his office. Ashli met him coming down the hall. Clad in red scrubs that were tight as a snakeskin, she tossed her bleach-blond hair and smiled at him with teeth like a horse. Stephen cringed inwardly as he subconsciously compared her look to the understated splendor of Claire's.

"Looks like we've got some doozies lined up," Ashli said, handing him two charts.

Perusing the first one, Stephen glanced up at her. "What's this?"

"Apparently she called the ER and they sent her over here, rather than having you come there. I guess it's not really super urgent?"

"Did you talk to her?"

"Uh, no. I thought since it was technically an ER case that you could just do it."

Stephen studied her a moment as though she were from another planet. Then, deciding against confrontation, he opened the next chart. It was apparently for his first standing appointment.

"You *have* talked to this one?" he asked Ashli.

"Oh, yeah. We had a nice chat."

Ashli turned on her heel and then sashayed down the hall in front of him, swinging her full hips from side to side.

Stephen scowled after her. He took another deep breath before entering exam room one.

Sitting on the exam table in front of him, kicking her feet, was a young woman who appeared to be about twenty. Her chin-length hair was faded maroon at the tips and dull brown up near her scalp. She had a lip ring that curled around her upper lip in one corner. *Like a miniature tusk,* Stephen thought.

The girl was poorly dressed in ripped sweats, old tennis shoes, and a gray jacket. Underneath those layers, however, was the unmistakable protrusion of a pregnant belly. She looked like she had swallowed a watermelon.

"Hi there. I'm Dr. Reyes," Stephen said, sitting down on his stool in front of her. "And you're Brandy. Is that right?"

"Yep."

"Well, Brandy, what seems to be the trouble? Are you having any problems with your pregnancy?" He glanced down at her chart. "It says here that your due date is next week."

"That's true, but I'm past ready to get this baby out." She rubbed her abdomen. "When I talked to my momma—she's out in California—she said to drink some Castrol. That's what she did with me to get her labor going."

Stephen thought he was hearing things. "Excuse me, what did she tell you to drink?"

"Castrol."

Stephen looked at her quizzically.

"You know. *Castrol.*"

It finally dawned on him what she was saying. "Castor oil?" Stephen was aware of the old wives' tale. He'd heard it many times before.

"That's what I said." She looked at him like he was completely stupid.

"Okay, but Brandy, I have to tell you that's just a myth. It doesn't work."

"I know that now. I drank half a quart of it last night and nothing happened."

Stephen's pulse quickened. "What do you mean you drank half a *quart* of it?"

"Well, my boyfriend's a mechanic, and he gave me a quart of Castrol yesterday out of his shop. I drank most of it, but when his momma found out about it this morning, she about had a cow. She's the one who called the emergency room, but they sent me over to you. She got into a fight with that nurse Carlos. She thought they ought to pump my stomach."

Stephen fought hard to retain his composure.

"Let me get this straight. You drank Castrol motor oil last night to induce your labor, but nothing has happened. No diarrhea, nothing."

"Nothing. No labor pains, either," she added sullenly.

"Well. Okay, Brandy, I think we'll just set you up in an observation room for a few hours; how does that sound?"

"I guess that's all right with me. I mean, you're the doctor."

His next patient was a woman of thirty-five. She had long, nut-brown hair and small green eyes.

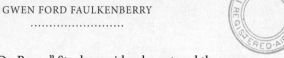

"Hi, Jennifer, I'm Dr. Reyes," Stephen said as he entered the room.

"You can call me Jen," she told him in an over-friendly manner.

"Okay, Jen, what seems to be the trouble? Ashli wrote on your chart that you've been bitten by an insect?"

"Not *an* insect, but *some* insects. Although I'm not sure if they're technically insects."

"Well, where did they bite you?" Stephen stood up from his stool to examine her.

"All up and down this arm."

She held out her arm for him to see, but Stephen couldn't make out the tiniest mark anywhere.

"The bites were really red yesterday. I called for an appointment but couldn't get in until this morning. I almost came to the emergency room last night; they were so painful."

"Well, are they hurting today?"

"On and off—I mean, they're not really hurting that bad right now, but I bet they will be later."

"I see." Stephen was beginning to wonder if everyone in La Jara had lost their minds.

"I brought them in, in case you need to do lab work or something on them."

"On what?"

"The woolly worms. The ones that bit me."

Jen slid off the table and went to her purse. Opening it, she retrieved a bell jar that had holes poked in the lid, presumably so her assailants could breathe.

"This is what bit you?" Stephen asked, disbelieving.

"Yeah. I was sitting under a tree in my backyard drinking tea, and these worms fell on my arm and bit me!"

Stephen took a deep breath. Looking back and forth from Jen's face to the three woolly worms obliviously munching a leaf inside her jar, he sat back down to write on his prescription notepad.

"I'm going to give you something preventative, for the next time you're outside."

"Okay," Jen said, her smile pasted on like the third runner-up in a pageant.

Stephen wrote "Bug Spray" on the pad and handed it to her before walking out of the exam room.

* * * * *

"Irene?" Stephen boomed into the phone when the receptionist answered on the other end of the line.

"Dr. Reyes?"

"Yes. Has Nell Patrick come in with Marsha Evans yet?"

There was a moment's pause before Irene said, "Well, yes. As a matter of fact they are here."

"I'd like to see them in my office."

"Your office?"

"Yes. I'm in my office right now. You can walk them back."

"Uh, okay." Irene was obviously rattled by his request.

Stephen's mood changed almost instantly when Nell walked into the room and hugged him. He was as happy to see her as he was sorry to see the shape Marsha was in.

"Thanks for getting me in today, Dr. Reyes," Marsha said somberly.

"Hey—no problem. When Nell speaks, I listen." Stephen joked with them, trying to lighten the heaviness of Marsha's situation. "But why don't you call me Stephen? Or Steve? We're neighbors."

Nell patted the younger woman's arm. "I'll just wait outside."

"Go right in here," Stephen motioned to the empty exam room

across the hall and then closed the door to his office. Marsha sat down in one of the wingbacks across from his desk, and he sat down behind his desk, leaning back and putting one cowboy boot up on its corner.

"Tell me about you," he said to Marsha.

She laughed uncomfortably. "I—I think I may be going crazy."

Stephen smiled at her reassuringly. "You have the right, if anyone does."

"I don't know why I'm here, really, Dr. Reyes, because I don't think anyone can help me. My daughter's death has changed everything, and no one can bring her back. I'm trying to cope the best I know how."

Stephen looked at the woman who seemed a shell of the person she'd been. He hadn't known her well before, but he could see that her honey-colored hair had grown an inch with no attention, and her clothes hung like they were two sizes too big. Her blue eyes stared back at him from their sockets as though from some dark, lonely caves, and a deep furrow ravaged her brow. Stephen was moved by the honesty of her words. "What are some things you're doing to cope?"

"Praying, reading the Bible, trying to stay in a routine. But that's hard."

"Does any of that help?"

"Maybe; I mean, I believe praying and reading the Bible do. But I've also come to the conclusion that I can't pray my way out of this. If I could, it would have already happened."

"Is your husband supportive?"

"Very. At first he was so deep down in a hole himself that he couldn't support anyone, but these last few weeks he's doing a lot better. It's strange." Marsha fiddled with her hands in her lap. "Seems like the worse I get the better he does. I mean, he's worried about me now and all, but he's doing better with his own grief for Sydney. He even got saved." A hint of a smile touched her lips before sadness resumed its position on her face.

"Hmm." Stephen pondered for awhile. Then he asked, "Have you considered grief counseling?"

"I've talked to my pastor."

"Has that been helpful?"

"I guess. As much as anything. It's like I just don't have any energy or taste for life." Marsha looked soulfully into Stephen's eyes. "I know everything happens for a reason. I know it's a sin to second-guess God. And I feel guilty about it. But I can't help it. I need my daughter back."

It seemed as if her eyes poured out buckets of tears. Stephen handed her a box of Kleenex, and she wiped the tears away.

"Marsha, I want you to be honest with me. Have you thought about taking your own life?"

Her silence filled the room. Then, after a moment, she said, "I've thought about it, but I wouldn't ever do it. I don't think I could go that far. I know God cares—and He's there. I just wish sometimes He would let me go to sleep and not wake up."

Stephen removed his foot from his desk and sat up in his chair.

"Marsha, I believe your feelings are completely normal, and the way you're dealing with things is better than many people. This is a healing process that is going to take time, but I want you to know that you do have a future and a hope."

"I believe that."

"I'd like to see you take an antidepressant to start building up some good chemicals in your brain. Sometimes when we have a traumatic experience, the good stuff gets suppressed and that makes it harder for us to go through the process of grieving and healing. Just a minute, okay?"

Stephen hurried down the hall to one of the clinic's medicine cabinets and pulled out several samples of Lexapro. Stepping back inside his office, he handed them to Marsha.

"This is six months' worth of medicine, and that may be all you need. Our brain's chemical makeup can be like a diabetic's, whose body doesn't produce enough insulin, and so she has to take insulin shots forever. Or, what seems likely in your case, that chemical makeup can be thrown off by an extreme experience, and medicine can help us over a hump until our bodies get back to producing what we need on our own."

Marsha nodded, like she was trying to understand.

"Why don't you take this for a few months, and let's see if it helps you get back on your feet. Then we'll monitor and adjust if we need to."

"I never thought a Christian should need anything like this," Marsha admitted.

Stephen smiled at her. "I hear that a lot," he said. "And medicine shouldn't be anyone's first option. But when a person is truly depressed, I believe it's a physical condition. It's not really about what we can do or not do to change it. God can use anything He wants—including medicine—to help us live our lives to the fullest."

Marsha rose to her feet and, for the first time, Stephen thought he read a little bit of hope in her expression. He opened the door. "Nell?" he called. No answer. "Nell?"

Finally Nell appeared, sleepily, at the door of the examination room. "I just about took me a little nap," she said with a yawn and a grin.

Stephen ushered them to the back entrance near his office, which he always used.

"Why don't you two go out this door, and don't worry about doing anything up front."

"Backdoor guests are best," Nell said, winking at him.

"Thank you, Dr. Reyes," Marsha said. "Thank you very much."

Chapter Thirty-one

Claire was excited—maybe even giddy, at least for her—about the prospects of the evening. It was two days before Christmas, and she and Abuelita had invited Stephen over for an early Christmas dinner. Instead of the traditional American menu of turkey and dressing and all of the fixings, which they'd do on Christmas Day, they decided to do something a little different. They were going to make Mexican tacos and chicken taquitos—Graeme's favorite.

"Graeme! Come help me with these lights!" Claire called up the stairs.

They had set up the four-foot tree—his own personal tree—in his bedroom. The day after Thanksgiving, when he was still on break from school, they had kept the tradition started when Rob was alive of decorating a "Graeme Tree." The Graeme Tree was an artificial Scotch pine flocked with fake snow and pre-lit with hundreds of tiny colored lights.

Claire had been so excited about that tree—much more excited than Graeme had been the first year he had it. She had found it on an after-Christmas clearance sale the year she was pregnant with him. During her pregnancy she had whiled away many evening hours cutting out and decorating little ornaments for him, many times joined by Rob who lovingly poked fun at her nesting instinct. By the next year, the oblivious four-month-old had a Christmas tree in his nursery, full of ornaments that documented his incubation and birth.

In the years after that, they added to the box of ornaments with mementoes from family excursions and tiny framed pictures of the three of them, which they hung on the tree with ribbons. There was one of Moira in a Santa hat and another of Rob's parents in a frame that announced "Proud Grandparents." Graeme's grandparents had also contributed a tiny set of bagpipes and a miniature Eilen Donan castle from their family reunion in Scotland. All of these had been converted to ornaments for the Graeme Tree collection.

The year Rob died, Claire didn't put up a tree—not even Graeme's. She felt bad about that. As much as she tried to keep Graeme's life and routine as normal as possible through that time, Christmas had been something she just couldn't face. Moira, as always, had picked up the slack by shuttling them back and forth between her house and her parents' and showering Graeme with gifts, but the truth was that none of them had really felt like celebrating. The memory of it stung her.

But this year was different.

"Graeme! Are you coming?"

"Just a minute, Mom!" he called from somewhere upstairs. He had disappeared that morning with the tape, his school scissors, and a roll of wrapping paper that Abuelita freely turned over to him.

Claire went to work stringing the lights on Abuelita's tree by herself. Opting away from the traditional tree they had when Claire was a child, with giant Easter-egg-type lights, Abuelita had somewhere along the line gone with a more southwest approach. She usually paid someone to do it, but this year Claire had the honor of stringing one thousand red chili-pepper-shaped lights on a seven-foot fir that had been delivered that morning. It was a job.

"What can I do to help, Mom?" Graeme finally appeared, with his hands behind his back.

"What's that behind your back?" she asked him.

"Oh, nothing." He leaned toward her. "You can't peek!"

"Okay, I won't."

"Promise you won't peek!"

"I won't! I promise!"

"Okay. These are yours and Abuelita's Christmas presents. When we're done I'm going to put them under the tree."

He set them on the coffee table for the time being, and Claire admired his handiwork. "My, what excellent wrapping you've done, Graeme."

The boxes were each a mass of crinkled paper and excessive tape. Graeme beamed up at her proudly. "I did it myself."

When they finished the chili-pepper lights, Claire checked in with Abuelita, who was rolling *taquitos* in the kitchen. The smell of green peppers and onions filled the air, and Claire inhaled appreciatively. "Yum."

"How does my tree look?" Abuelita looked up from a homemade corn tortilla and grinned at her.

"Beautiful—finally. What's next?"

"I want you to go to the storage area under the stairs—the same place you got the lights. I have a special surprise for you and Graeme."

"What is it?" asked Claire.

"You'll know when you see it. It's in a blue box with your name on it, on the top shelf."

Claire obeyed and ducked back under the stairs to fetch the box. She hadn't noticed it before since it was high above where the lights had been stored, but, using a stool, she got it down. She remembered it instantly. It was the box of ornaments from the Christmas trees of her childhood. Carrying it into the living room, she placed it on the couch and then sat down beside it, inviting Graeme to sit down with her.

"What are these?" he asked.

"These were mine. Abuelita and I used to put them on our Christmas tree when I was growing up."

"Cool!" Graeme, said, digging into the box. The first thing he pulled out was a medal. It was faded now, but the ribbon had been red, white, and blue, like something from the Olympics. The faux-gold medallion was engraved. "What's this for? Did you win a race?"

"Well," said Claire, "let's look at it." Turning the medallion over, she showed Graeme where it said "Geography Champion. Caspian, C."

"Caspian C! That's what Carlos calls you!" Graeme exclaimed. "What else is in there?" Fascinated for the moment by these trinkets from his mother's past, he rummaged through the box.

"Be careful, *hijo*," Claire cautioned him. She could see the little wheels turning in his head as he linked the adult he knew as his mother with the child she once was—a child just like him.

Graeme fished out another ornament. It was a picture of Claire in a frame she'd made at Bible School as a first grader. "Whoa!" he said. "This looks like me!"

One by one, they hung all of the "Claire" mementoes on the fir tree. There were other school awards that Abuelita had converted into ornaments, plus trinkets made in foreign lands, keepsakes of Claire's missionary parents. Her favorites were a handful that had been crafted from a kit with sequins and beads.

"These are really good!" Graeme said, holding up a lion and a clown.

"Well, they've seen better days, but those are pretty special. Abuelita and I made them one time when school was out for snow." Claire could still taste the hot chocolate they had made that day, with the star-shaped marshmallows.

"Can we do that if I'm out for snow?"

"I bet we can," Claire said, hugging him. "We need some new ornaments for this tree anyway."

She looked back under the stairs for another box but couldn't find any.

"Abuelita?" she called. "Are there any more ornaments?"

* * * * *

By that afternoon, when Stephen was scheduled to arrive, the Claire Tree sported an several new ornaments that Claire and Graeme had made from materials in Graeme's craft box.

"Abuelita, can you get the door?"

Abuelita looked at Claire sideways across the table they were sharing. With Graeme in the middle of them, they had decorated three dozen sugar cookies with green and red icing in various festive designs. They were just starting on the fourth dozen.

"I want to freshen up a little!" Claire explained, taking off her apron.

"Well, I suppose that does matter more to you at this point than it does to me," Abuelita said, pretending annoyance. She pulled her own apron over her head, repositioning the combs in the sides and back of her hair, and pitched it onto the counter.

Glancing at each other, Graeme and Claire scrambled quietly out of their seats and tiptoed behind Abuelita as she left the kitchen.

"*Hola*?" They heard her call from the empty doorway. Then, as she stepped forward onto the porch, they heard a loud squeal and then a "*Chistoso*! Dr. Reyes! *Baboso*! Put me down!"

From the foyer where they watched the spectacle, Graeme and Claire guffawed with laughter. Abuelita whipped her head around, taking notice of them for the first time.

"You knew about this?" Abuelita cried, kicking her legs in protest as Stephen held her up in the air.

Directly above them, hanging from the iron chandelier, was a huge clump of fresh mistletoe, tied with a red ribbon. The look on Stephen's face was pure Dennis the Menace.

"Kiss her! Kiss her!" Graeme began to chant, and Claire joined him, clapping. It was the first time in a long time that she could remember anyone pulling one over on her abuelita. This feat of Stephen's would more than compensate for her little OFS joke.

Stephen held his prey at eye level and planted a loud, sloppy kiss on Abuelita's cheek before releasing her. Back down on her feet, Abuelita laughed until tears flowed down her cheeks.

"You'll be sorry when I pee my pants!" she croaked between gales of hilarity, wiping her eyes.

* * * * *

After such an icebreaker, it was easy to settle into a celebratory mood. Abuelita led Stephen directly into the living room, where she proudly narrated the childhood stories behind each of Claire's ornaments. Claire was touched by how he listened, looking carefully at each one.

"These are really special," he said, giving Claire a side squeeze.

Next, Graeme showed him the presents he had wrapped himself. Stephen turned them over and over, inspecting his technique. After sufficient approbation, Graeme stood up on the couch to whisper in his ear.

"Promise me you won't tell!" Graeme warned when he was done telling his secret. He pointed his finger in Stephen's face.

Claire cringed a little at this, but Stephen seemed unfazed.

"You have my word of honor," he declared, placing his hand over his heart.

Graeme nodded in satisfaction.

Then Stephen asked, "Hey, buddy, will you help me get some things out of my truck?"

Graeme jumped down off the couch and they exited the way Stephen came in. While they were gone, Claire and Abuelita flew around the kitchen, filling glasses and setting the table. By the time Graeme and Stephen returned, dinner was served.

"That meal was really delicious," Stephen said to Abuelita. "I've never had such wonderful Mexican food."

"That's because you're not Mexican," she teased.

"Is that okay?" Stephen retorted facetiously.

"Hmm." Abuelita narrowed her eyes at him. "What are you, anyway?"

"I'm half Puerto Rican and half Irish."

"Well—" Abuelita cocked her head to one side. Then she reached across the table and grabbed his hand. "It's more than okay." She was no longer joking. "You are who God made you. And I'm glad God has brought you to us."

It was a gesture that nearly brought tears to Claire's eyes, though she couldn't explain why.

"So, Graeme, how about you help me with dessert?"

"Can we have it in the living room?" Graeme asked. "I'm ready for presents."

Abuelita smiled at him. "By all means."

While the adults ate cookies and sipped their tea and coffee, Graeme neglected his hot chocolate for the presents Stephen brought.

"These are all mine?" he asked, pointing to the pile they'd retrieved from Stephen's truck.

"All yours except the two that are marked differently. You can read your name, can't you?"

Graeme frowned at him. "I can read my name and my Mom's and Abuelita's."

"Okay then. Why don't you be Santa's elf and deliver theirs first?" Stephen suggested.

"I'm giving them mine on Christmas morning."

"Well, that's even better, but I won't be here on Christmas morning. Do you think it would be okay if I gave them mine now?"

Graeme thought seriously for a moment before he nodded his

agreement. "Yeah, I guess that would be fine." Then he dug in and shuffled through the gifts until he came to a small, thin box. "This one's for you, Abuelita!" he said excitedly. As he walked it over to her chair he said, "It's kind of little, though."

"You didn't have to get me anything," Abuelita said to Stephen. She tore the paper off carefully and opened the box that was inside.

"Oh! These are beautiful! I—well, I—Claire, look!"

Abuelita held up two of the prettiest combs Claire had ever seen. They were silver and inlaid with red coral and turquoise pieces.

"Thank you, Esteban." Abuelita walked over to hug him. "I guess you've redeemed yourself from that earlier assault."

Stephen, pleased with her reaction, said to Graeme, "Now find your mother's."

Claire sat down near the tree while Graeme found it. Her gift was in a clear bag with a black and white Oriental pattern, stuffed with red and green tissue paper. The first thing she pulled out was a book.

"The new Ian McEwan!" she said. "I've been waiting for this!"

"It just came out yesterday; I preordered it from Amazon."

"Thank you," Claire said, holding his glance for a long moment. He didn't seem to miss a detail.

"What else is in there?" Stephen prompted her.

Claire reached back into the bag and found Godiva chocolates.

"Mmm." Her eyes sparkled at him.

"We can share those," Abuelita teased.

"There's one more thing."

Feeling down in the bag, Claire's hand felt a small, hard object wrapped in tissue paper. She pulled it out and unwrapped it.

"Oh." She was stunned.

It was a blown-glass Christmas ornament in the shape of a butterfly. The clear glass shimmered iridescently in her hand, waiting to take on the color of the tree's lights.

"I love it, Stephen." Her voice was quiet. "How did you manage?"

She had admired it in one of the shops in Taos.

"I'm not telling *all* my secrets," he said with a grin as he rose from the couch to help Claire hang it on the tree.

She warmed at the touch of his hand, slowly inhaling the scent of wood smoke and cedar.

"Here's to new beginnings," he whispered only to her.

The butterfly undulated on its clear nylon string, reflecting red rays from the Christmas tree lights.

* * * * *

A week later, on a trip to the library in La Jara with Graeme, Claire decided on a whim to stop by the clinic and surprise Stephen. Seeing his truck parked in the rear lot, her heart skipped a beat.

Claire pulled up by the back door and left her car running.

"I'll only be a minute," she told Graeme, who was deep into a book on dinosaurs. "I'm sure he's really busy."

Graeme didn't even look up, but he grunted, "Okay."

Claire got out of the car and shut her door, locking it with the keyless entry pad on her key chain. Seeing her reflection in the window, she tucked her hair behind her ears and pulled down her red Razorback baseball cap. It was a very casual day, but Stephen insisted casual was what he liked best. She deposited her keys into her jeans pocket.

Stephen had told her to use the back door to his office anytime she was in town. He'd practically begged her to stop by and see him on her way back and forth to work, but she never had. Seemed like she was always in too much of a hurry. It was wonderful to not be in a hurry today. One of the perks of teaching at a college was the long Christmas break.

They'd had dinner the night before at Art and Soul, but she failed to mention she was taking Graeme to the library the next day. They'd gotten into some deep theological conversation about forgiveness, and it slipped her mind. *He'd never be expecting me today.*

Claire opened the door to a quiet, empty hallway. There was no nurse at the desk and no other movement to indicate that patients were in the exam rooms. The door to Stephen's office was open, however, and she could see a light shining from within. Expectantly, Claire walked up to the door.

Stephen was sitting at his desk with his back to her. He fingered something with one of his hands, and Claire could see it was the compass she'd given him for Christmas. Blue scrubs stretched over his broad shoulders, and Claire could see the faint outline of his muscles underneath it. His dark hair curled in a few loose wisps around the base of his neck in a way that had become so dear to her. She was suddenly warmed by a rush of emotions.

Claire was about to say, "Surprise!" when she noticed that Stephen was on the phone. Instead of disturbing a work call, she decided just to stand by the door and wait. She stared at the Georgia O'Keefe print on the wall in front of her. It was of a cow's skull, presumably bleached by the sun as it lay in the russet desert sand.

"Janet?" She heard his voice say. Claire certainly wasn't trying to eavesdrop, but the word was unmistakable. Her heart dropped to the floor as she recognized the name of Stephen's ex-wife. Claire felt as if her feet were pinned to the floor.

"Janet, thanks for not hanging up. I've been thinking about you so much. There's something I really need to say to you."

What could he possibly need to say to her? Claire's heart and mind were racing.

"I've realized how badly I treated you, how I neglected our marriage.

I was wrong. I see that now. I—I know I hurt you very deeply, and I am sorry. Can you ever forgive me?"

Stephen was laughing. *Laughing?* "Oh, Janet, I can't tell you how thankful I am. How happy it makes me that God has brought us both to this point. It's, well, it's amazing, isn't it?"

His voice sounded so happy, and yes, so familiar. *Intimate.* There was a pause. Claire could only imagine what Janet was saying.

Stephen continued, "You know, I think about that, too. Our shared history. How good it was in the old days and how crazy I was about you. I wish I could go back and do things differently—"

This could not be happening. What was that he had said the other night at Abuelita's? That he wasn't telling her all of his secrets? Was that some kind of sick joke? Claire knew she shouldn't ever have trusted him. Her impulse was to jump into the office and grab the phone—to tell Janet how he'd been schmoozing her, and worse, her little boy—but she didn't.

Claire had heard enough. She turned on her heel, face on fire and whole body blazing. Pushing through the steel and glass door, she felt an icy wind slap her across the face. There were tears welling up in her eyes, but she didn't want Graeme to see her cry. *No. Not again.* Claire pulled her cap down lower over her eyebrows and swallowed hard. Then she ducked into the wind, stepping out of the clinic and into the waning December day.

Chapter Thirty-two
....

It was New Year's Eve, and Stephen didn't know where Claire was. He had talked to her on Christmas Day in the evening while he was at Maria's. Rather than being together, they'd decided to focus on their families and their plans—she with Graeme and Abuelita and he with his parents, who had flown in from Florida. They were staying at Maria's in Salida, and Stephen was catching up with them as well as with Maria's husband, Manuel.

Claire, Graeme, and her abuelita, along with the members of the Old Farts' Society, had hosted a Christmas dinner at the community center in Romeo for anyone who wanted to come, just like they had done at Thanksgiving. On the phone that evening, Claire said the place had been packed with even more needy people than it had been the month before. She described how Abuelita had been in her element dishing out turkey and dressing, and they talked briefly again about "feeding the sheep." Claire sounded so energized by the success of the dinner and said they were going to do it again at Easter. Stephen promised to help.

He had worked three long days after Christmas, and they went to dinner at Art and Sol after that, on the twenty-ninth. He hadn't talked to her since then. Surely she hadn't left town without letting him know.

At dinner that night, over Martina's now-famous tamales, Claire had talked to him about taking a New Year's trip to Arkansas so Graeme could see his grandparents and aunt. It wasn't a sure thing, but she was looking into flights. During their conversation, Stephen sensed he was being tested—by the Lord and perhaps by Claire, too. Could he handle another man's family being a part of Claire's life forever? Should he even be thinking about forever?

Even though it was a tough subject, Stephen encouraged Claire to go. He knew how badly Graeme needed that connection, and he imagined the grandparents and aunt did, too. It was all the family had left of Rob. It was a tricky position for Stephen, but he determined never to stand in the way of that. He promised as much to Claire that night. Not that he wouldn't miss them being in town for New Year's. He'd gotten almost as attached to Graeme as he had to Claire.

He dialed her cell phone number again.

"You have reached the voice mail of Claire Caspian...," he heard after several rings. Stephen sighed his disappointment.

"Hey, Claire. It's me, Stephen. Just checking in. I'm hoping you're not gone." Stephen quickly corrected himself. "I mean, if you *are* gone I hope everything's going well for you and Graeme." He paused. "If you're around I'd love to see you. I'm on call tonight, but just as backup."

A computer-generated voice let him know his message time was almost over.

Stephen hurried, "As long as we stayed close to La Jara—like your place or mine—it would be fine. Call me."

Beep. "Your message has been sent."

* * * * *

Claire pressed the "Delete" button on her phone. It was the third message Stephen had left her since yesterday, and the third one she had deleted. Who did he think he was, playing her for the fool? Ironically, his first call had come just as she was driving away from La Jara the day before. Just moments after she overheard him making up to Janet.

She couldn't believe Stephen had the audacity to call her after that. But, of course, he had no idea she knew. He was still playing his game.

Claire had heard of people like Stephen, men and women who got some sort of thrill out of living double lives, manipulating others into believing they were someone they weren't. She read a book once about a pilot who had two separate wives and families on two continents. It was sick! Stephen was clearly the worst kind of narcissist. And to think she had almost fallen for him.

Claire was furious with herself and not too happy with God, either. After finally opening her heart up to the Lord, believing He was leading her, she'd been hurt again. How could He have let this happen to her and Graeme? Hadn't they suffered enough? She was tired of asking those questions. Maybe no one was listening anyway.

* * * * *

Feeling restless, Stephen decided to go for a run. He pulled on his shoes and clipped his phone to the waistband of his wind suit pants. He had to keep the phone with him at all times when he was on call for the ER, but in his heart he also hoped Claire might get his messages and finally call.

He rounded up Duchess and Regina and started down his driveway. They were reluctant partners today. The air was cold and crisp, and it burned his lungs. There were even a few snow flurries in the air. Stephen had gotten lazy over Christmas—eaten too much and run too little. Cold or not, this would do him some good. He decided to head towards the Evanses' house and do a five-mile loop.

* * * * *

"Claire! Would you mind getting the mail? It's starting to snow, and I haven't been out to get it today. I'm looking for a package."

"I'll go get it, Abuelita. Let me!" Graeme called from the living room where he was playing his new Wii.

Claire roused herself from where she was laying on the couch. "No, *hijo*, I don't want you down there by that road."

"Aw, Mom, you never let me do anything."

"I know. You're very deprived."

He frowned at her as she walked by but was soon back into a heated tennis match.

"Could the package be at the post office, Abuelita?" Claire asked as she strode through the kitchen, headed for her red wool coat that hung on a peg by the door.

"Well, I suppose, but I haven't gotten a notice. If it is, it's too late anyway. It's six o'clock."

Claire had lost all track of time. "So it is. I hadn't realized."

"*Hija*?" Abuelita turned from the pot she was stirring on the stove to face Claire, who was still standing in the doorway.

Claire looked at her, wishing she could shake the sadness she felt. She knew it burdened her grandmother.

"Is there any way this could be a misunderstanding? Shouldn't you give him the chance to explain?"

"I don't think so, Abuelita. I mean, what is there to explain? What I heard was very clear." Claire reached up and twisted a strand of her hair. "He had us all fooled—and me most of all. I'm sorry—for you and for Graeme."

"Oh, *pshh*." Abuelita waved her wooden spoon in the air. "Don't be sorry for me. Be sorry for him if I ever get my hands around his neck." She set the spoon down and formed her two hands into a circle, as if she were choking someone.

Claire had to laugh. "I'll be back in a minute," she said, as she walked out the door.

* * * * *

The sun was going down, and what had been flurries when Stephen started out had turned to larger flakes that were falling more consistently. The gravel road through Romeo's back country was covered in a thin layer of white already, and Stephen could barely see it—as though through a bride's veil. He was beginning to regret not wearing reflective clothing.

He pulled his collar up around his neck to try to keep out the cold and whistled to Duchess and Regina. He was revving up to turn his frozen legs on. If he could, he was going to sprint the rest of the way home. Enough exercise. If he couldn't be with Claire, at least he could be in front of his fireplace tonight.

In that moment, two things happened: Stephen heard his beeper going off on his phone, but above that noise was the loud rumble of a vehicle approaching way too fast for the conditions. He turned to see what looked like Stan Evans's brown truck coming toward him at high speed.

* * * * *

Claire wished, as she squinted her eyes in order to see the mailbox down by the highway, that she'd brought the flashlight. The painted bricks under her feet looked black instead of red. When she left the house she didn't realize how dark it was already. But with the sun going down and the snow falling, she could barely see Abuelita's iron gates.

That was something she hated about winter in Romeo—the shortness of the days. In fact, if Abuelita would go with her, she'd move to the Cayman Islands or somewhere it was sunny year-round. But Abuelita would never move, and Claire knew she couldn't run away from her problems. She'd tried that once, and it obviously didn't work.

She thought of Moira and Rob's parents back in Arkansas. What right had she to take Graeme so far away from them—to remove him so far from their lives? And them from his? And yet, her abuelita was getting old; they needed to be near her, too. Claire resolved to do a better job of keeping in contact with Rob's family. She would let Graeme go to Moira's in the summer, and next Christmas she would get plane tickets before they were all sold out. She owed that to Graeme, to Rob, to them all.

Opening the big black mailbox, which was encased in brick, Claire saw the package Abuelita must've been looking for. She reached in for it and for a bundle of letters that were held together by a rubber band. As she turned to close the mailbox, Claire heard a sound that was as loud as a freight train. It seemed to be blowing directly in her ear. There was a crash like thunder and then the mind-rending screech of metal on metal. Claire turned around, but all she saw was a bright light that blinded her eyes. She dropped the package and the bundle of letters onto the ground, where they were soon covered in a cloak of snow.

Chapter Thirty-three

....

The truck slammed on its brakes, stirring up a cloud of dust and snow that momentarily blinded Stephen.

"That you, Dr. Reyes?" Stan's deep voice called out of the open window.

"Yes—hold on just a minute."

Stephen staggered over to the window, flipping open his phone to answer the beeper.

"Dr. Reyes?" asked the caller's voice. "We've got a two-car accident on Highway 142. A pedestrian was hit. EMS is there now."

"I'll meet them at the hospital."

"Need a ride up to your house?" Stan offered, assessing the situation.

"That would be great; thanks." Stephen climbed into the backseat of Stan's blue Chevy, which was toasty warm. Marsha was sitting in the middle of the front seat snuggled up to Stan, and they seemed to be out for an adventure. "Where are you two headed on a night like this? And why are you in such a hurry?"

Stan gunned the engine and the truck leaped forward. *He could have been an ambulance driver.*

"Oh—it's so exciting!" Marsha turned around in her seat to face Stephen, her pretty face lit up like a Christmas tree. "Our pastor's wife is in labor! They don't have a four-wheel drive, so they called us to take them to the hospital!"

Stan barreled down his drive and stopped just short of Stephen's garage.

He looked at both of them for just a moment, feeling a wave of satisfaction. "Well, you guys be careful," he said as he exited the truck. "And thanks."

"We will. You, too."

Stephen let his dogs in, grabbed his keys, and jumped into his truck. In ten minutes he was in La Jara. Another five and he was suited up.

"Dr. Reyes, glad you're here. They want you take the patient down the hall," Carlos told him, and Stephen took the chart he was holding out.

Thankfully, because it was New Year's Eve, two other ER doctors had been at the hospital when EMS arrived. They had taken the most critical patients, whom Stephen understood to be an unrestrained male under the influence of alcohol who had been ejected from his vehicle and a father and his child. The drunk man, who could not be resuscitated, had been pronounced dead. The father, who had been driving the other vehicle, was already in surgery for a ruptured disc and spleen, while the child was being treated for a head injury.

Carlos handed Stephen a chart, explaining that he was to attend to the fourth accident victim: a pedestrian who had been injured by the colliding vehicles.

"I need to prepare you, though—" Carlos's voice trailed off.

Stephen's face went white as he read the chart. The name of the patient was Claire Caspian.

* * * * *

"Claire?" Stephen bent over the bed and stroked her hair. It had pieces of grass woven into it and felt damp all over. There was a huge knot on her head near her crown, and the hair around it was matted with blood. He felt the knot and saw that the blood was congealing—both good things. If anything about this could be called "good."

Though Stephen was told that Claire's situation was not critical, the wreck and the whole scene in the ER reminded him of Sydney Evans and that horrible night she died. He'd never forget having to tell her parents she was dead. Stephen shuddered.

Claire had multiple lacerations across her face, though none looked deep, and a black eye. Examining every inch carefully, he thought he could see the imprint of a brick on her cheek, like one had been thrown at her. Her bottom lip was bleeding. Stephen reached down to stop it with a piece of gauze. She flinched when the gauze touched the cut and opened her eyes slightly. He thought he saw the hint of a frown. Then she closed them again.

"Claire, this is Stephen," he said caressingly. "I'm here. You were in an accident, but you're going to be okay."

He took inventory of all of her monitors. Her telemetry, which was her heart's rhythm and rate, was normal. Pulse, 110. The pulse ox clamped on her finger showed 99 percent, which was good, and her blood pressure was 158 over 93. A little high, but understandable. It was okay for that moment.

Stephen pulled back the sheet that covered her. She was still fully clothed, in red flannel pajama bottoms and a long-sleeved Razorback T-shirt. There was not much evidence of the accident on her clothes, thanks to the long wool coat that had been removed by an EMT. It hung over a chair in the room and was covered in snow, mud, and grass. One of its wooden toggles hung by a thread.

Around the bottom of Claire's pants, the fabric was wet. She wore white socks that were stained with mud and gravel. Her feet were cold.

Stephen reached into his pocket and took out his knife to cut off the wet hem of her pajamas. Then he gently pulled off the socks and threw them into the trash. He rubbed her feet between his palms to warm them, and she moved her toes—a good sign that she could feel them. Removing his own socks, he placed them on her feet. His size twelves swallowed her eights, but at least they were warm and dry. He added a blanket to the sheet and pulled the covers up to her chest. She stirred slightly.

The chart said that Claire had been found in a ditch six feet away from the vehicles, which were locked together in a head-on collision. She was responsive, though only semiconscious. She was able to move her arms and legs. The story the nurses pieced together with the EMTs is that Claire jumped into the ditch to avoid being hit as the cars collided. They slammed into the brick mailbox right beside her, sending it careening into the ditch where broken pieces of it—as well as glass from the cars—struck Claire. The worst and biggest piece of the mailbox landed on her head. She had multiple contusions on her knees, hip bones, and elbows from the impact of the fall and was believed to have two badly sprained ankles. The greatest concern, naturally, was her head. It was predetermined that she had a concussion. No X-rays had been done.

It was Stephen's call whether to order radiography or lab, and he determined pretty quickly, since all of her vital signs were good and she wasn't on IV meds, to order a head CT scan. After the CT, what she needed was rest. To be observed, as they called it in the ER. She was definitely obtunded and not moving her arms or legs at the moment, but the feeling was there. Nothing seemed to be broken. Stephen sensed she was going to be okay, and great relief washed over him.

After ordering the CT scan and some pain medication for Claire, he sat down in one of the chairs. Running a hand through his hair, he breathed a prayer of thanksgiving.

"Dr. Reyes?"

Stephen looked up to see Carlos's anxious face at the door.

He walked to the door so they could talk softly through it without disturbing Claire.

"Does someone else need me?" Stephen asked, suddenly remembering he was on call for the ER and not only there to watch over Claire.

"No," said Carlos, "but Claire's abuelita is here. She wants to see Claire."

"Okay—let me go talk to her."

Stephen looked back at Claire, who seemed to be resting peacefully. Then he stepped outside the door. Abuelita was waiting at the end of the hall with an overnight bag, and she had a pained look on her face that didn't alter when she saw him.

"She's okay!" Stephen smiled, reaching out to hug her. "I've been with her the whole time, and I think she's going to be just fine. She's bruised—"

Abuelita flinched from his hug. "Is she awake?"

"No, she's resting. The EMT report says she was semiconscious when they found her. She talked to them—mentioned Graeme's name—and told them something about what happened. We believe she has a closed head wound. She's about to get a CT scan, and then I want to observe her for the rest of the night—to see how she does when she wakes up."

"Can I see her?"

"Of course. I'll take you in there."

Stephen thought Claire's abuelita was acting strange, but he also knew she was in shock.

"I'd prefer to go by myself."

She started to walk away from him, but Stephen caught her arm.

"Hey, where's Graeme?"

"Martina came and got him, if it's any of your business." Abuelita shook him off, eyeing his hand as though it was leprous.

Stephen didn't get it, but he didn't let himself take it personally. "Oh. Well, okay. I'll just go to my dictation room a few moments and get caught up. Then perhaps we can talk." Maybe she'd be more normal after she saw that Claire was okay.

It had been only thirty minutes, but it seemed like hours before Abuelita emerged from Claire's room. The attendant had come to take Claire on a gurney to radiology, and Stephen saw Abuelita follow them from where he was sitting at his workstation, doing documentation on the computer.

"Abuelita," he called.

She scowled at him. "She opened her eyes."

"That's wonderful!" He jumped up from his chair.

She put her hand up to stop him. "You mustn't go near her when she returns from the scan."

Stephen was getting frustrated. He motioned for her to come into the little room, and then he shut the door.

"I need to see her if she is awake. There are certain questions I need to ask as her doctor."

"Carlos can do it. Let him ask all of the questions."

"Is something wrong? I mean, other than Claire's accident? I don't want to be a bother to you, but I don't understand how you're acting."

"*No entiendes? Estoy hasta la madre! No tienes una corazón! Eres tan estúpido como un burro. Baboso! Cerdo egocéntrico!*"

Stephen wasn't completely proficient in Spanish, but he was pretty sure Abuelita had just called him a heartless, stupid, egocentric pig. "Whoa! Slow down! What are you talking about?"

"I'm talking about Claire. And Graeme. And you leading them both on. What kind of a sicko are you to get a kick out of hurting people—especially people who have been hurt so much already? You're a doctor! You're supposed to care about people!"

Abuelita suddenly looked very old. Her rouge was smeared, as was her mascara, presumably from crying. She tucked the hair that had fallen into her face back up with a comb, putting herself and her composure back together.

"I do care," Stephen said as sincerely as possible. "In fact, I love your granddaughter and her son. I would never hurt any of you on purpose. I honestly have no idea what you're talking about." He knew his voice was pleading.

Abuelita studied him, narrowing her dark eyes as though to reduce him down to nothing. Nothing but the truth.

"You have no intentions of getting back together with your ex-wife?"

"What?" Stephen felt like *he'd* been hit on the head with a brick. "No! None at all. She's married to another man." He ran his fingers through his hair, suddenly aware of why Claire had been avoiding his calls. "Where did Claire—and you—get that idea?"

Abuelita seemed to sense that he was genuinely astonished, and she sighed, mulling this over. "She went to your office to surprise you the other day and overheard you talking to your wife on the phone. She assumed—she believed—you were deceiving her. I told her she should let you explain. But she's so stubborn! I don't know why she jumped to such conclusions."

Despite his astonishment, Stephen couldn't help but savor the irony of Abuelita's words. He raised his eyebrows and a grin tugged at his lips. "Hmm. I'm glad *you* would never do that."

A smile crept around the corners of Abuelita's mouth, and her voice softened. "You have to understand, *hijo*, that Claire has been abandoned by many significant people in her life. Both of her parents and then her husband. All through death. They would never have willed it—but that is abandonment just the same. I'm afraid if you're going to love her you must take on this baggage, until the day she is truly able to lay it down."

"I want to—I will, gladly," Stephen said. "I thought she already knew I loved her, but I haven't told her yet. I've been waiting for the right time to say the words."

"Maybe that time is now."

* * * * *

While Claire was getting her scan, Stephen and Abuelita shared a cup of coffee in the lounge. Then the two of them walked back towards Claire's room. They met Carlos, who was just coming out.

"I'd say she's doing great," he said to Abuelita. "Called me her 'shining *caballero*' the minute I walked into the room."

"Oh, that's good," Abuelita said. "Was she hurting?"

"Said she was sore." Carlos looked at Stephen. "I gave her the Percocet you ordered."

"Good. That should help her rest."

"Yep, doc, she knew everything. Got all of the questions right." Carlos seemed very pleased with himself and with Claire.

"Well, okay, that's great. Thanks, Carlos. We'll go in and see her now."

Carlos stopped them. "Don't wake her up! She fell asleep while we were talking. Said she was really exhausted. I saw your note to admit her, but I thought we could just leave her in this room until she wakes again—I mean, if that's okay with you, Dr. Reyes."

Stephen nodded. "Of course."

Carlos ambled back to the nurses' station with the air of a small-town ER nurse. He knew everyone and could do a little bit of everything.

Stephen and Abuelita tiptoed into the room and found that Carlos was right. Claire seemed to be sleeping serenely.

Stephen stooped by her side and touched her face as Abuelita stroked her other hand. "I love you, Claire," he whispered in her ear.

Back outside, Abuelita quizzed him. "Are you going to be here all night?"

"I am. I won't leave."

"I was going to spend the night." She indicated her overnight bag, which was still sitting on the waiting room floor.

"There's no good place to sleep."

"Well, I think I'll go back home then, if you think she's really okay."

"I do. She just needs rest."

"You'll call me, *hijo*? If she needs anything?"

"I'll call you. I promise."

"I'll be back first thing in the morning."

Chapter Thirty-four

Claire didn't know whether she was dreaming or awake. Her head pounded against her skull like a prisoner trying to escape, and her bottom lip felt tight. Her body ached, and her ankles, when she tried to move them, felt as if they each weighed one hundred pounds. Her eyes burned as they adjusted to the semi-dark, slowly revealing her surroundings.

She was lying in a hospital bed with covers pulled up to her neck. The only light was a sickly, bluish fluorescent beam cast through a crack in the door. She looked around her. A man who appeared to be a doctor was sitting upright in a vinyl chair with his head resting against the wall. He was asleep.

Stephen, she thought in a flash of recognition. *What's he doing in here?*

She flailed her arms a bit to get them loose from the covers. Then she pushed a button on the railing of her bed that would set her up a bit.

At the sound of the inclining bed, Stephen roused.

"Claire?" he asked, emerging from dead asleep to full consciousness faster than Claire could've imagined possible. He sprang to her side. "It's me, Claire. I'm here. I've been here all night. You had an accident, but you're okay. You're going to be fine. Are you hurting anywhere?"

"My head."

Stephen pushed the button to call the nurse. "Bring us some Advil."

"Okay, Dr. Reyes. Be right there."

"Stephen, I don't understand."

"The accident? Do you remember anything?"

Claire shook her head in disgust. "Yes, I remember the accident.

I'm not talking about that. I don't understand why you're here."

The nurse came in with a pill and a drink. Claire swallowed it, and the water felt good on her parched throat.

"Can I have a little more of that?" she asked the nurse.

"Sure, hon, I'll be right back."

When the nurse left them again, Stephen said, "I'm here because I want to be with you. To take care of you."

"I don't need you to take care of me." Claire spit the words at him through her busted lip. She was starting to feel agitated.

"Claire, I—"

The nurse came back in with a big glass of ice water and a package of cheese crackers. "You probably ought to try to eat these with that pain medicine, if you can."

"Thanks," Claire said, taking them from her.

"You guys just call if you need anything. I'll be right outside at the station." The nurse left the room.

"Can I go home? Is my car here?" Claire asked Stephen.

He looked at her like she was from Venus.

"Claire, you have a concussion. We're observing you overnight. If you're fine in the morning, which it looks like you will be, I'll take you home first thing."

"I don't want you to take me home. Where's my abuelita?"

"She was here, but she left. She'll be back in the morning. You can go home with her then if you want, as long as everything checks out."

The lines in Stephen's face were deep. Claire could tell he was tired, and she thought she saw something else. He seemed wounded. But that only made her mad.

"Stephen, the ruse is over. I heard you call Janet; I know you're getting back with her. That's fine and I wish you the best. I just wish you'd drop the act of pretending to care about Graeme and me. We don't need you." As she said these words, a sharp stab of pain in her head engulfed her, and she lurched forward, raising her hand to the spot where she'd been hit.

Stephen's tone became more professional. "Claire, I'm going to go out now. I think you need to rest. I'll be just outside the room if you need anything." He lingered over the bed for a moment, staring at her. Then his voice softened. "You're wrong about Janet. And you're wrong about me." He tapped the side of the bed with his hand, and then he was gone.

Claire leaned back against the pillow and closed her eyes. She could feel the Advil kicking in, and the throbbing in her head dulled to a more bearable level. Like muted bass drums, the pain seemed to beat out a cadence of Stephen's last words. *Wrong about Janet. Wrong about me. Wrong about Janet.*

"Lord, am I wrong?"

Her words seem to fall and shatter to a million pieces on the cold tile floor.

"Are You even listening? Do You even exist?"

There was no answer but the low hum of a machine down the hall.

Emboldened by the silence, Claire sat up. "I don't think You do." There, she'd said it. "You're a figment of the imagination, something people make up to explain what they can't understand. But You know what? Even that doesn't work for me. Because You don't make any logical sense."

Claire was crying now. She could feel something in her dying, something she'd held onto for all these years, and she imagined it was the last of her innocence—the last vestiges of her faith. But on some level, she realized, it felt good. Honest. Every question she'd shoved to the corners of her brain was suddenly swept out into the open. Claire was cleaning house—getting rid of a hand-me-down religion that never had fit.

"My parents died a brutal death and so did my husband. Three of the most pure souls to ever walk the earth. And what did You do to prevent it? Nothing. My life—and Graeme's—have been changed forever by what we've lost. And where were You?"

Silence.

"I thought so. You're nowhere. We're all on our own. I could have been killed tonight just getting the mail, for crying out loud. Then Graeme would be an orphan!"

Claire thought about all of the conversations she'd had with Oscar about religion. He'd shown a tremendous amount of respect for her beliefs, though he never shared them. He'd abandoned his faith a long time ago.

"Why didn't I?" Claire thought. "What's taken me so long? Have I just not had the guts to admit it's outdated?" She rubbed a sore place on her side. "I've known for a long time, both personally and existentially, that Christianity doesn't work. Even so-called Christians can't get it right. Why have I hung on so long to the idea that it could?"

I'm not an idea, a distinct but inaudible voice said.

Claire stopped rubbing her side and sat very still. *Had she really heard something?* Her heart seemed to stop in her chest.

I am a Person, and I am your Friend.

Claire closed her eyes as fresh tears streamed down her cheeks. Her quivering chin dropped as she bent her head low, listening intently for one more sound of that voice. His voice.

I am not a man that I would lie. I am not matter that you can contain me. I am not a question you can answer. I am your Lover, and I am your Friend.

If anyone would have asked Claire, prior to that moment, if she had heard the voice of God, she would have given a pat answer. "No," she would have said, "but I believe He speaks through the Bible." She had said that to Oscar, in fact, many times, pointing out scriptures that she believed taught people how to live a moral life.

Let go, Claire.

"I can't. I want to, but I can't."

Let go, once and for all.

"I'm not strong enough. Not brave enough. What if something else bad happens? I'm afraid."

I understand, my love. But let go.

"I will not let go until You bless me! Until You promise that everything will be okay from here on out."

Let go and I will catch you. I promise I will always be here to catch you, no matter what.

* * * * *

Claire woke the next morning to see Abuelita fussing about the room. She was unpacking an overnight bag with a fresh change of clothes for Claire, and on the roller table there was a Styrofoam plate of breakfast tacos and fruit. A thermos was set beside it, and Claire could smell the welcome aroma of Ginger Peach tea.

"Good morning, Abuelita," she said, pressing the button to elevate her bed.

"*Buenos dias, hija.*" Abuelita kissed her on the forehead. "How are you feeling?"

"Sore, but fairly okay. I am ready to get out of here."

"Stephen gave the orders for you to be released, so after some breakfast, we'll go." Abuelita eased the table across the bed in front of Claire.

"Is Stephen here?" Raising herself up, Claire found that her head had turned into a fishbowl. She closed her eyes to steady herself.

"No, he left when I got here, just a few moments ago. I'm sure he's gone home to rest."

"He stayed here all night?"

"*Sí.*" Abuelita sat down on the edge of Claire's bed.

"Oh, Abuelita, I'm afraid I behaved very badly toward him. Again."

"Hmm," Abuelita said. "Well, that makes two of us, then."

Claire looked at her quizzically. "What do you mean?"

"I spoke harshly to him last night before giving him a chance to explain."

"Explain what?" Claire took a sip of her tea and let the warm, soothing liquid sink into her soul. "Please tell me everything."

"Well, first of all, Stephen is not getting back together with his exwife. She's remarried and is living in another state. He called her to apologize after talking to you about forgiveness." Abuelita cocked her head to one side and raised her eyebrows for effect as she stared at Claire. "He is very hurt that you would still doubt him after all the water under the bridge, but he loves you. He told me so himself."

Claire let out a big sigh.

"Second of all, you could have died last night down at the mailbox." Abuelita's eyes suddenly welled up with tears. "There was a terrible wreck right in front of the gates of the Casa. A man died, in fact. And had you not jumped into the ditch, you would have been crushed. Thank the good Lord you used those brains He gave you and jumped out of the way."

Claire suddenly remembered something with startling clarity. "I didn't jump," she said. "Somebody pushed me."

Abuelita leaned forward, sable eyes shining. "What do you mean, *hija*? No one else was there at the scene. Graeme and I didn't even know about it until the ambulance came."

"I don't know," Claire answered. She tried to piece together the fragments she remembered in her mind. "I was getting the mail and I saw the cars coming; there was a loud noise, and then I felt somebody push me out of the way. I don't remember what he looked like. The next thing I knew, I was in the ditch."

"Well, glory be. It must have been an angel."

* * * * *

On the way home, Claire asked Abuelita to turn down County Road 10. "It's where Stephen lives," she explained. "I want to leave him a note."

She scrawled on a piece of a Sonic napkin she found in Abuelita's glove box.

Stephen,

I'm desperately sorry. Please, please forgive me. I will never doubt you again.

Love,
Claire

She saw Nell's figure in the picture window as Abuelita's Cadillac passed the Patricks' house.

Turning into Stephen's drive, Abuelita said, "What a lovely place."

They drove up into the space between Stephen's house and the outlying barn.

"I'll just be a minute," Claire said, slowly getting out of the car. Both of her ankles were wrapped, and she hobbled up to the door.

When she finally got there, she tried to lodge the napkin between the door and its frame. Surprisingly, the door opened.

"Stephen?" she called, poking her head into the mudroom. There was no answer.

Claire looked absolutely awful, but she didn't care. Crossing the space in front of Abuelita as fast as she could, she motioned with her arms. "I'm going to try the barn," she mouthed.

Abuelita, who was singing along with Andraé Crouch, simply nodded.

By the time she reached the doorway of the barn, Claire was

painfully exhausted. The fish in her head were swimming, and her ankles screamed in protest of that much activity. She heard a rustling down toward the sheep's pen and dragged herself there.

"If I didn't find you here, I was going to lie down and die in the hay," she said when she saw Stephen down on one knee, feeding Woolworth from his hand.

"Claire?" He rose to his feet and looked at her, his eyes searching as from across a deep desert.

"You take that sheep feeding thing rather seriously, don't you?"

He grinned and came to her, and Claire fell into his arms.

Epilogue

....

The March day was everything they could have hoped for. The clouds, like gossamer curtains, drew back to reveal a cerulean Colorado sky stretching out in every direction as far as the eye could see. Even the mountains seemed to notice, standing taller and seemingly more erect. In the sparkling sunlight, the sky seemed to Claire as pure and spotless as a wedding dress. The train of it billowed on forever, like a royal robe unfurling its jewel-like hues.

They had chosen this place because it was sacred to them—this sky was the dome of their love's cathedral. It was here in the San Luis Valley that they met and fell in love, here they courted, and here they planned to live their lives. So it only made sense that here, in this place, they would also be married.

Many people had pitched in to make this day happen—and now they were all gathered under a bower of oaks on Stephen's ranch in Romeo. Claire scanned the crowd of white chairs laced with pink tulle and ribbon and spotted Jesús sitting proudly beside Mickey. He beamed up at the bride's only attendant, Martina, who was standing and holding a white rose near the natural stone altar.

Martina looked lovely in a pale pink dress with a princess neckline. The bodice and skirt were satin with lace overlay. Its long, soft lines accentuated her graceful figure, and the color of the fabric seemed to make her skin glow. Her hair was up and held in place by a ring of faux pearls. Elegant curls framed her face, and the loose tendrils beside her ears fell like black filigree over pearl drop earrings. She smiled at Claire like one who had always known and loved her, and they shared a moment of secret delight.

Near Jesús and Mickey were Dr. Banks, with his neat grey ponytail, and Jerry with his wife, Sue, who was very pregnant and radiant in a yellow linen dress. Across the aisle from them were Nell and Gene Patrick on a row with the Evanses. Nell was wearing her best Sunday dress, a flower print, and Gene and Stan were both in suits. Marsha looked like spring had come into her heart. She held Stan's hand in one of hers and smiled thoughtfully as she patted it with the other.

Stephen's sister, Maria, in all her vibrant beauty, was on the front row ahead of them. She was wearing a silk turquoise tent dress that came to her knee with a pair of tiny silver ballerina slippers. Her hair was swept up in a loose French twist and adorned with a peacock feather. Manuel, her distinguished-looking husband, sat beside his wife with his arm around her, reading the program.

In front of them, opposite the altar from Martina, was Joe. Claire thought she had never seen him look happier nor more alive. Not even the night his team won the big game.

Joe was steady and strong in his black tux with tails. Though his eyes seemed to exude an energy barely contained, he didn't fidget. He just stood there, sometimes looking to heaven and humming his own tune. Every once in a while he would glance over and smile at Stephen.

Ah, Stephen. Claire's pulse quickened at the sight of him. Who would have imagined they would be here together on this day? She remembered another ceremony and another groom she would always cherish. But today there were no comparisons. Everyone and everything—past, present and future—were bathed in the sunshine of grace.

Claire watched Stephen from her hidden position in the back. He shifted his feet in the black dress shoes that matched his tux. She noted the broad shoulders she'd learned to lean on, the strong set of his jaw. He had a white rosebud tucked into his lapel.

Stephen's eyes, looking towards the mountains, were tender and reverent. He held his hands loosely at his sides, and she could still see the gentleness in them, the gentleness that had caught her eye on the day they had met. He smiled warmly at Joe, and Claire could just barely make out the chip in his front tooth.

At two o'clock sharp, Frieda's brother, a recognized protégé of Wynton Marsalis, stood and played the "Bridal Chorus" on his horn. The small gathering of people rose to its feet in honor and anticipation. Gabriella Isabella Rodriguez strode down the aisle in multiple layers of satin and lace, tossing rose petals out of a satin basket.

When the music's energy heightened, Claire caught her breath. The moment had finally arrived. She smiled wholeheartedly at Frieda, who was as warm and sweet as Mexican chocolate underneath her veil.

"It's time," Claire said and handed Frieda the bride's bouquet of roses.

As Frieda stepped forward on the arm of her father, who would also perform the ceremony, Claire ruffled the train out behind her friend. Then she took a seat on the back row, sliding in beside Abuelita and Graeme, who had saved her a place.

* * * * *

When the ceremony was over and Joe and Frieda were pronounced man and wife, Frieda's father turned to Joe and grinned. "Now, Joe," he said, pausing for effect. "Finally, Joe—you may kiss your bride."

Joe released Frieda's hand, returning it gingerly to her side like he was afraid it would break if he let it go. Then, using both of his hands, he carefully lifted the veil from Frieda's face and kissed her ever so tenderly.

The crowd broke into applause, standing to its feet.

Frieda then reached up, grabbed Joe's face in her hands, and planted another kiss—a bigger one—on his lips.

The crowd went as wild as it had at the championship game.

The Reverend Franklin yelled, "Ladies and gentlemen, may I present to you Mr. and Mrs. Joe Riggins."

The trumpet sounded, and Joe and Frieda practically ran down the aisle amidst more jubilant cheers. Stephen escorted Martina behind them and then came to find Claire where she was standing with Graeme and Abuelita. The plan was to head to Art and Sol for a fiesta-style reception.

As Claire and Stephen walked hand-in-hand toward his truck, Abuelita beside her and Graeme on Stephen's shoulders, Graeme pointed to the sky. "Look!" he cried. "A butterfly!"

And so it was, the first Monarch of the season, wafting ahead of them on the cedar-scented breeze.

POST CARD
Love Finds You

Want a peek into local American life—past and present?
The *Love Finds You*™ series published by Summerside Press
features real towns and combines travel, romance,
and faith in one irresistible package!

The novels in the series—uniquely titled after American towns with unusual but intriguing names—inspire romance and fun. Each fictional story draws on the compelling history or the unique character of a real place. Stories center on romances kindled in small towns, old loves lost and found again on the high plains, and new loves discovered at exciting vacation getaways. Summerside Press plans to publish at least one novel set in each of the 50 states. Be sure to catch them all!

Now Available in Stores

Love Finds You in Miracle, Kentucky by Andrea Boeshaar
ISBN: 978-1-934770-37-5

Love Finds You in Snowball, Arkansas by Sandra D. Bricker
ISBN: 978-1-934770-45-0

Love Finds You in Valentine, Nebraska by Irene Brand
ISBN: 978-1-934770-38-2

Coming in February, 2009

Love Finds You in Humble, Texas by Anita Higman
ISBN: 978-1-934770-61-0

Love Finds You in Last Chance, California by Miralee Ferrell
ISBN: 978-1-934770-39-9

Coming in April, 2009

Love Finds You in Maiden, North Carolina by Tamela Hancock Murray
ISBN: 978-1-934770-65-8

Love Finds You in Paradise, Pennsylvania by Loree Lough
ISBN: 978-1-934770-66-5

summerside
PRESS